ECHO of A HERO
SPIRITS of POWER

PEARSON MYLES

SPIRITS of POWER

PEARSON MYLES

ECHO OF A HERO

SPIRITS OF POWER

In loving memory of Jorjette Millie Myles

ECHO OF A HERO
SPIRITS OF POWER

PEARSON MYLES

ONE

BOOM *BOOM BOOM.*

Explosions of color lit the city. Different shades of crimson, orange, and ebony complexions filled the streets. Night fell once again. The black veil of the sky augmented the lights below. Throughout the streets, laughter rang, echoing all around; other sounds drowned out by the merry mood. Except none of these images were true. Clouds of smoke and ash blocked out the sky, and instead of laughter, the sound of screams and cries vibrated through the streets, mingling with blood, fire, and debris.

BOOM BOOM BOOM.

Fire consumed the city of Villhilium as plenarie citizens screamed while trying to flee the destruction. Buildings and streets exploded into piles of brimstone and fire as the city's fortifications blew apart. Plenaries tumbled down the crumbling town square, taking refuge inside underground shelters. The chaos outside cracked the largest shelter's foundation, dust falling from the roof as the room shuddered. Sitting in the center of the room, a projected image of the city phased in and out of focus. Gathered around the map, the remaining plenarie officials and commanders reported the rapid deterioration of Villhilium.

"We have another breach in the east wing of the city!" called a frantic general.

The commander turned to one of the surviving members of the council. "We must assume the enemy is closing in," he said grimly.

The people huddled in the room cried out as the building shook once more. The doors of the chamber burst open as a single soldier limped in. His face scarred and scorched, the plenarie's right arm dripped tears of blood. Hobbling up to the commander, he weakly gripped his robes. "They have us surrounded, sir! The city is under heavy fire from the enemies' missiles and artillery. Most civilians were evacuated, and we are preparing a shutdown of the portals in the arch tower."

Desmond Viridian, one of the few high-ranking officers remaining, beckoned his lieutenant. "Summon the senior sentinels of the city. Tell them to meet me at the vault."

The middle-aged woman nodded as she ran into the chaos outside. When he glanced one last time at the map of the city, his stern expression grew darker seeing the black pinpoints of the invaders swarming the city. The vault room wasn't far away. Desmond wasted no time sprinting out of the shelter and into the archives building across the town square. Standing close together in the building's desolated foyer, the remaining sentinels of the capital looked to their leader.

"With all due respect, sir, shouldn't we be at our posts to help evacuate the city?"

Desmond locked eyes with the speaker. Felicity Chiffon, a young mother but a fierce warrior, had only recently been appointed the honorary rank of sentinel. She and the Darkthistle family were the guardians of Villhilium's armory district. A loyal friend of Desmond, Felicity awaited his response with vigilant eyes.

Desmond cleared his throat. "Where are Erick and Steven?"

This time an older, balding man stepped forth. "The market place and barracks have all been destroyed, sir. Along with all their inhabitants, including Erick and Steven."

Desmond exhaled his grief. Wiping his brow, he walked over to Felicity and laid his hand on her shoulder. His gaze softened with more compassion than he could express in words. "Felicity, find your family and the Darkthistles. Head to the arch tower and seal the portal to one of the old outposts behind you."

Felicity clutched his hand tightly before leaving. The archives building shuddered a little as the sound of screams grew louder. Gazing up, Desmond's eyes turned to slits as he watched the sky grow blacker. The city's purge would end soon.

"Alizarin, Fuchsia, and Bazaar, with me." Desmond gestured to the last sentinel. "Marigold, same as Sentinel Chiffon. Retreat to the arch and take anyone you can."

Desmond and his three followers dived deeper into the wrecked building toward the secret vault. It wouldn't matter, though. Within hours, any secrets this building had would either be revealed or destroyed. Filled with hidden relics and objects of immense power, the raging war above somehow left the room nearly unaffected, with only dust and cobwebs to pester it.

"Dismantle everything you can," Desmond ordered as he overturned a crate.

Unless nailed down, the sentinels crushed, smashed, and destroyed everything in the room. Various inventions, weapons, and tools lay scattered across the floor in fragments while they hurried. They could not let their enemies claim any additional assets, even a single object from the room could help them advance their weaponry.

The task almost completed, Desmond signaled them to stop with only one package left untouched. Some relics, more powerful and dangerous than others, could not easily be destroyed. He never intended to destroy this small box; its purpose outweighed the sensible notion of smashing it before others could steal it. Strange how an object so small and delicate could be so important, but Desmond knew that its size did not matter.

He handed it to Bazaar who had a bag ready. Checking one more time to make sure they had destroyed every box and device possible, everyone rushed out of the room as Desmond sealed the door for the last time. Their timing had been almost perfect. Almost. Just as the final lock clicked, the walls and roof shook again as rocks came crumbling down.

"Take cover!" he yelled.

A shower of rocks and pieces of roof rained down as everyone tried to shield themselves. When the dust settled,

Desmond struggled to his feet and helped Alizarin up. Scanning the caved-in hallway, his heart stopped at the sight of Fuchsia's crushed corpse under the pile of rubble behind them.

"Keep going," he said, his voice thick and strained. "We need to reach the tower before it's too late."

They picked their way through the wreckage and climbed out of the stairwell. After Desmond checked to make sure Bazaar still had the bag, he turned right into what remained of the building's foyer. The front doors of the archives opened to a direct path to the tower where they could make their escape.

"Come on!" he encouraged.

The room shook even more as something moved in the shadows. The atmosphere was eerie with no other sound except their own heavy breaths. Over the sound of their breathing, a new noise echoed. A deep, rattling voice that cackled in the darkness.

"Relegator!" Desmond shouted, calling the invisible enemy by its name.

Alizarin let out a bloodcurdling scream, his cries swiftly silenced by the gruesome popping sounds of his body being stabbed over and over. His armor torn apart, he dropped to the floor twitching as the dark voice laughed. Before they joined their friend, Desmond and Bazaar sped out of the room and into the desolate outdoors. Just a block down, the arch tower stood out like a beacon of hope. Grabbing Bazaar, Desmond spat, "Get to a portal and seal all the arches! I'll distract him."

He had no time to argue as the shadow leaped from behind and impaled Desmond. Bazaar bolted with the bag and disappeared into the cloud of smoke that flooded the streets.

Dropping his head to see a clawed hand coming out of his chest, Desmond fell to his knees and choked. The crimson-stained fist turned and then pulled out, leaving a gaping hole in the center of him. His head dizzier by the second, Desmond used all the energy he had left to twist around. Standing above him loomed a relegator—not *a* relegator—*the* relegator! The first one.

Relegators in general had identical, black armor. But their leader separated himself with his one-of-a-kind, fear-inspiring suit. A sable pillar of foreboding, Solon Blak towered above everyone. The armor widened at the shoulders with powerfully built arms and legs ending with barbed claws on the tips of his fingers and toes. His face, a horrible mask resembling a corpse, bore the vivid details of a skull from the empty-looking eyes to the absent nose and exposed teeth and jaw. All the light around him seemed to vaporize into darkness as he stood there with smoke and energy ebbing off him.

Solon reached down and ripped Desmond's pendant out of the center of his chest. Without the device, the last of Desmond's armor melted away as he crushed the oval ornament in his claws. "Pathetic," he stated. "You plenaries are nothing without these."

Desmond coughed up more blood. "Traitor! You will never win."

The murderer only chuckled. "Ah, but I already have. You should have listened to me when you had the chance, Viridian. Because of their ignorance, the plenaries will be slaughtered."

Desmond struggled to stand. The first relegator stretched

high above him, but he would not show any fear. He knew what came next. "The plenaries will survive. You and your relegators will pay for what you did."

Solon Blak slashed him with a final and intense stroke. "You are so right."

Desmond Viridian fell limp to the ground as his killer stepped over him, looking down the path at the tower with narrowed eyes.

Bazaar would never know that Desmond didn't make it. A lone relegator tackled him from behind and decapitated him so fast that the assault hadn't registered. His headless body slumped forward as the bag was ripped from his lifeless grasp. The relegator shook it upside down, the case inside tumbling across Bazaar's bent arm. Clutching the box in its bloody hands, the relegator gurgled a shriek as a blade pierced through its throat.

Pulling his sword out of the relegator's neck, Leonard Blu, a lone plenarie guard, kicked the relegator's body away from the box. Hastily grabbing the item, Blu tucked it gently within the bundle in blankets he cradled in his arm. He ran back toward the tower, tucking and rolling just as another relegator sailed above him. Blocking the entrance, Solon's fingers still dripped with Desmond's blood.

"There is no escape," he hissed.

"You're a fool if you think you can win. The humans will crush you once you're no longer any use to them!" Blu roared.

Solon stretched a pointed finger at the bundle. "I will

slaughter your child first. Everyone in this city will taste my vengeance."

Clutching the bundle tighter, the protective father raised his sword. "I will kill you before you touch her!"

Solon snarled as he charged at Leonard. The guard leapt to the side and stumbled through the entryway, barreling into the tower. Built in the center of the city, the arch tower was the only connection from Villhilium to the old outposts. The ancient plenaries created the arches to travel throughout the realm. Only a few arches remained in this world. Because of the Excretion Act, most of them were destroyed.

The circular room on the first floor of the tower housed the seven arches—portals that accessed the outside world. Lined against the back wall in a semi-circle, two arches resembled nothing more than rubble, and four portals were shut down. The last portal slowly closed as Leonard ran toward it. He cried out in pain after getting knocked off his feet. His baby and the box tumbled out of his arms and rolled next to the arch. On the ground, the baby cried as Blu felt Solon's grip snake around his foot.

"No!"

Thrown off the ground, Leonard flew into the wall with a sickening crack. He crashed to the floor motionless, his still face drenched with blood. Kicking at the corpse, Solon seized the box and examined it. The killer's gaze shifted as the baby's loud cries drew his attention. He nudged her with his foot and tilted his head at the infant. She would never see her father again. The last thing the infant would see was the foot that crushed her mercilessly. Solon raised his foot to stomp when the last portal flickered. A flash of green and silver exploded into the room as a man zoomed out of the arch and rammed the relegator, knocking him down.

Like every plenarie solider, Alton Malachite wore silver armor with an oval pendant that had the letter P in its center on his chest plate. His face completely covered, the helmet concealed the anger that blazed in his eyes. Green light glowed under the plates and throughout the cracks of the armor as well as on the coat of arms. With a quick jerk, Alton kicked the box into the arch behind him as it vanished into the portal.

"No!" Solon shrilled. "What have you done with it?"

Holding his thrashing enemy down, Alton pulled his right fist back while pinning his left hand on the relegator's throat. A narrow blade slid out of his armored right wrist, extending to Solon's chest.

"This purge ends tonight with your death," he spat viciously.

Solon only laughed. "You fool. Humanity already made its choice. Even if you kill me, they will finish what I started. Fear has turned them against you."

Alton punctuated Solon's statement with his sword.

Pulling his blade out, he watched it shrink away back into his wrist. Solon's body remained on the ground limp, as Alton walked over it and to the sprawled guard. He pressed his fingers against his neck. Nothing. The man's sword lay beside his corpse, an heirloom of an old plenarie family. Alton picked it up, untying the dead man's scabbard and tying it around his own waist.

He stepped over Solon, reached down, and lifted the baby

into his arms. As he peered through the entrance, he watched a wave of fire blow the city apart, soaring toward the tower in a giant orange wave. Alton had one foot in the portal when he heard a choking cough behind him. Solon Blak bent his head up at him. "This... is far from over. I will find you and kill you both. You hear me! I'll... find... you."

Solon's helmet hit the ground with a metal clunk. His threat meant nothing. At least not today. Alton clutched the child tightly as he ran through the portal just as it closed. Fire consumed everything, and then the city disappeared in smoke and ash.

Running through a portal was strange; pure energy of white light surrounded the rider zooming across the void between the dimensions. A lack of concentration on the destination would send the traveler into the void dissolving into nothingness. Plenaries never worried about this; they could bend the power of the portals to their will with the help of their pendants. If trained enough, they could even access a portal without an arch.

After Alton teleported and tumbled through the other side of the portal out of an arch, he righted himself and stretched to his full height. After concentrating on his helmet, it faded away. He ducked his head and inspected the baby; she'd fallen asleep in his arms. Holding her in the crook of his elbow, Alton turned around and watched the portal blink out of existence. No one would be using it to make a return trip.

The outpost housing he'd traveled to appeared vacant.

This was the last escape route. Other survivors would have made it to one of the other outposts. In a hall filled with blank doors, Alton wandered around until he found a bedroom. He laid the baby on the bare mattress tucked in a corner to rest. Once he unstrapped the scabbard, he leaned the sword against the wall by the bed.

It belonged to her father, and now it was the only thing she had left of her legacy. He didn't even know the infant's name. When he inspected the hilt, he recognized the coat of arms with a lapis lazuli jewel carved in the center. The Blus were an ancient family line of warriors and fighters. Perhaps one day she would learn of her heritage. His back pressed against the wall, Alton slid down until he sat on the floor and rubbed his eyes with fatigue.

"Hello, do you require my assistance?"

Alton jumped as he grabbed the sword and swung around. At first he saw nothing, and then the figure came into view. *A felera*, he thought. One of the servant keepers of this place. Spirit-like creatures, felera served as humble caretakers under the orders of designated masters. As a plenarie, this made him her superior by default.

"Who's here?" he croaked, his throat cracked from dehydration.

The felera smiled kindly. "You two are the only ones."

"Can we reach out to the other survivors?" Alton asked.

"All communications have been cut off," she answered.

Setting the sword back down, he sat on the edge of the bed and turned to look at the baby girl. With a fuzz of hair just visible on her head, she couldn't be more than a year old.

"You will be taking control?"

Alton blinked in confusion. "What?"

The felera hovered closer. "As the eldest plenarie here, you are by default the appointed protector of this outpost."

Not for long, he thought to himself. Once he could reach out, surely more survivors would take refuge here. How many made it? Had any escaped the massacre? *Not now*, Alton thought. Now was not the time to depend on others. He needed to step up and take control. The future of the plenarie race could depend on him. It *did* depend on him. Right here, sleeping before him, lay the future of his people. He would do better. Raise her the way her own parents might have.

Looking at the wall across from him, Alton saw his reflection standing in the mirror before him. In dirty, battered armor, his orange hair spiked up, streaks of premature gray had already started to sprout. Wrinkles of stress circled his eyes and across his soot-covered brow. The last few years of the purge had certainly done a number on him.

With a quick twist and pull, Alton removed the circular pendant off his chest plate. His armor began to glow as it faded away, a unique ability plenarie armor possessed. Their pendants could summon their own armor or make it vanish at will when they removed it. When they placed the pendant coat of arms on their torsos, protective armor appeared and covered their bodies completely.

When his armor disappeared, Alton brushed his bare fingers across the child's soft brow. "I want a full tour. Show me everywhere and everything there is to know about this place."

The felera nodded. "Of course. And how would you like to be addressed?"

Gazing at the child, he replied, "I am Alton. Alton Malachite. The appointed guardian of the Sacrarium until deemed otherwise."

"Sacrarium?"

"Yes, a Sacrarium," Alton repeated. "A place of sanctuary and a home to the remaining plenarie people.

The spirit dipped her head once more. "As you wish, Alton Malachite."

Leaving the baby to rest, Alton followed the felera out of the entrance chamber. If he was going to run this place, he would have to make-do with the company he had.

"I'll have to give you a name," he said.

The felera turned to smile at him. "Very well. Is that yours?"

Alton looked where she pointed. A few feet away from the arch sat the bloodstained box the infant's father had been holding. He hadn't thought much of it, possibly just a treasure the man tried to save. Picking it up, Alton had no trouble opening the beaten-up box. The object inside glowed brightly in multicolors.

Impossible, absolutely remarkable.

Alton didn't dare touch the orb bare-handed. Closing the box, he offered it to the felera. "Take this and place it in the safest chamber here at the Sacrarium."

Following his command, the felera vanished with the box. Just then, Alton heard the crying of the baby echoing down the hall. *I am not just survivor,* he thought. *Looks like I am a father as well.*

TWO

ᴀꜰᴛᴇʀ the destruction of Villhilium, the plenarie population all but vanished. As the years went by, more survivors were discovered and then never seen or heard from again. Over time most of the world learned to ignore and forget about the plenaries altogether. Nearly two decades after the last city of the plenaries was destroyed, the clocks struck three o'clock on a Friday in Newark, New Jersey.

With school out for the weekend, students hastily left the premises without a second glance. As middle-schoolers flooded out of the building, two kids lagged behind their friends. One of them shoved red-marked pages of homework into his backpack while the other walked alongside him. The results from his latest math test did nothing to help the boy's sour mood. As he walked with a glum expression, his friend kept trying to engage in conversation.

"Austin. Austin! Are you even listening?"

He barely was. "Hm?" he replied.

Today marked the third week of Austin's bad streak. One more low score on an exam, and Austin Bennet would be in for it. Detention sounded reasonable compared to the consequences of his next screw-up. A twelve-year-old with the common distaste for studies, Austin didn't consider himself an academic prodigy.

In general, he kept a low profile in school and with his classmates. This left him few people he personally called friends. He didn't mind it because he had Kate. Kate Summers, his best friend since early childhood, was turning thirteen next month but already had the persona of a mother. She helped him with schoolwork and often critiqued him in a maternal way. Coming out of his self-pity, Austin turned to her and flinched. Kate's emerald eyes narrowed and burned into his.

"Jeez, Kate! Quit burning holes into my head!" he exclaimed.

Kate had a friendly personality, but everyone knew to stay on her good side. She could be ferocious when she was pissed. Hands on her hips, she raised one of them only to start knocking on Austin's head. "Hello, McFly! Did you hear me?"

"Okay, okay. I'm listening," Austin reassured as he backed out of her reach.

Giving him one last death glare, Kate smiled and folded her arms. "So do you want me to come over and help you with that assignment or what?"

Austin shook his head. "Not tonight, I'm going to the movies with my mom. I'll see you tomorrow, okay?"

"All right. Tell her I said hi!" Kate shouldered her backpack and ran off, waving back as she went. When he noticed the battered sedan pull up, Austin threw his bag in the back seat and rode shotgun.

"So, how was school?" Denise Bennet asked him.

Austin avoided her eyes and stared out through the window. "Good. Nothing new, really."

For a while, no one talked. He glanced at his mom once and found her hands gripping the steering wheel tightly. Not a good sign. Driving up to the exit that led to the plaza where the movie theater was, Austin frowned when they missed the turn.

"Uh, Mom? We missed the turn back there."

Her voice even, Denise said, "We're not going to the movies tonight."

"What?" Austin finally turned around and looked at her.

"Your principal called me at work today."

The knots in Austin's stomach tightened. "He did?"

Now they headed home as his mom merged into a different lane. Frustration ebbed off her like steam. "Apparently a couple—no, a lot—of your teachers have expressed some concerns with your grades and homework. Why didn't you tell me you were failing Social Studies?"

"It was one paper! I already told Mrs. Hennig—"

"And you talked back to Mr. Colt in his class yesterday?" she added.

Austin tried not to explode. "Mr. Colt kept going on and on about the Excretion Act and how great the relegators are! I just asked him why the world thinks the plenaries were so bad."

His mom swerved the car as a truck cut them off. "Austin!

You know you can't talk about plenaries, especially not in school. Are you trying to get yourself arrested?"

"No. I just think they really weren't—"

"I don't want to hear it. You're never going to bring them up again, understand?"

"Yes, ma'am." Austin sighed. "Am I grounded?"

"I don't know yet, Austin," his mom huffed impatiently. "I have too much to worry about right now. Just go to your room and do your homework."

"What about the movie? You promised we could go!" he protested.

"We're not going anywhere until your grades pick up and *stay* up." Denise looked over at him. "I mean it, Austin. I've let it slide too many times. Not anymore."

"You always do this," Austin snapped at her. "You always cancel stuff at the last minute! You never have time for me!"

His mom spluttered, and blinked away angry tears. "I am trying to take care of us. Paying for the mortgage is expensive, and I have to work double shifts at the hospital just to pay for your education."

"I wish I was with Dad," Austin muttered.

Denise wiped her eyes, her chin trembled as she stared straight ahead. After she cleared her throat, she croaked, "Austin…"

Austin ignored her. His arms crossed and blue eyes stormy, he kept his back facing her. She reached out to touch him when the truck ahead of them blew a tire. It sounded as if a gunshot punched through the air as the vehicle spun out of control and crashed into them. Both cars collided, metal crunching against metal, and they tumbled across the road. By the time the ambulance and police cars sealed off the accident, fire surrounded the vehicles and both drivers were dead. In the remains of the sedan, they pulled a young boy out of the car. Unconscious, Austin's crushed body heaved as he struggled to breathe.

THREE

REUEL never expected the purple glitter.

Today's patrol had been slow, and Reuel wanted nothing more than to head back to headquarters. Before he could call it a day, someone made a call about a disturbance downtown. Probably a prank call, but Reuel needed to check it out anyway. Taking some on-duty relegators with him, he traced the call to an alley between a diner and a boutique shop. Crowds quickly parted around them, avoiding eye contact with the group as they approached the location.

Staring at the empty strip of road, the relegator shook his head, unsurprised. Reuel wanted to call it when a canister flew out of the air and bounced against his leg.

"Get down!"

BANG!

Glittery purple paint splashed everywhere as chaos shook the street. While citizens ran away from the commotion, the relegators scrambled around, their visors blinded from the blast. Reuel threw off his helmet, his black armor sparkling with paint. No casualties or injuries this time, if you didn't include Reuel's pride. Looking around, he gawked at the words painted on the wall. A giant purple flower glistened on the bricks with two words written beneath it.

We resist

A symbol of the insurgence, Reuel immediately recognized. This one belonged to an elusive plenarie who dubbed himself "The Orchid." For the last eight months, purple flowers had been painted where the rebel targeted relegators. Some attacks ended with casualties, others just victimless call signs to other resistors. Reuel's new mission was to bring this revolutionist down. When he tumbled out onto the curb, Reuel caught a glimpse of a hooded figure fleeing the scene before vanishing into the crowd.

"He's getting away! After him." he roared at his squad.

The relegators continued to slip and crash into each other, trying to get the ridiculous paint off. Cursing as he bolted down the street alone, Reuel shoved past bystanders with his target barely in sight.

There was no pain when Austin accidentally smashed his toes against the door. Straightening his wheelchair, his second attempt to pass through the doorframe succeeded.

Outside the diner where Kate worked, he wheeled himself down the sidewalk to get some fresh air. Parked on the sidewalk, Austin checked his foot while he waited to cross the road. If anything was bruised, he couldn't tell.

After the accident, he lost all feeling in his body from the waist down. According to the doctors, he would never walk again, bound to the stupid chair for the rest of his life. His damaged legs came with another loss. This September would mark the fifth year since the car crash, the same month his mom died. Their final moments together had been wasted, arguing about Austin's grades and school. And the last thing he'd said to her was that he wished he was with his dad. Guilt rotted inside Austin like cancer. The hollowness overflowed the emptiness stretching from his waist down.

He watched as his left hand trembled again. *Another irreversible injury*, he thought bitterly. Austin tried to hold it still, but the effort proved pointless. After he crossed the road, Austin was thinking about trying the comic book shop when an explosion shook his chair. A shower of purple paint doused with glitter erupted out of the alley ahead of him. People screamed and shoved past Austin, trying to escape the mayhem.

When Austin spotted the relegators, he laughed. Drenched in the stuff, the relegators bumped and tripped over each other comically. No one offered to help them; everyone feared and respected them too much. One of the relegators shouted at his associates, commanding them to find the culprit.

It's The Orchid. Austin grinned. A defector of the system, someone who fought for the plenaries in a society fearing them.

When it came to flipping it at the relegators, Austin loved The Orchid's style. Back in his room at Kate's, Austin had a wall of pictures capturing the rogue's handiwork, but he had never been so close to an actual attack before. Adrenaline boiled inside Austin as he tried to take a video. In the confusion, someone crashed past him, knocking the phone out of his hand. It cracked on impact and skidded on the concrete pavement.

When he reached down, a stranger's knee flew out of nowhere, smashing into Austin's face. He cried out, his eyes watering, swelling quickly following the pain. Gritting his teeth with one eye shut, he tried again to grab his phone, but nobody noticed him struggling to keep himself from falling out of his seat. A second before he lost the fight, someone caught him and gently pushed him back into the wheelchair.

"My phone," he groaned. "I've got to get my phone...."

His good Samaritan snatched up the device and returned it to him. Rubbing it against his jeans, Austin frowned at the cracked screen.

"You should be more careful, you're lucky all you got was a black eye."

"Yeah, I will be," Austin mumbled, returning the phone to the safety of his pocket.

The helpful stranger rolled his chair away where the crowd wouldn't hit him. Austin glanced at his helper, but his good eye couldn't focus on the girl's face. A relegator, the one who was yelling, caught her attention and she quickly slipped on Austin's jacket that he had hanging on the back of his chair and flipped the hood up. The relegator rushed past them without a second glance, and the girl relaxed with a long exhale. Her guilty behavior evaporated after she checked their surroundings, her hand clutching something in her pocket. When she slipped her hand out, Austin noticed the purple stains on her fingers.

"Take care now," she bid him farewell.

Austin blinked and she vanished. Rubbing his good eye, he turned left and right. The citizens returned to their own business, as if the attack never happened. The relegators blocked off the alley but the girl's chaser hadn't returned. When he double-checked himself, Austin realized she had stolen the jacket.

"Hey! I liked that jacket!" he yelled at no one.

The next day, Austin's routine followed the same old pattern. He got up, ate breakfast, then took a bath. Kate helped him into his chair and pushed him back to his bedroom. Even handicapped, Austin always managed to create a mess. His piles of old clothes and crumpled papers covered the floor, and his blankets were pushed to the edge of the bed with his pillows scattered around the place. Kate tidied the bed in seconds, then piled up his dirty clothes and threw them into the laundry basket. Austin always joked that she would make an excellent maid.

Kate worked fast, helping him dress nicely and forced a comb through his rowdy hair. Ignoring Austin's pained protests, Kate looked him over and gave her nod of approval. After she steered him out to the car, they drove together to the cemetery. With a promise of coming right back with a tight hand squeeze, Kate dropped him off to run a couple of errands.

Today marked the ninth of June, the birthday of the late Denise Bennet. Weeds grew around the small tombstone. While they obscured it, the name carved on the stone would always be etched into Austin's mind. Rolling his wheelchair closer, Austin tried to set a bouquet of flowers by the grave, but he dropped them clumsily. He cursed his shaking hand. Returning his attention to the stone, Austin wet his lips before he managed to speak.

"Hey, Mom." He paused for a moment. "I just wanted to wish you a happy birthday, wherever you are. What else, um, I'm done with school for the summer. My math teacher said I finished really well. I think I got Bs and some As in my other classes too." Austin blinked hard, his vision blurring in his good eye. "I know you would've been proud."

The wind rustled around him. In the past few weeks, the dreary skies with their iron-gray clouds and musty winds reflected Austin's mood. Looking at the sky, he saw even darker clouds forming. Today had been surprisingly clear, but now something in the sky intrigued Austin. Thunder boomed like a cannon as the sky grew blacker.

Crack!

Lightning accompanied the sound of teeth-rattling thunder; something about it bothered Austin. Instead of striking the ground, they seemed to bounce off each other in the air.

Crack! Crack!

"What the hell?"

As the lightning beat against itself again, it exploded in a shower of yellow and dark purple light. Austin dismissed it as fireworks until two large bolts hit the ground past the trees on his left. The lightning strike lit up the cemetery in a colorful spectacle, then the thunder silenced and the lightning storm instantly vanished.

Turning his chair around, Austin craned his head to see where the lightning had struck. A tiny voice at the back of his head warned him against checking it out, but curiosity got the better of him. He passed more tombstones to where the energy burst had struck beyond the trees. When he approached the spot, he scanned the perimeter for any seared surface, yet there was no sign of any odd lightning or impact marks.

Shaking his head, Austin was turning to leave when he suddenly flew out of his wheelchair from an explosion. Wind howled in his ears as the booming of thunder returned instantly with the crackling lightning. His ears rang and his vision blurred when he opened his good eye. For a moment, Austin thought a tornado had appeared as the trees next to him creaked and shook while the storm clouds spiraled down around the open area. As the ringing in his ears subsided, he heard an outcry from an indistinct voice mixed with the sounds of the storm. The sound was drowned out by another ear-popping blast. A burst of purple and yellow lights blinded Austin as he tried to shield himself from the danger.

After another outcry, everything around Austin went eerily quiet. He no longer felt the wind whipping around him, or the ground shaking from the freak storm. Peeking through his trembling hands, he couldn't stop shaking as he glanced around. The storm had vanished completely. Crawling back up into his chair, he took a few raspy breaths to calm down.

After steadying himself in the seat, he looked to his right and then to his left.

Austin cried out, blinded by yellow light when the force of energy collided with him, flipping him high into the air. Lightning pierced his body, tearing through every fiber. His blood boiled and burned under his skin, smoking in agony. As the strange power surged through him, his skin regrew and knitted itself back together. Austin's body glowed with yellow energy as he crashed to the ground unconscious.

FOUR

THE streets of Craiova teemed with life as the morning breeze beckoned citizens and tourists alike to walk around its landmarks and busy markets. Accustomed to the colder summers, people of different races and cultures milled around without noticing the cloaked woman slipping through the crowded streets, drawing her hood further down to conceal her face.

Stopping between a local café and a bank filled with tourists hurrying to exchange currency, Emily turned into an alley that appeared out of nowhere. The alley provided shade for the traveler who continued down the worn path. At the dead end stood a rustic door, crudely fitted to the carved stone surrounding its bent frame.

Emily knocked once on the door and it creaked open, its rusty hinges groaning in protest. Silently passing the bouncer, she was identified as a regular at the secret establishment. The deteriorating complex, otherwise known as a bar, remained hidden from the eye of the humans just outside. Only certain clientele could enter the establishment.

Sitting in the dimmest corner of the club, Emily unveiled herself, but her identity remained elusive within the darkness concealing her face. The bartender, a gruff man with a hardened face and a burly frame, wasted no energy welcoming her. By now he knew well enough that the woman under the hood hadn't come for a drink, but rather to meet an associate he feared.

The door of the bar flew open as Emily's cohort arrived. He barely fit through the door as he took heavy steps to the corner where the only other customer sat. The bartender took his cue to leave, stepping away from the grimy counter and vanishing to the back room so the visitors could work out their business without interruption. Emily chose the veiled attire to avoid recognition. Solon Blak, on the other hand, had no intentions of disguising himself.

He donned obsidian armor, wearing a charcoal and gunmetal gray-colored mask resembling a skull. The eyes behind the pits of the helmet glistened black. Just as black holes pulled anything into their endless voids, his eyes shared the same quality and were unnerving. They trained on Emily without wavering or betraying any emotion.

Displaying no sign of fear or hindrance, Emily spoke in an amused tone, "I wasn't expecting you for a few more weeks. To what do I owe the pleasure?"

The breath behind Solon's mask rattled passively as his voice pierced the air like the edge of a sharp knife. The words he spoke sounded just as frightful in his ghoulish aspect.

"Another plenarie outpost has fallen. I procured another subject for you to drain his power."

Removing the gloves she wore, Emily knitted her hands together as she set them on the table. "Did you bring him?"

With inhuman agility, the black spectrum disappeared then suddenly reappeared holding the crumpled body clad in battered armor. Dropping the body beside her, Solon gestured to it. "Drain him. All of it."

Kneeling beside the unmoving captive, Emily laid her bare hands on his temples. Orange electricity sparked from the body as it danced up her arms. She didn't flinch or cry out as the energy passed from the motionless teenager to her. When the electricity finally subsided, she stood up, sighing as the stolen energy settled inside her. Her accomplice extended his arm, his hand holding a colorless orb the size of a tangerine. She grasped it in her hand and willed the electricity to pass into the small object. Colorful static flickered around it as the orb glowed orange.

Placing it back into the hand of its owner, she returned to the table pulling on the gloves she'd removed for the process. "Another part for the machine?"

Solon examined the orb in his hand as he replied, "One of the few left to acquire. Until my pawns come into play, you must remain discrete."

Emily bowed her head. "Sure, but what about the Template View?"

"That is no concern of yours, my dear," he growled.

"You still don't know how to get it, do you?"

Solon pocketed the orb as he chuckled. "Patience. I will

be in touch."

In a whirl of black smoke, the phantom vanished with the body of the plenarie. The bartender shuffled up once the discomforting figure had left. "Mr. Amari is here to see you, ma'am."

Lifting her hood back up, Emily waited for the bartender to bring the man in. Shorter than the last visitor, he wore fine clothing hanging loosely on his skeletal frame. He had damaged facial features with disheveled, salt-and-pepper hair. Sitting across from her, he vigorously wiped the table's grimy surface with a handkerchief before resting his hands on it.

"You look tired," she pointed out.

Folding his hands together, Amari shrugged. "My last errand was a little taxing. Hardly any time to rest, let alone to bottle more of this."

"How much do you have?"

Pulling a vial from his pocket, he rolled it across the table. "A month's dose. Take it sparingly if you can."

Plucking it gingerly off the table, Emily tucked it into her gown as she tossed him a small bag. Amari caught it between his spider-like fingers. He shook it, making the contents jingle inside. Satisfied, he slipped it away as well, the trade now complete. "You'll be off, then?"

Rising, Emily replied, "Yep. You'll be heading back to America?"

"Of course. Business is booming after what happened in June."

He lingered to order a drink as his buyer exited the bar into the street. Emily blended back into the crowd as she walked down the road. A second later, she disappeared completely, leaving a flicker of red where she once stood.

The months of June and July came and went as the first week of August dawned. In the late morning, Austin snored in deep sleep, drooling on his pillow. After what happened to him in June, he'd dismissed it as a hallucination or a crazy dream. Kate had found him by his wheelchair, alone and unharmed, without any sign of the storm or anything Austin had seen that day. Kate told him he must have fallen out of his chair and probably hit his head. That's the story he repeated to himself whenever he thought about it.

Overnight, he had been dreaming of flashes of light and blurred images that made no sense. Instead of the sound of birds or the neighbor's lawnmower waking him up, Austin snorted awake to the smell of something burning. He opened his eyes just as he landed on the floor with a hard thump.

"Ouch!"

Austin tried to sit up, but his head cracked painfully against something wooden. Blinking the sand and stars out of his eyes, he recognized the baseboards under his mattress. *How did I get under here?* he thought. Pulling himself out from under the bed while swearing silently, he stood up, rubbing the bruised part of his forehead. He ached all over and his feet twitched with pins and needles. Wiggling his toes, he yawned and stretched his arms, and then he stopped and did a double take.

"What the—"

He moved his feet! After he pinched himself multiple times, Austin took a wobbly step and fell flat on his face. Gingerly pushing himself up, he took a brave breath and stood back up. A little shaky at first, his legs didn't just move, he actually *felt* them! The hairs on his legs bristled and tingled when he touched them. They might have been a little stiff, but Austin balanced on his feet without support. Before he started jumping around, his nose wrinkled. The stench of smoke filled the air. That's when he noticed the bed was on fire.

"Holy crap!"

In the middle of his bed—right where he slept—a smoking scorch mark the size of his body continued to burn. Hastily stripping the sheets off the mattress, he stomped on the flame-damaged linen until the fire died out. Discarding the remains of his top sheet, Austin inspected the bed for any other pyro damage. Nothing else showed any sign of being charred or blackened. Checking himself, he sighed in relief, seeing his pajamas hadn't burned off. That would have been humiliating. Austin yelped when someone pounded a fist on the other side of the door.

"Austin? You awake? *Hello?* Can I come in?" Kate's voice rang.

Austin quickly kicked the sheets under his bed; that problem could wait. Right now, he needed to wrap his head around the fact he could actually flex his legs. Kate's persistent knocking suddenly shook him out of his reverie as he panicked. *What will Kate make of this?* Just as she barged in, Austin flopped back onto the bed. She wore her waitress's apron with her shiny black hair tied back in a ponytail. Kate wrinkled her nose and frowned. "Are you burning something in here?"

"No, I think the neighbors are grilling again," he lied, staring at the ceiling.

Whether she bought it or not, he couldn't tell. Kate walked over to the window and swung it open. Without warning, it crashed back down just as she pulled her hands back. Another hazard in the house Austin and the Summers lived in. The floorboards creaked and the shingles rattled on windy nights. The old house also came with windows perfect for guillotining. Shoving it back up repeatedly until it stayed open, Kate stepped back, letting the fresh air and sunlight seep through. Carefully stepping over the contents of Austin's messy room, she opened the closet and threw him a pair of jeans and the cleanest shirt she could find. Kate pushed his chair beside the bed after helping him change.

Austin shook his head at the chair. "I think I'm going to stay home today."

"No one's going to be here, you sure you'll be all right?"

Austin's lips twitched. "I'll be more than fine."

"Okay, then." Kate made sure his phone had a full charge before leaving for her job.

Kate liked to pull her own weight when it came to money, so she took a part-time job to save up for next year's college classes. On Fridays and Sundays, she worked at Pappi's Diner where Austin usually got a late lunch. While he waited for her shift to be over, he would either read or catch up on his homework. But not today. Austin had a more interesting day ahead of him.

Alone again, he gently slid off the bed and examined his

legs. Scrawny to say the least, his legs' muscles had shrunk since the accident. Now when he checked them, they looked stronger and sturdier. Padding through the house, Austin itched to go out and walk around the city. He threw on a hoodie and flipped the hood up. If anyone he knew caught him, they'd be in for a shocking surprise. *Better not freak anyone out just yet,* he cautioned himself. After he pushed his feet into his less-worn sneakers, Austin steeled himself with a big inhale and walked out the front door for the first time in five years.

After spending most of the afternoon working his legs into overdrive, Austin's feet ached walking home. Kate would be done with work soon, and Austin had to get home before she did. If any of the Summers found the house empty, Austin would be in for it, legs magically healed or not. He was debating whether to run or jog home when the street exploded.

BOOM!

Falling onto the concrete, blood dripped from his chin. Across the road, one of the smaller apartment buildings bled black smoke. Fire roared from its shattered windows while people screamed and fled from the destruction. In the chaos, there were no signs of any firetrucks or relegators. While citizens barreled out the door of the burning building, the fire expanded. On the third floor, Austin spotted people, trapped and hanging out the windows, crying out for help.

Surely someone would save them, right? But the longer Austin waited, the more he realized no one would make it in time. Austin bolted to the building. No one stopped him from running into the flaming apartment as he flew into the danger. Coughing as smoke irritated his throat, Austin covered his head with his arms and leapt up the stairs three at a time. Only one family remained on the third floor. The apartment door crashed with a crunch after Austin kicked it down.

"Gah!" His ankle throbbed painfully. Austin had to be careful, he was pushing his legs beyond their limits. Huddled together by the bathroom, a wall of fire trapped two parents and a single child behind it. "Hang on!" Austin shouted over the hissing flames.

The room shook and cracked while Austin struggled to breathe. He tried to find something in the room to help the family, but the fire scorched everything. Just as Austin saw a chance to leap through the fire, another blast threw him backward. Groaning as he stirred, Austin screamed as a giant plank of wood came crashing on top of him.

The collision never came.

Squinting through one of his eyes, it looked as if the world paused like in a movie, frozen in place, unmoving and silent. The plank hovered in the air, only a few inches away, not moving at all. The fire in the room no longer spread. Everything around him was transfixed, but Austin could still move. A faint yellow blur shimmered from his body as he scrambled up. Austin's limbs moved slower as if he were treading water.

Then some instinct inside him snapped into action.

He ran to the family, frozen in a mannequin-like way, their eyes wide in fear. One by one, he zoomed the parents out of the apartment and onto the safer street. Time slowly sped back up. Every step he took drained him more, the pain in his leg spreading like the flickering fire. Wheezing and choking, Austin blinked smoke and debris out of his watering eyes. By the time he reached the child, the hallway floor leading back to the stairs crumbled.

Austin scooped up the child, frantically glancing around for some other way to escape. The flames burned brighter and faster than before. Within a few seconds, the whole building would collapse. Blood pounded in Austin's body, his heart hammering and cramping without air. A high-pitched whining noise screamed in Austin's ears.

I think I'm out of time.

Running with everything he had and shielding the child in his arms, Austin smashed through the living room window as the room behind him exploded. Falling from three stories, Austin crashed onto the roof of a parked car. After the quick impact, he rolled off the vehicle and sprawled onto the road. He watched sparks and ash rain down around the area as he gulped fresh air.

The child had no injuries, but Austin's body shook from the pain. His legs twitched in spasms, like knives digging into his wrists and heart as well. His shoulder was probably shattered. The parents of the little girl swooped down and snatched up their child, crying and babbling without any regard to Austin. Sirens wailed in the air. *Great,* now *they come,* Austin grumbled. When the firetrucks and relegator vehicles arrived, all the residents of the destroyed apartments swarmed them.

Everyone had their own story to tell of the accident,

most of the crowd lining up for the ambulances for medical attention. No one had serious injuries, the only person who needed it the most limped away into an alley. His hood still up and his clothes caked with soot, Austin leaned against the wall trying to move in haste. Not entirely sure why he snuck away, he followed the voice in his head telling him to run.

FIVE

DROPLETS of rain sprinkled from the sky as the storm died
out. A group of rain-washed relegators shook themselves off
as they entered the Alliance Tower, a giant skyscraper serving
as the headquarters for the relegators in New Jersey. With
their daily task of parading through the city as protectors
completed, they shed the hero façade away from the public.
Down in the private barracks, they unmasked themselves and
changed into casual clothes—all except one. Reuel remained
in his resplendent black armor, his unamused expression
hidden behind a reflective visor.

One of the other relegators, a girl named Beverly, exhaled
with a relaxed smile after removing her helmet. "Ugh, finally.
I want to know who the idiot is that designed our armor. I
can barely see out of it. The stupid bucket is tighter than my
choker."

"It's not the helmet's fault you have a big head, Beverly.
Just trade it for one of the men's larger sizes," Dustin, another

relegator, cracked at her.

Beverly complemented Dustin's suggestion by chucking her helmet at him. Reuel slipped out of the room before the fighting began; he never involved himself in his peers' daily drama. After turning a few corners to make sure no one followed him, Reuel finally made it to the elevator taking him to Floor 14. The only sound came from the echoing of his footsteps on the vacant level. Closed off for construction, the space was the meeting place for Reuel and his superior.

Reuel sensed the other man's presence before he materialized behind him. With his face enveloped in black metal, Solon Blak's eyes glistened in the dark. Reuel knew little about the relegator. Solon came and went as he pleased, and no one ever mentioned him around the Tower. All Reuel needed to know about the relegator was that he was powerful and capable of anything.

When he walked beside him, Reuel folded his hands behind his back and moved with a stiff spine and raised chin. After the silence stretched long enough, Solon halted, standing before a closed-off section of exposed wall. The unfinished window displayed the city in a framed picture at night. *An admirable view*, Reuel thought to himself, but he sensed Solon stared beyond the cluster of buildings and streets.

"We are on schedule as planned, the machine only needs a little more time," he informed Solon.

Solon barely nodded. He conjured a tech-pad out of thin air and passed it to Reuel without looking. The screen displayed screenshots of footage taken from a security camera. Swiping through the photos, Reuel's forehead creased. "I heard about the apartment fire on my way back from patrol. By the time one of our squads arrived, the whole building was in ashes."

"Take a closer look at the third picture."

Reuel obeyed. The screenshot caught the third floor exploding just before the whole thing crumbled. Eyes narrowed, he zoomed in on the picture. The image was poor quality, but he could just make out the silhouette of a person jumping from the wave of fire and rubble. Checking the other photographs, the same figure was captured entering the building and leaving the scene holding victims. "No glint or sign of armor," Reuel pointed out. "Not likely to be a relegator."

"Perhaps," Solon mused. He continued to stare out at the view.

Reuel shuffled his weight from foot to foot. Examining the images again, he finally asked, "You think it might be one of the plenaries?"

"We are going to find out." Solon turned around, he looked down at Reuel with his unsettling stare.

"I could send someone to investigate," Reuel suggested, "but I'm so close—"

"The Orchid has wasted your time long enough," Solon cut through. "I want you to focus your resources on this."

Reuel's jaw tightened. The Orchid outsmarted him week after week, but he'd been patient and bided his time. So close to success, only to be diverted to a new assignment. "As you wish," he ground out.

"I know I am not the only one who has taken notice of our mysterious hero. If we find him, then he will lead us to other hidden plenaries, including The Orchid." Solon walked to the elevator. Following him, Reuel said nothing as he continued. "Keep your eyes and ears alert. Find this person and learn everything there is to know about him. Report to me when you have discovered something."

"Where will I find you?"

Solon's next words unsettled him. "*I* will find *you*."

Solon Blak melted back into the shadows. Alone again, Reuel checked the tech-pad's pictures. After sending the images to his own device, he jammed his thumb against the down arrow on the panel. With a single ding, the doors opened and he slid through. Reuel would not fail this time. Determined to find this person, he would bring him down along with all the plenaries he could find, especially The Orchid.

Austin could barely stand when he made it back to the house. Stumbling past the front door, he limped through the living room into the kitchen. He found an ice pack in the freezer and moaned after pushing it against his bad shoulder. After he pulled his hood down, Austin wiped his face and puffed out a pained breath.

Smash!

Austin flinched at the sound of shattering glass. Behind him in the doorway, Kate's jaw dropped and her mug's pieces scattered on the floor. With a cringe, Austin looked down at himself. His clothes had soot and dirt stains everywhere— and he could walk. Her mouth opening and closing, Kate pointed a shaking finger at him. "A-Austin? Are you… are you *walking?*"

Austin could've lied or told the truth. Instead, his eyes rolled back and he crumpled to the kitchen tile. When he came around in the middle of the night, he found himself in bed, clean and patched up. Kate flew through the door and pushed him back down when he tried to get up.

"*Shhh,*" she hissed. "Don't wake my mom up! She can't see you like this."

"Kate! You'll never believe what happened," Austin babbled.

Kate quickly shoved her hand against his mouth and whispered, "*I said be quiet!* Are you trying to get in trouble? What's going on, Austin? I just saw you limp in covered in dirt and ash! How are you walking, and where on earth did you go?"

Pulling her hand away, Austin spoke to her quietly. "Look, Kate, I'm just as confused as you are. I just woke up this morning and bam! I could move my legs."

"So why did you look like you just climbed out of a chimney?"

"I was heading home, but then I saw this building on fire…"

"Austin," Kate smacked her forehead, "tell me you didn't—"

"Something happened to me, Kate," Austin examined the back of his hands. "Everything just slowed down. And I could still move, but like, fast. Really fast. I just ran in there, it was like an odd impulse or something." He looked up at Kate and smiled. "I saved them, the people trapped inside. No help, no relegators. Nobody died. Do you think—"

"No, Austin." Kate shook her head stubbornly. She got up and raked her fingers through her tangled hair. "This can't happen. What if the relegators find out about this? If they even suspect you are *something*, they'll take you in. You might never be seen again! Or worse—"

Grabbing Kate's wrists, Austin calmed her. "No one's going to take me in. I promise I won't let anyone find out it was me. If we don't tell—"

"Austin, your hands!" Kate yelped, jumping off the bed.

He had to bite his tongue so he didn't scream out loud. Austin's hands shook, but not the way they usually did. They shook and vibrated uncontrollably.

"Stop it. *Stop it!*" Austin willed.

He managed to calm his right hand, but his left hand continued to vibrate like a smart phone on steroids. It blurred when it moved and he could almost see through it. Eventually, his left hand subsided its crazy spasms. Both hands now sat still, but he could sense the energy teeming through as he opened and closed them. Kate had her back pressed against the wall as far away from him as possible. Her sheet-white face exploded with shock and fear. "What was that?"

It reminded him of what had happened to him inside that building. Austin's hands had been moving the way he guessed his whole body had when everything slowed down. "It's like what happened before, but this was just my hands. Last time was… well, something crazier."

He thought about that night in June with the strange lights.

Whatever that light had been, it affected him in some way. That had to have been it. Austin reminded Kate about that night and told her about this morning's episode with the burning sheets.

His best friend said nothing for a moment. Finally, she asked him, "Is there anything else you can do? Can you control it?"

Flexing his fingers, Austin looked up at his friend. "Let's find out."

SIX

HIS name was Austin Bennet.

Reuel identified the mysterious figure on the third morning of his new assignment. After countless hours of creating search algorithms and pulling some strings, he discovered a secondary feed of video of the street with a clearer image. Using his own access code to search in the Alliance Tower's database, the search brought up tags and files matching the new camera photo.

Twenty suspects narrowed down to twelve. Twelve shrank to five. And then, only one profile remained on Reuel's screen. A seventeen-year-old named Austin Bennet stared back at him as he examined the file. An ordinary-looking teen with chin-length, straw-colored hair and electric-blue eyes, the boy had been labeled wheelchair-bound. According to the database, Austin survived a car accident years ago, losing his mother and his ability to walk.

That part made Reuel frown. The pictures matched up, but

the person leaping from the fire wasn't paralyzed. So Reuel continued to search. Bennet now lived with another family, according to the file. The Summers had one daughter, a girl name Kathleen, who was just a little older than Austin. He tagged their address, but before paying them a visit, he needed to update Solon on his progress.

No. I *will find* you.

Solon's words always left an unsettling twinge inside Reuel. Solon hadn't found Reuel yet, and the relegator had no desire to be caught off guard again. Heading to the familiar meet-up on Floor 14, Reuel prodded his tech-pad with brisk fingers as he continued to learn more about Austin Bennet.

"Ready?" Austin called out.

"Ready!" Kate squeaked with nervous excitement.

Austin stood in the middle of the street behind their house while Kate retreated behind her safety wall of garbage cans. With Kate's parents out working most of the day, they could run their experiments without either parent noticing their strange behavior. On their third day of testing, Austin already showed progress. Breathing deeply, he urged his hands to vibrate. When they vibrated, which was the easy part, he tried to move the rest of his body. With a startling crack, he lurched forward a few hundred feet in a matter of seconds.

"Whoa!"

Doing it again, this time Austin flew forward even further. With the faintest idea of what this meant, he ran with all his might and shot down the alley like a bullet. Looking down at his feet, he saw two blurs kicking at an alarming rate.

"Woo-hoo!" he yelled. Besides being fast, in this state his brain processed information faster than he could blink. The effects only lasted when he ran, unfortunately. He didn't need to worry about obstacles. As he moved, anything that flew by him froze in a sluggish state of motion, allowing him to avoid collisions. Whipping around and skidding to a stop in front of Kate, Austin grinned.

Cautiously approaching him, Kate clapped her hands together and squealed, bouncing on the balls of her feet excitedly. "Ohmygoshohmygoshohmygosh! This is *totally* unreal. I'm freaking out right now!"

Going back inside, they locked themselves in Kate's room, continuing their ongoing discussion of theories. While she paced the room back and forth, Kate bit her lip as she did whenever she concentrated. "But how does that even work? I mean, scientifically speaking, this is impossible. You could burn up, your brain might go into shock, or the whiplash could break your neck."

"Except it hasn't…" Austin scratched his chest and cried out. *"OW!"*

"What?" Kate jolted at his outburst. "What's wrong?"

The skin on Austin's chest burned. He fell to the floor, writhing and screaming, as his body smoked and glowed. Kate tried to help but tumbled backward as he thrashed around. Energy tore through him. It burned itself inside Austin's veins, overloading his nerves with spikes of pain. And then, suddenly, the attack subsided. The pain faded while his body gradually ceased burning and shining.

Austin carefully sat up, moaning as he pulled his shirt up to look for any injury. Right over his heart, a strange scar spread out like tree roots. The raw-red skin around it stung his bare flesh. It resembled arcs of lightning spreading out. The cuts themselves still flared, glowing as if sunlight had been trapped beneath the stretching cracks on his body.

"Austin, your body! What's happening to you?" Kate asked.

"I don't know. It hurts, Kate. What do I do? I can't let your mom see this."

Once the pain ebbed away, the marks on his skin cleared and resembled veins across his chest. The only explanation Austin could think of came from the recent use of his powers.

"Wait, if I keep using my powers, will I get more of these scars?"

Kate shook her head in uncertainty. "Well, that sucks."

"We'd better hope it doesn't get any worse." Austin pulled his shirt back down, wincing. "I think I'm going to go back to the cemetery. See if I can find any clue to what's going on."

Kate dropped the foreboding face and perked up in an instant. "Can I come?"

Before they left, Kate insisted Austin put on a disguise. He didn't see the sunglasses and dark hoodie as inconspicuous, but it reassured Kate enough. It didn't take long to get to the cemetery. Within five minutes, he and Kate stood where he had clashed with the mysterious light energy. As before, the ground still showed no sign or mark from lightning.

After searching for over an hour, Kate stretched and dusted her jeans off. "Well, maybe it's been too long, or maybe things like this leave no mark?"

Austin had just given up when his eyes caught a reflection. For a moment, he glimpsed a figure in shiny armor some distance away. "Kate!"

"What is it? Find something?"

Austin pointed to where the man stood, but as he did, the figure appeared a little closer. Turning to Kate, he could see her eyes focused on the spot where he stood. "That's got to be a relegator, right?"

Kate nodded timidly. Now he appeared even closer. Besides the irregular attire, the man seemed to teleport from one spot to another. A flicker of bright purple light sprouted from where he last stood. Unusual, even for a relegator. An unsettling knot in Austin's stomach warned him against letting him come any closer. "Kate, I think we sh—"

Too late. The figure stood before them in an instant. Up close, Austin noticed that the man wore silver knight armor. *Weird*, Austin thought. Relegators all wore identical black armor, so the only explanation must be that this man was either something new or…

A plenarie.

Austin gasped. He had never seen armor as unique as this. It had a blended combination of past, present, and futuristic designs integrated into interlocking pieces with glowing purple light shining between the grooves of the man's suit. The stranger barely reached Austin's chin, but he still intimidated him with his fierce stance.

"Identify yourself. Which one of you has a pendant?" he asked.

The voice had an interesting combination of pitch and modulation. It reminded Austin of the unsettling and commanding voice of Darth Vader from *Star Wars*.

When neither Kate nor Austin replied, he shrugged. "Whatever, I'll wing it."

And with that, he vanished in an instant. With a crack and a pulse of light he disappeared with Kate.

"Kate!" Austin sped after the teleporter and his best friend. The teleporter moved fast. Faster than Austin maybe, but he pushed himself as he ran after Kate and her captor. Soon he could see a faint trail of magenta bolts of lightning sprouting where the teleporter appeared. Once Austin caught up to him, he couldn't help but marvel as the purple lightning and electricity flew off the teleporter's armor when he popped from one spot to another.

Austin couldn't see the man's face, but he could imagine his surprised expression at Austin running beside him. Both immediately stopped running, skidding to a stop in the middle of a street. Across from one another, they sized each other up. Kate pushed herself away from the plenarie, running to Austin and throwing herself into his arms. "Austin! What on earth is going one? Who is this guy? Why—"

"Dang it, I was so sure he was the human," the teleporter sighed.

Shielding Kate behind him, Austin spoke to the stranger. "Look, man, I don't know what's going on, but I don't want any trouble."

"Maybe not," the mysterious man chuckled as he shrugged, "but I'm here to take you in, willingly or not."

Austin posed in a fighting stance. "Guess you'll have to make me."

Again, the stranger laughed. Cracking his neck, he said, "I was hoping you were gonna say that."

SEVEN

AUSTIN made the first move by throwing a punch at the teleporter's face. Arms folded, he merely sidestepped while Austin stumbled past him. Making a quick recovery, he tackled the teleporter, throwing his shoulder into his chest. Austin might as well have tried to football-tackle a fire hydrant. Groaning, he caught the stranger swearing under his breath. When he got back on his feet, he adjusted his stance. Austin threw a left hook, but the teleporter blocked it with ease. "Dude, you can't beat me. I'm only—"

Crunch!

Austin swung his knee and bashed him in the stomach. He buckled, but the teleporter did not cry out. Dashing away, Austin zigzagged down streets and corners with his chaser in hot pursuit. As Austin ran, a flash of purple sparked next to him. The teleporter vanished and reappeared by his side, chasing him.

"Gonna play dirty, then? Fine!"

He slammed into Austin, throwing both of them off their feet. After the tussle, the teleporter had Austin pinned, pressing his arms down with his chrome gauntlets. Austin tried to struggle, but his attacker's grip wouldn't break. His leg jerked to kick him, but his attacker moved to push it down.

Exactly as Austin had anticipated.

With his free hand, Austin nailed him in the chin, throwing him off. The man hissed with a pained grunt and fell off. Jumping to his feet, Austin braced to run, but the teleporter yanked his legs off the ground, causing him to fall on his face. His cheek scraped against the pavement, blood trickling down his face as it smeared around his jaw. He dragged his aching body back up and faced the stranger. Legs a little wobbly, Austin shoved the pain down and clenched his fists. Across from him, the teleporter rubbed the spot Austin had punched and recomposed himself.

He spoke in an unimpressed tone. "Eh, not bad—but there's room for improvement."

"Well," Austin spat through gritted teeth, "try to keep up, Tin Man!" With adrenaline and seething rage fueling him, he zoomed in the opposite direction, trying to draw the teleporter away from Kate so he could lose him and get back to her. Looking back, Austin couldn't see any sign of the him. "Ha! Not fast enough, you—"

CRASH!

The teleporter tackled him from the right, knocking him off his feet. Austin bounced, flipped, and tumbled until he came to a rough stop with a bone-crunching crack. The pain shocked him so much he couldn't breathe. Finally, Austin let out a ragged gasp. "Ouch."

His body ached all over and he could taste blood in his mouth. Besides his legs, his left wrist hurt him the most, sprained or maybe even broken. Austin tried to sit up but immediately regretted it. He'd bruised some ribs as well. Austin spat blood out of his mouth as he watched the teleporter approach. The man squatted beside Austin and tilted his head. Picking him up forcibly, he vanished from the street, carrying Austin with him. Fuzzy images flew by him as Austin tried to squint to clear his vision. They came in and out of darkness as the man transported them through the air to an unknown destination.

The teleporting plenarie came to a quick stop and laid Austin against the wall of an abandoned alley. He backed up from Austin and touched an oval pendant on his chest, which illuminated a bright purple. After a minute, the plenarie dropped his hand to his side and faced the opening of the alley leading out into the street. In a sudden flash of blue light, another figure dressed in knight-like armor stood beside him and his captor.

Another plenarie?

Taller and a little slimmer than the first, Austin noticed more differences between the two plenaries' armor. His attacker wore a silver-colored suit of armor with purple light glowing between the plates. The center of the chest plate displayed an oval pendant with a silver P on top of the shining purple surface. This second stranger wore the same chrome armor, but bright blue light glowed in the design. Light ran throughout the kinks of the suit with a matching blue emblem that illuminated around the letter.

"Where's Braylin?" asked the shorter plenarie in his enigmatic voice.

The second plenarie replied in a similar, deeply adjusted tone. "We were together when we got your signal…"

In another illumination of blinding light—this time white—a third plenarie arrived. Braylin towered over his friends with intimidating height and muscular stature. Instead of blue or purple light, white-gray energy shone through his armor's cracks. His voice sounded modulated as well, but his tone had the deepest pitch out of the three. "Sorry, I got teleported to the wrong alley. Did you—oh!" Braylin took notice of Austin. He approached the second plenarie as he spoke. "So it's him, then? We need to take him somewhere safe before the relegators catch up with us."

His friend agreed. "We need to be sure. Orchid, see if he has a pendant."

Austin's eyes bulged. *Orchid? As in* The *Orchid?*

The first and shortest of the plenaries knelt beside Austin and patted him down. He pulled out Austin's phone and wallet. To Austin's disappointment, his phone was snapped in two. After checking the items, Orchid returned them. Then he saw the light coming from under Austin's shirt and pulled it up to take a closer look. The lightning-shaped scars appeared the same if a little longer. They shimmered and pulsed a little as the plenarie touched it. The Orchid looked up at Austin, his voice sounding startled. "Whoa! I wasn't expecting that."

Braylin inspected it too. "We can check it more at the Sacrarium. Take him."

The Orchid threw one of Austin's arms over his shoulder while the blue plenarie did the same. Stepping out in front of them, Braylin pulled off his chest plate's oval emblem. Austin watched as the plenarie's armor glowed and faded away. Once it vanished completely, Braylin pulled the rim of it outward. Its silver rim suddenly expanded with a click. He placed it on the ground and stepped back. A round window of misty white light created by the oval piece opened on the ground in front of them.

Holding him tight, the two plenaries jumped into the cosmic hole with Austin. Surrounded by the blinding light, Austin wondered how much more of the glow his retinas could take. The three landed up a solid surface with the white light evaporating instantly after. When everything came back into focus, Austin turned over and gagged out his breakfast, then lay back down on the frigid floor.

Austin's environment changed from a street to a small and sparse room with an old-looking archway in the center. As he looked up, the three plenaries gazed down at him with who-knows-what expressions on their helmet-hidden faces. Two of them helped him up while the third brought a chair alongside him.

"*Sit.*"

Easing himself into it, Austin spoke to the plenarie named Braylin, the one he assumed to be the leader. "I don't appreciate the manhandling. Where am I?"

Braylin plucked his oval trinket off the ground and pocketed it. He spoke in a kindly, authoritative voice. "Sorry for the confusion, mate. My name's Braylin. Braylin Grey."

Braylin had a chiseled jawline with golden-tan skin. His tousled brown hair was slicked back with sweat and his face smeared with grime. Behind his ears, Austin noticed a glimmer of silver catching the light. Without armor, Braylin wore dark trousers and a white shirt.

The other tall plenarie shook his head. "Enough with the introductions, Braylin. Let's just get to the bottom of it already."

Braylin frowned as he looked at his friend. "How about we wash up, have something to eat, and then do the questioning? I need to get some food in me after our little scavenger hunt. And you can take off your helmet, Aviana. There's no point in intimidating him. We need to show hospitality."

The plenarie with the blue markings removed his helmet. No, not *his* helmet—*her* helmet. Austin raised his eyebrows in surprise, then his jaw dropped. Pretty didn't cut it; Aviana radiated beauty and poise. A Wonder Woman with ebony, waist-length hair that complemented her darker skin tone. Drop-dead gorgeous, no makeup required.

"Get him cleaned up. He won't sit at my table looking like roadkill." Aviana walked past, muttering something about formal and orders. Braylin's steel-gray eyes followed Aviana until she moved out of sight. He stood back and sized Austin up. "I bet he'd fit in some of Wade's old clothes. Check his injuries and then show him to the showers. I'll meet you there with a fresh pair of garments."

The Orchid nodded and faced Austin. The atmosphere between them thickened with an awkward silence. Orchid still wore his helmet so his voice sounded unnaturally pitched.

"May I?" he gestured.

Austin held his injured hand back. The Orchid made an impatient tutting noise. "Look, man, I was only trying to bring you here. Things just got… out of hand back there."

Austin still wouldn't let him see his hand. The plenarie changed tactics and spoke in a calmer, friendlier tone. "Please? I'm trying to help."

Skeptical, Austin let The Orchid look at his left hand. He worked gently as he pressed and inspected the bruised part of Austin's wrist. "You got a name?"

"Aust—GAH!"

The Orchid squeezed his wrist with a small crack.

"Sorry, I had to apply some pressure to the bones in your wrist. Can you repeat that? I'm guessing your name isn't really Austgah."

Austin carefully flexed his wrist. "Ow. Austin. And you're The Orchid, aren't you?"

The Orchid's helmet shone for a moment before opening and disappearing just as Braylin's had. Austin had guessed wrong again. The Orchid had been a girl this whole time? He'd been so sure that "she" had been a "he." Wait a minute, the girl! Austin forgot about her. The one who'd saved his phone and stolen his jacket.

"You can call me Maisie." She smiled.

Without the helmet, Maisie's voice came out higher and sounded sweeter than before. She had a delicate, freckled face with a button nose. On her cheek, she wore a band-aid with skulls and crossbones. Unlike her friends, Maisie's wavy hair glimmered a light, reddish-blond. Strawberry blonde, that's what Kate would've called it.

"Sorry about the roughhousing," Maisie apologized. "I did my best to pull my punches—ish. I'm not sure who raised you, but kneeing someone—especially a girl—isn't really good manners."

"Sorry." Austin winced a little as she checked his ribs. "I just thought—the armor—I mean… I didn't know you were a girl," he finished lamely.

Maisie prodded a rib as she snorted. "Is it that hard to tell? There goes my feminine identity."

What little color he had left drained from Austin's face. "I didn't mean—"

"I'm messing with you." Maisie smirked as she clapped his shoulder.

"Ouch!"

"Sorry!" she grimaced. "Just being facetious."

While she attended him, a medical kit popped out of thin air. Once she'd patched him up, she stood back to admire her handiwork. "Okay, you're good to go! Now, if you turn around, you'll go down a hallway and take the second door to your left where Braylin will be waiting. I'll see you later!"

When he got to his feet, the pain faded from his wrist as he moved it. Turning around, Austin made his way to the hallway. He looked back one more time to find his hero The Orchid smiling and encouraging him to go on. Dozens of questions he wanted to ask her swarmed his mind. He pushed the thoughts aside and walked down the hall, taking the second door on his left. Bright lights illuminated the room as he entered. In the middle of the room, the shower resembled a narrow pillar with a curtain wrapped around it. Austin didn't expect the floor to be soft grass as he trod on it. Parting the curtain, he heard Braylin's steps behind him. He nodded his thanks after he took the fresh pair of clothes.

"You'll feel much better after a shower," Braylin assured. He stepped out of the room as he spoke, "We'll be eating soon. When you are finished, just leave your old clothes outside the shower for the felera to take away for washing. The kitchen is the door on your immediate right when you come out."

The door closed with a silent thud, leaving Austin speechless in the nature spa. *Felera? What on earth is a felera?*

EIGHT

ONCE he dried off and dressed himself, Austin left his old clothes where Braylin had requested. After changing he stepped out and entered the room on his immediate right and gasped. "You've got to be kidding me!"

Austin thought he'd stepped back in time. The room dwarfed the Summers' kitchen with its enormous size. Coming from the guy whose best friend obsessed over the houses on HGTV, this place dominated the competition. The gourmet kitchen rested on top of a marble patio, overlooking a garden littered with Grecian statues, pillars, and ponds. Near the edge of the patio, a long and low, beautifully carved stone table stood with six turquoise cushions surrounding it. Past that, white, reflective marble met bright green grass dominating most of the room's floor, giving the space an earthy look.

A large pond sat in the center of the garden with four silver lampposts shining brightly in the four corners of the room. Giant oak trees bunched together also outlined the room and surrounded parts of the pond. The ceiling arched outward in a dome inlaid with stained glass in various colors. Light shone through the glass, giving the pond and anything reflective a dazzling shower of colors.

"*Ahem.*"

Austin jumped when he realized someone watched him. The elaborate room still dumbfounded him, but now his attention magnetized to the girl standing behind him. No longer in armor, Aviana wore a short-cut silk dress that complemented her willowy figure. The dress's baby-blue color matched the ribbon tying her hair back in a long braid. Without her hair covering it, Austin noticed Aviana had a white spot around her left eye. More of these spots scattered across her bare skin. *Some kind of skin condition,* he thought.

He admired how Aviana didn't try to hide them. She wore oven mitts while holding a large pot filled to the brim with steaming contents. After he quickly glanced away, Aviana walked past him and set it down in the center of the table. The girl ignored Austin while she set the table and brought in more dishes for the meal.

"All washed up, are we?" greeted Braylin.

He gestured for Austin to sit beside him by the end of the table. Austin copied Braylin who sat up straight with his leg crossed over the other, waiting attentively. Braylin had changed his shirt for a clean, collared button-down. He'd washed the grime off as well, making him as clean as the room they were seated in. Braylin made a gesture in the air as a customer would when calling for the check.

Austin's eyes grew round in surprise as a floating pitcher

of water materialized in the air. He almost asked how it floated when he discovered its cause. The see-through shape of a woman held the pitcher, her features blurring while she moved. She came in and out of focus due to the shimmering light of the room and her transparency. The figure filled Braylin's outstretched glass with water before vanishing again. Taking notice of Austin's wide-eyed confusion, he explained, "Felera."

"That's felera?" Austin asked.

"*A felera,*" corrected Braylin. "There are dozens of them here at the Sacrarium."

Austin nodded numbly. "And what are felera exactly?"

"She-spirits, servants, the housekeepers of this place, or whatever you want to call them."

"Ooo, pasta!" called out a familiar voice.

Maisie's choice of clothing surprised Austin more than her sudden appearance. While Braylin and Aviana dressed formally, Maisie went to extra lengths to stand out from her peers. She wore a long-sleeved, black crop top with the words *Flawless* written on the front in bold, white letters. Her gray leggings were torn at the knees, and after their earlier tussle, he assumed it was from rough wear.

Taking a seat across from Austin, Maisie pulled a large bowl toward her and eagerly served herself. Behind Austin, Aviana returned with the sound of a disapproving sniff. She sat furthest away from him at the far end of the table.

Taking initiative, Braylin broke the silence. "I think we got off on the wrong foot. Why don't we start over with introductions?"

Maisie wiped her mouth with her sleeve and waved to everyone. "Hi, my name is Maisie Orchid, I'm sixteen years old, and it has been three weeks since I last—"

"Just names, Maisie," sighed Braylin. "And you already know me as Braylin Grey," he continued. "And Mrs. Social Butterfly over there is Aviana Blu."

Aviana's smile never touched her cheeks.

Clearing his throat, Austin introduced himself. "I'm Austin. Austin Bennet."

"How about we skip the formalities and just ask him about his Post-Genesis?" Aviana huffed impatiently.

Austin frowned. "Post-Genesis?"

"The process where you first changed and received your abilities," Braylin defined.

Austin pressed his lips. The weird storm back in June, waking up with the bed burning, the scars on his chest, and now this Post-Genesis? After he told the plenaries about what happened to him in June, they snuck suspicious glances at each other. Braylin explained that the relegators had noticed Austin and wanted to bring him in for questioning. A friend of theirs had hacked into the relegators' database and tipped them off.

"And that's when I sent Maisie to find you," Braylin finished.

The room shook as dust sprinkled down from the roof. A loud crashing followed the disruption and echoed down the hall. Shaking her head, Maisie sighed, "Alton."

Austin flinched as another loud boom shook the kitchen. "Who's Alton?"

Austin followed Maisie down a few unmarked corridors until they arrived at two wooden doors slightly ajar. Maisie's shoulders tensed as she spoke to Austin. "Before we see what monstrosity awaits us, there are a few things you need to know about Alton. First off, when he died, his spirit possessed and enchanted his armor, so he's an animated suit of armor. Second, be light on your feet in case something blows up."

"Blows up?"

Out of all the rooms Austin had seen so far, this one took the cake. Definitely by far the most stunning—and dangerous. First off, he couldn't see the original floor or walls. The room housed dozens of giant glass spheres. The spheres, Austin realized, were actually smaller rooms all connected by narrow, rotating bridges in the center of the gigantic chamber.

Austin imagined a giant clock making all the clicking and ticking noises echoing around them. Maisie led him to the closest sphere connected to the bridge they currently walked on. Avoiding looking down, he followed her into the smaller room where the disturbance must have originated from. The room they entered was an interesting combination of a library, laboratory, and garage. Science equipment lined the walls with engineering tools decorating the worktables. One of the shelves was smashed on the floor, its contents scattered around the wreckage. Carefully stepping over the mess, Austin choked after inhaling smoke.

Maisie pinched her nose. "Alton? What did you blow up this time?"

Following the trails of smoke, they came to a blackened wreck of books, seared metal, and sparking bits of broken technology. Almost completely buried in the pile, Alton struggled to pull himself out. Austin helped Maisie grab the hands sticking out of the mess and tugged.

"Thank you." Dusting himself off, Alton noticed Austin and jumped. "Goodness! Did someone reincarnate? Who was it this time? Braylin? Aviana?"

"No, no, Alton. This is Austin. Austin, meet Alton."

Austin didn't know what to make of Alton. He wore the same armor as the other three, but it was scorched and damaged. Unlike their well-fitted and polished suits, Alton's armor was a patchwork nightmare. Plates and other pieces were tarnished and the colors faded. Everything mismatched in size and was poorly fused together. Through the rusted holes and cracks, a weak green light flickered inside the armor.

Austin shook Alton's least oil-stained hand. "Hi, so you're a plenarie too?"

"I once was," Alton chucked in a reedy voice, "but my last body perished years ago." He indicated his crudely reconstructed body. "This armor serves as a vessel for my spirit. I'm an enchanted shade, an echo if you will, of one of my past lives."

"Alton is our craftsman. He designs our gear, is the founder of the Sacrarium, and is the keeper of the Athenaeum." Maisie waved a hand at the impossible room. Her nose wrinkled as she tried to contribute more to her friend. "Plus, he's good if you just need someone to talk to if you're bored," she added. "What were you working on this time?"

"I wanted to test the durability of the new set of armor I am working on. Unfortunately, I'm still having trouble strengthening the energy conductors in the grooves of the suit," Alton explained. His battered helmet creaked sideways as he pointed at Austin. "Wait, if you are not one of the plenaries here, who are you?"

Maisie spoke first, "We aren't sure ourselves. The relegators had him on their radar, but we used Amari's tip to find him first. Austin appears to be a human, but he's gone through Post-Genesis and has this crazy thing on his chest."

Alton rubbed his dented chin, peering at Austin. "A human you say? May I see this 'crazy thing' you speak of?" After seeing the scars growing on Austin's chest, Alton flinched back, bumping into a table. "Impossible! Aren't you in pain?"

"Well it—"

"We should start by conducting some tests," Alton told Maisie. "I do not know how deep it goes, but maybe we can avoid opening him up."

"O-Opening me up?" Austin stuttered.

"Maybe we should use your memory cap," Maisie suggested. "If we can see into his mind, then maybe we can understand it better."

Austin took a step back. "Get into my mind? What—"

"I will get the tools, you can take him to the room," Alton instructed Maisie. "We should—wait, where did he go?"

Maisie swiveled around but found no one. Austin had disappeared.

NINE

AUSTIN sprinted across the bridge and barreled down the hall without looking back. He had no clue where to go, but there had to be a way out of here. When he flew past the doorway, Austin recognized the kitchen, but he couldn't find an exit. Stumbling through other rooms, Austin bounced off someone blocking his path.

Braylin looked down at him in surprise. "Austin? Is everything all right?"

Austin dived past Braylin and kept running. *I've got to find the way out! Why don't they have a giant Exit sign?* He tried a room with no door and found himself in the first room he'd stepped in. The archway in the center glowed with the same misty white light from earlier. *Perfect. A dead end.* His back to the arch, Austin listened as they came closer and closer to the room. When they found him, Austin could feel the portal's energy tingle on the back of his neck as he stepped back.

Maisie found him first and panicked. "Austin! Move away

from the arch!"

"Stay back!" Austin ordered. He jolted in pain as his scars flared up and he slipped backward into the arch.

"Don't—"

In a *pop* and flicker of light, Austin vanished into the arch.

Maisie and the other plenaries gaped at the empty archway. Pushing through the others, Aviana inspected the arch herself. Looking at her friends, she lifted an eyebrow. "Did the human just kill himself?"

Screaming like a banshee, Austin was sucked into the white energy going faster than his stomach could handle. Covered in upchucked pasta and the rest of his food, he tumbled through colorless space. He hyperventilated as the void around him went on infinitely.

I'm dead. I'm dead. I'm totally dead.

He tried to stop spinning, but the effort proved pointless. The cartwheeling Austin gave up as he closed his eyes, his whole body shaking uncontrollably. Austin lost track of time, trapped between destinations.

Then he was hit by an airplane.

Technically, a plane didn't hit him, but Austin smashed against something made of metal incredibly fast and wheezed as the breath flew out of him. When he came around, he lay on a carpet against the vibrating floor. His head under a seat, Austin patted himself down and sighed. *Not dead.* But as to how he could be inside an actual plane under a chair, he had no clue. Groping the floor around him, Austin grabbed on to something round and narrow.

"Oh goodie, you're awake! Could you let go of my ankle? There is no need to be too intimate yet."

"Gah!" Austin jumped up and bashed his head against the bottom of the seat. "Ow!"

Someone pulled him out and dropped him into a cushy chair. Rubbing his aching forehead, Austin blinked a couple times before all the black spots disappeared. He flinched as warm fingers brushed across his brow. His forehead's throbbing pain vanished instantly.

"There, that should feel much better."

Austin's hand rubbed the spot where the fingers had touched. "Um, thanks. What—whoa!"

The woman sitting across from him could not be any more bizarre. Unnaturally tall, her eyes blazed white with no pupils or color, and she had skin fairer than ivory. The snowy locks on her head reminded Austin of animated fire, twisting and swirling with a faint shade of pink to them. They bounced and swirled over her shoulders, back, and all the way down to her ankles. She had sharp-tipped ears, and her smile would have been sweet if her teeth weren't silver and pointy like a shark's.

"My name is Lada. Ignore the teeth, dearie, I promise I will not bite." She smiled, seeing his expression. "It is a delight finally making your acquaintance, Austin."

"You know who I am?"

"Of course, I have a sharp eye when it comes to potential," Lada simpered, looking pleased with herself. "Your progress is slower than I had hoped, but the wait will be worth it, I am certain."

"Listen, lady, I'm kind of on the run from these people who want to dissect me. So…"

Lada leaned over and cupped his chin with her hand. "Do not worry, dearie. I was not planning on intervening so soon, but *somebody* had to pull you out of the void! No matter. We can talk again when you are more prepared. See you soon, Austin Bennet."

The plane and Lada disappeared around Austin as he fell through the air. He picked up speed again while everything around him turned white as he shouted, waving his arms around frantically.

Lifting an eyebrow, Aviana looked at her friends. "Did the human just kill himself?"

Suddenly the archway sparked to life as the white energy returned. A tiny sound gradually grew into an echoing scream as Austin shot out of the arch, ramming into Aviana and knocking her to the ground with an exclamation. Sprawled on top of the girl, Austin groaned before realizing who he'd landed on. "Oh, hey."

"Get off me!" Aviana snarled, shoving Austin off.

Back on the floor again, Austin gulped down some air after his horrible arch-experience. Crawling to his feet, he brushed himself off and looked back at the glowing archway. The arch's portal shut down before Austin could even consider escaping through it. He took a quick glance around, but Braylin blocked the only other way out. Palms up, Austin backed away nervously. "Can I call a truce? How about a truce?"

"Sacrarium," Braylin said. When Austin gave him a blank look, he reminded him, "You asked us earlier what this place was. It's a Sacrarium. It means safe place, or sanctuary. This is a *safe place*, Austin. No one is ever going to hurt you here."

Austin pointed at Maisie. "You and that—that other guy were talking about opening me up! Doing tests and… stuff."

"We were talking about *avoiding* that, dummy!" Maisie rolled her eyes. "Look, Austin, you have questions that need answering, so do we. And the relegators are after *all* of us. We can help each other out here."

Austin pointed to the arch. "I appreciate you not killing me and all, but I just left Kate alone for who knows how long. It's not you guys, it's just I don't want to get pulled into whatever this is. I'm asking you to let me go. Please?"

Sighing, Braylin curtly nodded. "Okay then."

Austin moved aside so Braylin could approach the archway. He pulled out his oval-shaped device and held it out toward the arch. Detecting its presence, the archway came to life again with the same energy creating the portal. Grabbing Austin's shoulder, Braylin looked him in the eye. "I'll help you get back. Just hold on, okay?"

Austin nodded. Before he could say good-bye to the others, Braylin pushed him through the portal without warning. When they came out on the other end, they'd teleported to the street where the plenaries first found him.

"Thanks, Braylin. Take care, okay?"

He tried to walk away, but Braylin tightened his grip on Austin's shoulder. His gray eyes burrowed into Austin's blue ones. "Things will never be the same for you, Austin. Just know that we'll be keeping a close eye on you."

"Uh-huh. Can you let me go now?"

Braylin released his shoulder and clapped him on the back. "Stay safe, mate."

He dissolved in another flash of light, leaving Austin alone on an empty street. It must have been late judging by the setting sun. How long had he been gone?

"Kate," Austin shouted. No one replied as he spun around in the spreading darkness. "Kate!"

Still nothing. Patting his pockets, Austin forgot his phone had been destroyed. Its remains were at the Sacrarium, probably thrown out by now. The thought made his heart sink. A hand-me-down from his mom, one of the few possessions of hers he still had. Not anymore. Austin's eyes stung. After shaking his head, he tried to remember what street they'd been on when he and Kate got separated. Unsure, Austin cursed and bolted down the street.

TEN

AUSTIN heard the sirens before noticing the fire. The entire street had been blocked off; two firetrucks barricaded the property surrounding the Summers' house. Slipping past the crowds and roadblocks, Austin stared at the flame-consumed remains of his second home. After the fire was smothered, a recovery team picked through the blackened shell of the first floor. No relegators arrived at the scene.

Hidden in the shadows, Austin overheard some of the firemen passing by. No bodies, everything in the house had been vaporized and reduced to ash. Both parents' cars were parked in the driveway—and Kate's. No one discovered the cause of the fire, but Austin didn't need powers to know what happened. The plenaries beat the relegators to him, but they forgot about Kate and her family.

Austin snuck away from the scene. After losing him, the relegators targeted the people closest to him. And they burned them. Alive. Destroyed the only home Austin had left and murdered the people closest to him. Tomorrow, the news would call it an accident. An oven left on or some wiring malfunction. The relegators' tracks covered, they would move on without a second thought. To the relegators, Austin had vanished. To the world, he had died with the Summers.

He had nowhere to go. Alone in the world, Austin ran into a dark alley and slid behind a rotting dumpster. Wrapping his arms around his legs, he buried his head between his knees and squeezed his eyes shut, heaving dry sobs. First his mom and now the Summers. Just because the relegators hadn't— the relegators! Austin's jaw tightened, his nails dug into his palms until the pain cleared his head. *They* were responsible. *They* caused his misery. Austin would make them pay for this. He rubbed the sleeve of his jacket across his eyes, then jumped up.

Out of the alley with his hood raised, he stormed down the street, his new goal clear in his mind.

Kate's wrists wouldn't stop throbbing. The tight cuffs bit into them but didn't draw blood. The chain connecting them was attached to the table she sat behind. Sore from the metal chair she slumped in, Kate remained silent while she waited alone in the empty white room. Austin had vanished along with that teleporter who'd tried to kidnap her. Left in some run-down street with no idea where her friend had vanished to, Kate walked several blocks home only to be blindfolded and abducted the moment she arrived.

Now Kate understood why Austin didn't appreciate the

relegators so much. Besides the table and extra chair, a mirror stretched across the wall to her right. If anyone was watching her behind it, she gave them the best hand gesture she could flip while cuffed to the table. Tapping impatiently on the steel surface, Kate blew a frizzy strand of hair out of her face. Her mind wandered, the thought of her parents and what happened to them freaked her out. They'd been in the same truck when the relegators took them, but Kate wondered where they kept them now. Wherever Austin had disappeared to, Kate hoped he stayed hidden. That teleporter could only be trouble, but he probably had it better off than Kate did.

Voices! Kate flinched in her seat as the hidden locks behind the door in front of her clicked. Shoulders back and chin up, Kate held her breath and stared straight ahead. When the door opened, two figures whispered to each other out of sight. When their discussion ended, one of them stepped in and sealed the door behind him. He took a seat in front of Kate and dropped a folder onto the table. "Kathleen Summers?"

Reuel couldn't be more pissed off. After updating Solon on the figure, he'd uploaded the profiles of Austin Bennet and Kathleen Summers to the relegator database. The plan had been to visit the address and bring them both in for questioning if necessary. Just before he headed out with his squad, a relegator stopped him, panting and wheezing from his dash to find him. The database had been hacked.

"They must've cracked our password!" The relegator had wrung his hands nervously. "One of our files was downloaded thirty minutes ago!"

When Reuel's group rushed to the Summers' home, neither Austin nor Kathleen were there. He howled in rage, but then the parents pulled into the driveway. Kathleen arrived not even twenty minutes later.

"Take them," he ordered his squad.

They'd blindfolded Kathleen and her parents and taken them away. When they returned to the Tower, Reuel ordered for an interrogator from the department downstairs to speak with her. Waiting outside the interrogation room, Reuel twitched with annoyance listening to the girl rattle the handcuffs behind the door. Finally, the interrogator waltzed out of the elevator with Kathleen's file in his hands. Reuel rushed to speak, but the relegator raised a finger at him to wait. Reuel's anger bubbled. His peers would have recommended he take up yoga or another hobby to calm his temper.

"Okay." The relegator looked up. "What do you want me to ask her?"

Reuel unlocked the door and explained to him, "Start with some basic questions, then find out what she knows about her friend and if he's in league with anyone."

"Have someone in mind?"

Reuel waved him into the room. "Nobody just *hacks* into our database. The plenaries are behind this. They have to be."

"If you say so, boss." The interrogator shrugged. Reuel turned on his heel and stomped down the hall with his shoulders hunched. The relegator assigned as the interrogator shut the door behind him and eyed the girl glaring at him. An only child, according to the file. Seventeen years old and an honor student at her high school, Ms. Summers had been labeled as the best friend of one Austin Bennet. With a well-rounded figure and a slim waist, she looked average in height. Her skin glowed a rosy-pale complexion, she also had shoulder-length, jet-black hair. Eyes hard and sharp as jade, her lips never moved while he took a seat across from her and dumped her file onto the table.

"Kathleen Summers?"

She continued to glare at him accusingly.

He'd forgotten about his helmet and pulled it off. Kathleen's eyes softened a little, seeing the scars on his face, but she remained silent. "Let me get those." He leaned over and unlocked her handcuffs. Rubbing her wrists, she pushed her chair back and crossed her arms. "My friends call me Scratch," he offered her his hand. Kathleen only stared at it. Undeterred, Scratch reached for her file instead. "Daughter of Clarissa and Richard Summers?"

No reply.

Scratch pretended to examine her file again. "Listen, I'm just here to ask you a few questions. Once my superior gets his answers, I promise to make sure you're released promptly."

"Bull."

Scratch closed the folder. "Excuse me?"

Kathleen repeated herself. "That's bull. You can drop the nice guy act, I'm not going to give you anything."

"It's not an act, I'm told being nice is part of my charm." Scratch smiled at her. Kathleen almost did too, but she quickly frowned back. He tried again, "You want me to cut the crap? Fine. My boss wants me to ask you what you know about

Austin Bennet. He's your best friend, right?"

"I don't know where he is."

"That wasn't my question."

Kathleen kicked one of the table legs. "Why are you even asking me? You're the ones with the drones and the cameras. I bet you have a printed copy of my public records too."

"It's digital, actually," Scratch confessed. "Sure, we know a lot about you, but there's some information—recent information—that we can't get from a Facebook profile. Your friend is in trouble, Ms. Summers. If we don't find out what's happened to him, he could be in danger."

"I got nothing to tell you." Kathleen turned her palms up.

Scratch showed her a photo, it was an enhanced photo of Austin jumping from a burning building. Kathleen's mask of indifference cracked. She took the photo and squinted at it. "Where did you get this?"

"Did you know that relegator armor can withstand up to nine-hundred degrees Fahrenheit without even heating up? Your friend here isn't wearing armor, Ms. Summers. The only person who could survive that kind of heat with barely a scratch is a plenarie. Now, Austin has a public record. We have his whole life documented, but records can be forged. So I must ask you this: How well do you know your friend?"

Kathleen's indifference fractured. "We've been best friends since we were little. He's not a plenarie. He just... there was..."

When her chin trembled, Scratch handed her a Kleenex. "We're only here to help you, Ms. Summers," he said to her kindly. "We can help Austin too. But if we're going to help him, you need to tell us everything you know. If he's connected to the plenaries in any way, now is the time to tell me."

Blowing her nose, Kathleen took another glance at the picture. "You won't hurt him?"

Scratch crossed his heart and smiled. "Cross my heart and hope to die."

ELEVEN

AUSTIN had the strangest dream. He knew it could only be a dream, but he had a serious case of déjà vu. At first, he only saw darkness, and then memories surfaced. Not exactly memories, but his brain couldn't be making this up. The visions scrambled in fractures, as if someone took scissors and cut pieces out of a strip of film and tried to play it through anyway. In his sleep, Austin watched a city burn, a strange glowing orb, and then the archway at the Sacrarium, only the room had changed and the arch appeared older.

But then multiple voices screamed in his head, turning the images red as his brain ignited under the flame of pain. Shouted by people Austin did not recognize, fractions of phrases—sentences mixed with the visions.

"Can't stop me, Chiffon!"

"Wait! Stop. Ryker. Ryker!"

In a flash of yellow light, someone yelled what Austin had heard, back during the storm in June. Suddenly, the pain from that night returned as he screamed in the dream. Waking up in a cold sweat, Austin breathed heavily as he blinked. For a moment, he forgot where he was. Then he remembered. The plenaries, the fire, and Kate dead. Homeless, he had to sleep on a bench using his jacket and newspaper to keep warm. His clothes smelled of garbage and his stomach wouldn't stop growling. The scars on his chest kept tingling, but since the plenaries had found him, Austin refused to use his powers. Now he considered otherwise.

Getting revenge wouldn't be as easy as Austin thought. Being broke didn't help, and he only had the clothes on his back. Technically, he should be dead; that's the story the public knew. When he thought about it, maybe being out in the open hadn't been the smartest move. Austin would have to find a shelter or some kind of refuge before he got caught again.

This is a safe *place, Austin. No one is ever going to hurt you here.*

That's what Austin needed, a sanctuary. Trustworthy or not, the plenaries could help him make the relegators pay. And he'd turned them down. Austin cursed himself; he had no way of finding or contacting them. How did they find him in the first place? Braylin hadn't explained much. He mentioned keeping an eye on him. Where they watching him right now? Austin did a quick three-sixty.

No shining figures or people here. Then he spotted them. Not the plenaries, but five relegators scattered around him, advancing quickly. Austin slowly walked away and then broke into a full sprint out of the park. They openly pursued him now. Austin tried to will his body to move faster, but he couldn't concentrate. Three of them herded him into a vacant street, the other two not far behind.

"Stay back!" Austin held his hands out threateningly.

The relegators circled him like vultures. Each one wielded their own adze, a small, cylinder-shaped device. A typical relegator gadget. Energy from the device could be manipulated into a tool or a weapon. In this case, Austin counted on the latter.

One of them held out handcuffs. "You're outnumbered here, kid. Don't make this harder than it needs to be."

Austin didn't move. The other two relegators found them and joined the closing circle around him. When he didn't comply, the leader jerked his chin and one of the other relegators grabbed Austin from behind and restrained him in a full nelson. Another one stepped in front of him and socked him in the nose. Austin spat blood as his vision swam in and out of focus. He tried to fight back, but he couldn't control his powers.

Concentrate your power, Austin!

Running out of time as they dragged him away, Austin butted his head back and freed an arm. He touched the relegator's wrist and focused on the energy inside him. His chest stung as the relegator slackened his grip on him, yelping from getting zapped. The rest of the relegators swarmed him instantly. They kicked him onto the ground and he cried out as they punched him.

"Get away from him!"

The relegators stopped, startled by the new arrival. On the

ground, Austin winced as he dragged himself up. Decked out in her plenarie armor, Maisie faced the relegators with her fists on her hips. Some of the relegators gasped, but the leader only chuckled. "Nice try, pint-size, but there's five of us and only one of you."

"You're right." Maisie nodded. "If there were five more of you, I'd say it would be a fair match."

"Grab her," the relegator leader commanded.

Maisie disappeared in a spark of purple. The relegators froze, muttering nervously to each other. In another spark Maisie appeared beside Austin, taking two relegators down with a single sweep of her foot. The chaos continued, and the relegators tried to tackle Maisie together, but she moved too fast. She teleported back and forth, kicking torsos and bashing heads together *Three Stooges*-style. While the fight raged on, Austin crawled away before someone stepped on him. He would have jumped in and helped her, but Maisie fought without breaking a sweat. She battled three at once when the leader snuck behind her.

"Watch out!" Austin warned her.

"What?"

The relegator jumped the off guard Maisie from behind. He used his adze to stab her, but it shattered against Maisie's armor. The small blast threw them both to the ground. The relegator recovered quickly, but Maisie groaned on the asphalt. Before Austin could reach her, the last three standing relegators held Maisie down.

"You two restrain her. Reuel will be pleased with this find. I'll get the boy," the leader said gleefully.

Another order never came from his lips after Austin slammed his knee into the relegator's face. He caught one of the other relegators by surprise and punched him in his less-protected throat. But when he turned to the last relegator, Austin's eyes crossed, coming eye-level with the relegator's adze.

"Move and I'll blast a hole between your eyes!"

Crack!

The relegator screamed as Maisie's leg connected with his right knee. She grabbed his weapon and snapped it in two. For good measure, she threw an elbow into his face, knocking him unconscious. Austin gaped at the girl as she marched up to him. "You distracted me!"

"Sorry, I was only—"

Maisie yanked off her helmet as it dissolved into purple energy and vanished. She rubbed the back of her neck and complained, "I'm gonna have neck pains for a week. What were you doing? I totally had them!"

"Sorry," Austin mumbled, avoiding her eyes.

Maisie waved a finger at him threateningly. The heat in her tone evaporated as she dropped her hand and held Austin's chin, turning his face left to right. "They got you pretty good."

Austin wiped his nose. His fingers came away with more blood. "The… the relegators burned my friend's house down." His voice came out flat, a distant and empty sound. "They *killed* Kate and her parents."

"They're not dead, Austin. The relegators were waiting for you at the house. I watched them load your friend and her parents into a truck and drive off. The house caught fire shortly after. They probably staged it to cover their tr— *Now* where are you going?"

Half-hobbling and half-running down the street, Austin grimaced as his knee throbbed. *Perfect. Another injury.* Ignoring Maisie's protests as she ran behind him, he pushed forward. "What does it look like I'm doing? I'm going to find Kate and her parents!"

"And I thought Aviana was the stubborn one," Maisie grumbled as her armor melted away and disappeared. "Fine! Let's *at least* check that knee first. I'll help you find your friend, but you have to work with me here. Deal?"

Austin didn't have any better options. "Deal."

TWELVE

AUSTIN and Maisie stopped at Coco's to check his leg. Coco's Cappuccinos held the title for best coffee bar in town; it even had karaoke nights for both extra entertainment and income. Packed with customers, Maisie and Austin managed to squeeze through the afternoon crowd to get inside. Here they wouldn't have to worry about being spotted by any more relegators. Scooting next to Austin in the booth, Maisie patted her lap. "All right, let's see whatcha got."

"Say what now?"

"I mean your leg, dummy. Let me see the knee."

"Oh, right." Austin gingerly lifted his leg and rested it on top of Maisie's lap. He almost gagged at the swollen knee cap.

Maisie brushed the purpling knee with her nimble fingers. She pulled out a small glass vial from one of her jacket's many pockets. The clear liquid inside the vial swished around with a purple tint to it. Austin winced as Maisie drew her finger along his knee. She worked gently and talked minimally while nursing it. Finished, she shoved the stopper back on the empty vial and pocketed it. "There. The swelling should go down. I might need to reapply some more later, but you should be able to walk on it just fine."

"Thanks. So how do we find Kate and her parents?"

"I know someone who could find her easily," Maisie said as they walked out of the coffee bar. "I don't know where Amari is now, but Jay can help us. Follow me."

The address led Maisie and Austin to the other side of town. She explained to him that relegators had devices to detect the energy their powers gave off when used, so they couldn't risk using them and would have to walk instead. By the time they found the place, darkness shrouded the sky. Outside the club, a muscled biker with his arms and head painted in tattoos shook his head, arguing with an indignant girl with bangs and maroon-colored hair.

"How do we get past the bouncer?" Austin whispered to Maisie.

"We're not trying to get past Jay. We're here to talk to her."

"That g— Hold up, *she's* the bouncer?" Startled, Austin gaped at the girl.

Jay shooed the brawny man away, and she didn't reach half his height. "If I see that ugly mug of yours around here again, I'll rip off one of your arms and club you like a Whac-A-Mole!" The biker muttered something before shouldering past Austin and Maisie. When the bouncer caught sight of Maisie, her amber eyes narrowed. "You got some nerve coming back here." Jay cracked her knuckles. "I guess I didn't pound you hard enough last time."

Even Maisie had to look down at Jay. "Aw, do you say that to your other girls?"

Austin covered his mouth and snickered. The short girl whipped around and sized him up. "Something funny, shorty?"

"Shorty? You're one to talk, fun-size." Austin snorted.

Jay gave him a crooked grin. In a matter of seconds her body shot up until she towered above Austin and Maisie. Small muscles grew and became tight and lean, the little girl façade vanished. Plucking Austin off the ground by the neck of his shirt, Jay pulled him in, their faces only inches apart. "Watch it, shorty, or I'll wipe the pavement with your backside." After dropping Austin on the sidewalk like a sack of flour, she shrank back down, returning to her child-size stature. "Can't you see I'm busy?"

"Some relegators kidnapped his friend." Maisie pointed at Austin. "They took her parents too, and we need help finding them."

"Good luck with that." Jay turned to go back inside.

"Wait!" Austin charged after her. He found her inside in the middle of the club. Disco lights blinded him while music blared in his ears. When he touched Jay's shoulder, the girl raised a fist at him warily. "Easy there! I'm sorry I called you fun-size, all right?" he yelled over the music. "Look, I'll do anything. Just help me save my friend."

Jay dropped her fist. Her eyes scanned the room before they stopped at a corner where people danced. With a jerk of the chin, she pointed someone out to him. "See that dude over there with the gray sweater? He works inside Alliance Tower. Maybe you can get him to tell you if they're keeping your friend there." Austin tried to walk over but Jay yanked him back by the shirt. "You owe me one now, got it?" Austin froze, then quickly nodded. Satisfied, she shoved him toward the corner. "Now get lost."

By the time Austin managed to weave himself through the cluster of partiers on the dance floor, Maisie was already there, talking with the guy and laughing. She stood on the tips of her toes and whispered in his ear. Something inside Austin grumbled at the sight. The guy melted into the crowd when Austin reached her. Maisie seemed quite pleased with herself. "Good thing I came along. What would you do without me?"

"What did he say?" Austin questioned her. "What did *you* say?"

Maisie grabbed his hand and maneuvered him out of the club. Back on the street, she glanced around before she pulled her pendant out and placed it on her chest. Her armor glowed as it reappeared over her body. "Your friend's being interrogated inside Alliance Tower. If we go now we just might be able to sneak in and bust her out of there."

"Alliance Tower? That place will be crawling with relegators!"

"I know, I know. But we're running out of options," she reminded him. "Time to put that speed of yours to the test. Are you up for this?"

Austin didn't hesitate. "I am."

Kate's second day of interrogation sucked. Scratch had been replaced with a less good-natured relegator who bombarded her with question after question. She always countered with the same answers, but nothing satisfied the new interrogator. After a whole day of being grilled by Mr. T-1000, Kate massaged her droopy eyes and ached in the same chair in the same blank room. Still cuffed, Kate's chain had been freed from the table. Even with this amount of freedom, the cubicle-sized excuse for an interrogation room still trapped her. Escaping crossed her mind, but to do that the door would have to be opened.

Oh, and maybe all the relegators in the building would have to be gone.

No one answered any of *Kate's* questions. *Did you find Austin? Where are my parents? Are they safe? Are you questioning them too? Why can't you let me go?* The list went on and on, but they left Kate with nothing. After kicking her chair over for the dozenth time, Kate squatted in the corner and hugged herself.

That's when the locks on the door clicked.

The interrogator again? Kate glanced over her knees, but no one stood there, just the open door. Cautiously getting to her feet, Kate approached and peeked out the steel door. No one guarded the empty hall. Down the end, she could make out the silver doors of an elevator. Was this a trick? Or a trap? Even if it wasn't, Kate had no idea how to escape this place. She didn't even have a clue *where* she was. The decision made her hyperventilate.

Ding!

Kate squeaked and slipped back into the room as the

elevator opened. When she looked again, the elevator was empty. *Totally a trap.* She shivered at the thought. After going back and forth about it, Kate finally bolted to the elevator. The doors shut themselves as she jumped in. Instead of buttons, a digital screen with floor numbers blinked on the wall. Beneath the floor numbers, the rest of the screen filled up with text.

Took you long enough.

Kate stared at the screen. With a shaking finger, she used the digital keypad to write back. *Did you unlock the door?*

The last message disappeared. In its place, the text now read, *Yes. I'm also controlling the elevator.*

Kate bit her lip. She typed again on the screen. *Can you help me escape?*

For a moment, the screen only showed her question. Then one word flashed on it: *Yes.*

The elevator gradually eased downward. It descended level by level until it stopped on the fourth floor. When the doors opened, Kate didn't see any relegators ahead. Another hall lined with door after door. Glancing back at the screen on the wall, Kate waited for more instructions. Instead she got one more sentence.

Good luck.

The Alliance Tower stretched high above the buildings around it. One of the tallest skyscrapers in the city, Austin knew the building was designed for relegators' and Alliance officials' uses alone. Walking through the front doors was out of the question. Armed relegators guarded the ground floor and patrolled the entrance.

"Can't you just teleport us inside?" Austin whispered to Maisie.

Maisie scoffed, "Gee, why didn't I think of that? Oh wait, now I remember—because I can't. I can only do *short-distance* teleporting. We'd have to be standing right in front of a window."

Window. An idea came to Austin. "I think I got something." Looking back, he knew this had been a monumentally bad idea. He took Maisie inside one of the neighboring buildings and ran up the stairs to access the roof. The property barely reached a quarter of the Tower's height. When he peered over the edge, Austin shivered. Nobody could survive that fall. "With your powers, can you teleport people with you?"

Maisie's eyes darted from Austin to the Tower, then her eyes rounded with understanding. "No way! Bad idea—correction—terrible idea. Are you insane, Austin?"

"No, but I got nothing else," Austin admitted. "Well?"

Maisie glanced over the edge again. "I don't know... I've honestly never tried before. So you want to run and jump across the roof to the Tower and have me what... teleport us through the wall?" She looked at him incredulously.

"Exactly." Walking to the opposite side of the rooftop, Austin turned around and faced the Tower. Her jaw tightening, Maisie muttered under her breath and followed him. Every impulse inside him was screaming against the idea, but Austin ignored them. Narrowing his vision, he focused his mind on where he wanted to go. Run. Jump. Teleport. Easy-peasy. Maisie climbed onto Austin's back, wrapping her arms and legs securely around him.

"Hold on," he ordered.

"Do you always tell girls that before they climb on?"

She tried to sound cheerful, but Austin caught the tremor in her voice. Taking another breath, he closed his eyes and relaxed. Then his eyes snapped open. They kicked off like a rocket, zooming across the roof and running out of space in milliseconds. Austin poured everything he had into the kick as he sprang off the building and leapt at the Alliance Tower. They plummeted toward the ground barely three-quarters to their target.

"Maisie! NOW!"

Purple sparks flashed around Austin and Maisie as darkness shrouded them. The scars on Austin suddenly flared up as Maisie's electricity coursed through him. After a moment of pain and a rush of energy, the shadows vanished. They fell out of the void and tumbled into an unmarked corridor inside the Tower. Sprawled on the floor, Austin found himself nose to nose with Maisie. "You all right?"

Maisie jumped off him like she'd been shocked. "Let's move before they know we're here."

Austin cupped his ears as a blaring siren screamed in the hallway. The lights flashed crimson as it continued to wail. So much for being incognito. "That didn't take long."

Maisie grabbed Austin's hand and ran down the hall to an elevator. "No, it's too soon! Something else must've triggered the alarm."

THIRTEEN

KATE'S breakout failed instantly. Under five minutes, she bumped into a relegator and triggered the alarm. Brilliant. Now she sprinted for her life, gasping and wheezing as she darted back to the elevator. More relegators stepped out of the elevator, and when they noticed Kate, some of them froze while others shouted and chased after her. Barely ahead of her chasers, Kate cut another corner and jumped into a janitor's closet.

She managed to knock over every broom and cleaning tool in the closet and tripped to the ground. Soaked in liquid soap and brown mop water, Kate coughed and blocked her mouth with a hand as the relegators charged past the door. When the sound of their footsteps died out, she opened the door a crack and checked her surroundings. Down to her right, Kate's eyes stopped at a familiar symbol of a staircase sign.

Kate's sneakers squeaked as she rushed to the other door. Flying up the staircase as fast as she could, Kate passed the sixth floor before cramping up. "I—hate—stairs!" she panted before going up again. By the time she made it to the eighteenth floor, she all but dragged herself up the steps. Floor number eighteen was a maze of corridors and storage rooms full of dusty paperwork and office supplies.

Wielding a plastic Swiffer she'd taken from downstairs, Kate crept through room after room. The way out would be through the first floor, but she couldn't escape while the relegators guarded it. Besides, her parents must be here somewhere, and she wouldn't leave without them. Whatever floor they interrogated on, Kate couldn't remember the number. Higher than four, she guessed, but by now the relegators would all be on high alert.

Good luck. Who'd tried to help her escape? Maybe if she got back into an elevator, Kate could talk to her mysterious ally again. When she found the lift, the alert had reached the eighteenth floor. Typing frantically on the digital screen, Kate tried not to scream.

H-E-L-P M-E!

The monitor only replied, *Unauthorized input. Enter identification number to continue.*

No good, Kate was on her own.

Behind her, a relegator shouted to his comrades as he opened fire on her. Kate shrieked and jammed her finger over and over on the *close door* button. The doors were peppered with dents and blast marks as Kate hit a random button taking her to a lower floor. "No! Take me higher. Take me higher!" she screamed as she tried to undo her mistake. The elevator stopped on the twelfth floor. Alarms still rang over and over, and the lights blinded Kate as she heard another elevator open.

"Hurry! We can check—"

With a scream, Kate swung her Swiffer and smashed it against something made of metal. Someone yelped and crashed into another person coming out of the second elevator.

"What the— Kate?"

"Austin!" Kate dropped her mop and almost tackled her friend to the ground.

Her best friend held her for a moment before breaking away. "Are you all right? Did they hurt you? What did they— uh, why are you covered in Windex?"

"Behind you!" Kate shrieked.

The person in silver armor wore a helmet masking their face. Kate remembered seeing this person before Austin had vanished. Touching their helmet, the mysterious teleporter sighed, "Good thing I decided to put the helmet back on."

"It's okay, Kate. She's with me, but we need to find your parents and get out of here," Austin shouted.

"They're shutting the elevators down," Austin's accomplice interrupted. "They're trying to cut us off, we need to leave right now!"

Kate looked at her friend. Austin's eyes flickered back and forth, thinking on the spot. More relegators stormed up the nearby stairs. Within the minute, there would be no escape for any of them. The doors to the stairs flew off their hinges as black-armored soldiers swarmed out. Taking Kate's hand, Austin also held the armored person's glove. "Can you teleport us down?"

"Teleport?" Kate watched as the relegators surrounded them.

The silver figure touched Kate and they all slipped

through the floor, wrapped in a lightless void. The three of them continued to descend level after level, coming in and out of space until they reached the second floor. Dropping their hands, Austin's ally crumpled to the floor.

"Maisie!" Austin slipped his hands under the person's arms. "Kate, grab her legs and head for the stairs."

The first level mainly served as a garage. Austin and Kate were carrying Maisie toward the closing exit when a black van swung in front of them. A relegator transport vehicle. The van's side door flew open as a masked relegator waved at the trio. "Took you long enough! Let's go!"

Relegators flooded into the garage and spotted the van. While more arrived, Austin crawled in first, pulling Maisie in after him. As the relegator flopped into the driver's seat, he shifted gears and gunned it. Before Kate fell out, Austin grabbed her by the sleeve and yanked her into the van. Tires screeched as the relegators shot at the vehicle.

"*Close the gate*" one of the relegators screamed far behind them.

The gate was already closing when the driver slammed his foot on the gas. The van bounced and wobbled as it zoomed over the rising barrier and skidded onto the road. Yanking the steering wheel to the left, the driver yelled over his shoulder, "We got company. Hang on!"

Sure enough, four identical relegator vans swerved behind them. They swerved between lanes of cars as the driver tried to lose his chasers. After another sharp U-turn, the driver still couldn't shake them and swore. Kate spun around in the back of the van. On the floor, Austin had his head against the armored person's chest, his eyes wide with panic. Rolling by his foot, a fire extinguisher caught Kate's eye. She heaved it up with a grunt and inched it toward the back doors of the van. "Austin, help me with this!"

Austin checked his friend one more time before joining Kate. While Kate fumbled with the handles on the doors, Austin lifted the extinguisher above his head with a grunt. With a click one of the doors flew open. As the second door swung open, Austin yelled and tossed the metal cylinder at the closest vehicle. The extinguisher broke through the van's windshield, shattering it and pulverizing the driver.

"Kate!" Austin flung her backward as the hit van spun out of control and crashed into one of the others chasing them. Saving Kate threw Austin off balance just as their van hit a bump. Tumbling out, he barely caught onto the right door's handle. Austin dangled in the air, parallel to the road, yelling as the door swung him right and left. When the driver made a hard right, Austin's door threw him back into the van as it slammed shut.

"Guys, we got a problem!" the driver pointed.

Kate crawled to the front and squinted through the blackened windshield. The relegators had set up a blockade, cutting them off from the upcoming highway. They were trapped. Instead of braking, the driver drove faster. "You three need to vamoose. Get out of here while you can and get underground!"

The relegator's voice sounded familiar, but Kate couldn't remember who it belonged to. His armor matched the other relegators', except for the shark tooth bracelet he wore on his wrist. "Who are you?" she blurted at the relegator.

The road was getting shorter; they would either be car debris or prisoners of the relegators in a minute. In the back, Austin shook the girl he called Maisie. When she came around, Maisie moaned. "Where... how..."

Austin whispered something to her, Kate picked up the words "teleport" and "sacrarium." When Austin's eyes met Kate's, he reached for her hand. Thirty seconds. Kate turned back to the driver. "What about you?" Twenty seconds.

"Kate. *Now!*"

"Go!" the relegator shouted at them.

Ten seconds. Kate's hand slapped Austin's just as purple sparks erupted around them. Zero seconds. The van crashed and flipped as they dissolved into nothingness.

FOURTEEN

THE first time he'd teleported, Austin threw up. This time, he got covered in *Kate's* puke. After they traveled through the white light instead of Maisie's short-range black void, he recognized the small room with the archway in the center. Austin wanted to take a moment to rest, but a furious voice interrupted his bliss. "Maisie Orchid! You are in so much trouble. Sneaking out again and—oh no, not another one."

"Nice to see you too, Aviana," Austin groaned, he looked over and remembered. "Maisie!"

Aviana flew to her side before he even moved. She twisted off Maisie's pendant and brought a finger to her nose after the armor vanished. Nodding, Aviana scooped up the smaller girl with ease and glided out of the room. A head of brown hair poked out around the corner. "Austin?"

Austin waved from the ground. "'Sup, Braylin. Can you give me a hand over here?"

With Braylin helping, he pushed off the floor and sat up. His head a little dizzy, Austin survived his trip mostly unscathed. A shower sounded wonderful right about now. Beside him, Kate rubbed her head and hiccupped. After wiping her mouth, she dusted off her jeans and observed the room. When she noticed Austin, she barreled over and hugged him tightly. "Austin! Oh my gosh. The relegators kidnapped me. They questioned me and took my parents. My parents! Austin, what am I going to do? Everything that happened—I—I—"

"You must be Austin's friend," Braylin gently interrupted. When she noticed Braylin, Kate stopped talking instantly. Austin had never seen her eyes as round as they were now. Kate blushed scarlet as she shook hands with Braylin. Not even five minutes and Kate already had a crush.

"Hi!" she quickly responded in a high voice. "I—I'm Kathleen. Kathleen Summers, but you can call me Kate."

Braylin nodded. "You can stop shaking my hand now."

"O-Oh," Kate stammered. "Sorry! Wait a minute—you're a—you're not a—"

"Plenarie?" Braylin bashfully half-raised a hand. "Guilty."

Austin didn't know if Kate was about to run or glue herself to Braylin. Before she could do either, he spoke to Braylin, "The relegators burned our house down. We don't have anywhere else to go."

Braylin patted him on the shoulder. "We can talk about it tomorrow at breakfast, but for now you both should take showers and get some rest. You two look like you could use some new clothes too," he added with a frown.

After a change of clothes and washing off, Austin followed Braylin to the hallway where the bedrooms where. While he helped Kate find some new garments, Braylin told him to pick out one of the spare rooms. Alone in the extensive hall, Austin had no idea which of the bedrooms were unoccupied. The first door he approached had no knob to turn. Just a blank slab of metal without detail, with the exception of a purple-colored oval that matched Maisie's pendant.

The door to his immediate left had the same symbol but colored silver. *Braylin's,* he thought as he walked further down. The next one had a yellow pendant imprint on it when he approached it. *Huh, now whose room is this?* he wondered. Just like the other doors, it had no handle or hinges. How were you supposed to open them? Laying his hand on it, Austin pressed the door gently, and to his surprise it slid open like the motion-activated doors at the grocery store.

Walking in, the room lit up in his presence. The floor was polished wood and the walls were painted sunshine-yellow. It added a vibrant light to the area even with its overhead lights providing a sufficient source of brightness. A bunch of corkboards decorated the walls with various pencil sketches and photos pinned on them. An artist or maybe a photographer's room by the looks of the pictures and dusty camera sitting on the cluttered desk.

A thin layer of dust coated everything. An unkept bed in the corner had blankets kicked to the edge of it like it hadn't been made in months. While Austin looked around, he noticed a single picture frame sitting on the bedside table. Picking it up and blowing on it, he sneezed as he inhaled some of the dust particles. Austin recognized some of the picture's subjects: A little shorter than her present self, Maisie tugged at her hair tied in a French braid, looking annoyed by it.

Aviana appeared the same if only happier. Her dark hair flowed over her back and her eyes and smile radiated warmth. On her sides, two boys Austin didn't recognize linked their arms with hers. The taller one had blond hair with a devilish smile. His body aptly muscled, he wasn't as big as Braylin. He actually reminded Austin of himself, more or less. His eyes, a blazing-blue, stood out like Maisie's sea-green ones. Braylin, to the boy's left, had changed the most out of the three Austin recognized. His longer hair had a wilder look to it. Standing beside the boys, Braylin shadowed both of them with his stature. All the boys sported simple white shirts and pants while the girls wore lilac dresses.

The last boy, the one on Aviana's right, stood out as the mildest of the group. With short black hair and a blue-green eye color, he had sharp features with a thinner build than his friends. His skin appeared pale, but his cheeks glowed rosy-red with a meek grin, giving him a sheepish smile. In the picture, he appeared to be hugging Aviana while trying to grab the other boy playfully.

In the photo, they all formed a jovial group of friends with a family-like bond. Setting the frame down carefully, Austin turned to leave and bumped into Aviana standing in the doorway. She hadn't made a sound when she entered, and her mouth betrayed no hint of a smile like the one she wore in the picture. A hint of bitterness and loathing lay in her eyes as they bored into his. "How did you get in here?"

"Sorry!" Austin quickly apologized. "Is this your room? I didn't mean to look around, but the door just—"

"No. What I mean is you shouldn't have been able to get in. Nobody has been able to since…" Gesturing to the area, Aviana sighed as she explained, "This was Wade's room. After he disappeared, it locked itself and none of us could get in."

Austin remembered Braylin had let him borrow some of Wade's clothes, but he hadn't given it a second thought afterward. "I'm sorry. I—I'll just leave then."

Aviana didn't move as he hurried past her. Returning to where Braylin left him, he bumped into Alton. Guiding Austin to one of the unoccupied rooms, he asked Austin to touch the door for him. Apparently, the doors needed bare skin, and since Alton was made of armor not flesh, the door denied him. The room matched Wade's setup but with bare walls and less furniture decorating it. Sitting on the edge of the bed, Austin admired his new bedroom. Alton stood in the doorway with his head tilted at Austin.

"What is it?" Austin asked.

Alton shrugged, a surprisingly human gesture for an enchanted metal suit. "You remind me of him. Wade, I mean."

Before Austin could think to ask him why, Alton creaked him a good night and disappeared into the hall. Alone again, he was about to search for the bathroom when Kate poked her head in. She'd gotten her own pajamas. Lucky. Sitting on his bed, she patted for him to scoot beside her. "So. First we see a plenarie, then I get taken by relegators, and now we're having a sleepover with the world's most dangerous enemies?"

Austin chuckled. "Crazy, right? How are you holding up?"

Kate wrapped her arms around herself. "I feel like we've been uprooted. I—I miss my parents, Austin. I didn't want to believe we'd have to leave our lives behind, you know?"

Austin shuddered at the thought. "Things aren't going to be the same," he confessed. "But once these guys help me out and fix whatever's going on with me, they can help us find your parents. Then we'll disappear and the relegators will never find us."

"It doesn't seem that simple," Kate worried.

Austin promised, "It'll all work out, you'll see."

Kate nodded with an unconvinced frown. She left with a quick "Good night," and returned to her own room as the door closed behind her. Crawling under the blanket, Austin closed his eyes as he drifted into sleep. Images streamed in his dream, filled with the voices from the night before.

While Austin and Kate remained in their rooms, Aviana took Braylin and a recovering Maisie into her room for a private discussion. Pacing back and forth, she spoke to her friends. "I wanted to speak with you two to figure out what our plans are for Austin and his friend."

"It's obvious, isn't it?" Maisie frowned. "We're going to help Austin figure out what happened to him, and while they're here they can help us."

Aviana shook her head. "We're getting sidetracked. We

need to redirect our attention to finding our friends and killing Solon Blak."

"Which is what we are doing," Braylin slowly drawled.

"Oh really?" Aviana snapped. "Because I thought we were playing *house* with the humans!"

Maisie stepped up to Aviana and rose to her full height. Even standing less than a head shorter, Maisie's ferocity matched the taller girl's. "Helping Austin with his powers is just as important as stopping Blak. Don't you think he might be scared? I know I would be if I went through Post-Genesis without knowing what it meant. And imagine how Kate feels. She doesn't have powers, but she was dragged into this as well! You might be too proud to say it, but I will: we need all the help we can get."

Aviana's face reddened to the shade of a beetroot; she looked as if she might explode. Before she did, Braylin spoke gently, "Don't let your temper get the better of you, Aviana. This isn't going to help Wade."

At that, Aviana silenced herself.

Folding his arms, Braylin grunted irritably. "Now's not the time to lose our heads. We'll talk about this another time, okay?" After Aviana conceded, he opened the bedroom door and yawned good night to Maisie. Before he left, he glanced at Aviana over his shoulder. "Good night, Aviana. You should get some rest."

"You can't tell me what to do, Grey."

"No." Braylin shrugged, smiling sadly at her. "We both know only one guy ever could. Sleep tight."

Aviana closed her door. "Yeah, g'night."

FIFTEEN

AUSTIN *ran down a vaguely familiar hallway. Stepping down a staircase, he entered a circular room with three additional doors. In the center of the chamber, an orb glowed in different shades of bright lights. Standing beside it, hidden in shadow, someone watched him enter and clenched their fists.*

"I didn't want to believe it," Austin fumed in a different voice.

"I guess one of us was wrong about the other," snarled the other man.

The scene changed in a flash of white as multiple images flew through his mind, burrowing themselves into his thoughts. There was a sword, a staff with a glowing stone perched on the top, a strange torch with enchanted fire, and there was that same orb again. Why did he keep seeing it?

Austin, wake up!

Now Austin stood on a street. Squinting his eyes, he could make out a vast structure ahead of him. Something eerily familiar about it. Energy shot out of the dark pillar's roof, and an army of relegators marched from the structure into the heart of the city. The street evaporated around him as Austin floated on a surface of clouds. He found himself running very fast, chasing a blackish-purple streak ahead of him.

"You can't stop me, Chiffon!" the blur jeered.

Then together, Austin and the person he pursued fell to earth. A flash of yellow and purple blinded him as Austin's body fractured with unstable energy. Looking at his hands, they began to dissolve before his eyes into yellow energy. To make matters worse, a strange knife pierced his chest. Pulling it out, it faded away as the gash in his chest burned his body.

"No! Ryker? RYKER!" he yelled.

Another blast of light flashed before Austin woke up. Gasping and coughing, he wiped his brow drenched in sweat. Despite the terror and trauma the vision caused him, it already slipped back into his fading subconscious as he rubbed his groggy eyes. Moaning, he lay back down, trying to fall back asleep. He jerked awake as he heard someone cry out.

"No! Please no, stop it!" someone screamed.

Jumping out of bed, Austin burst out of his room. The voice came from down the hall on his left. Running down, he passed Braylin's door slightly ajar. Kate poked her head out of her room.

"Austin?" she mumbled, still half asleep. "Wuzgoingon?"

"Shh. Just go back to bed, Kate. I'll check it out. Just go back to sleep," he whispered.

Nodding, she disappeared behind her door as Austin walked farther down the hall. The screams echoed behind the door with the lighter purple symbol.

Maisie's room.

The door opened at his touch. In the dark, he could make out the outlines of two figures.

"Austin?" Braylin asked in a low voice.

Austin inched forward. "What's wrong, Braylin?"

Braylin motioned for him to come closer. A couple feet away, Austin noticed Braylin cradling someone curled up—Maisie. Maisie, the perky, talkative one of the group, shook hysterically, eyes wide in sheer terror as she repeated to herself, "No, no! Please stop—I didn't want to—no! I can't...."

Braylin, the gentle giant, hushed in a soft tone, "It's okay, it's okay. I'm here, Maisie. Look, look who it is, Maisie."

Slowly, Maisie's breathing subsided as her eyes fluttered. They glanced at Austin before clearing into focus. Her quivering lips formed a weak smile. "H-Hi, Austin, j-just a little nightmare is all."

Austin jumped as a cold hand touched his shoulder. "Austin? May I speak with you for a moment?" Alton whispered.

Glancing one more time at Maisie, he followed Alton out into the hall. Alton did not look back as he led him farther down the hallway. Passing through the double doors of the Athenaeum, they walked on one of the narrow bridges to the smaller spherical room Austin visited the other day. Alton sat on his desk, beckoning Austin to join him. He noticed the splintered remains of the exploded shelf had been cleared away.

Pushing the thought aside, Austin sat beside Alton. "Alton, what's going on? What's wrong with Maisie?"

He could almost picture Alton rubbing his eyes in exhaustion. His metal shoulders sagged as he heaved an unnecessary sigh. "I'll explain that in a moment, but first there is something you need to know: Humanity has been lied to. Before the Excretion Act, before the purge of our people, humans and plenaries lived together peacefully. Unfortunately, a few of us were not content with the way things were. Years ago, a plenarie named Solon Blak thought our people's passive ideals were obsolete. He believed that humanity was a disease, a mistake. In secret, he gathered our people and argued how we could achieve so much more in this world, and how humanity only held us back.

"Solon called us to rise against mankind and wipe them all out. The elders of the plenaries rebuked him; they had no interest in jeopardizing the peace. But some of us followed Solon, agreeing that we could not continue as we were. That is when Solon reimagined his scheme.

"He approached the leaders of humanity and claimed he had come to them as a humble servant. He lied, warning them how the plenaries were rising up against mankind—to wipe them out. His spies had already infiltrated their government and whispers spread about an uprising. To the newly founded United Alliance, he offered his services of protection in exchange for his life and the lives of his followers."

"Did he help them write the Excretion Act?" Austin asked.

"Yes. The same document ordering all plenaries to be hunted down, and the first commissioning of relegators—

Solon's idea of course. Any plenarie was to be killed and their pendant destroyed. Plenaries had always been a mystery to humans—they knew so little of our ways—but now the United Alliance could write whatever they wanted, knowing they had Solon's relegators as protectors. And humanity believed it. Solon's relegators grew while our people were slaughtered. Decades later, humanity thinks we are all but extinct."

"What happened to Blak?"

Alton looked down at his own metal palms. "He was killed, along with most of his original followers. At least I thought he was."

"If this Solon guy created the relegators," Austin frowned, "wouldn't we have heard of him? And if *his* relegators died, where did the rest of them come from? All the United Alliance ever mentions about the relegators is that they're here to protect us. They never say where they enlist them or even train them. Are they robots?"

"No, you wouldn't have," Alton replied. "It is true, Solon was never recorded or mentioned to the public. Why would he be? A servant to humanity perhaps, but a plenarie nonetheless. It is also why they never told you the truth about relegators."

"What do you mean? The truth about them?" Austin questioned.

"Austin," Alton hesitated, "the United Alliance had to come up with a plan to produce more relegators without risking their own population. The number of plenaries could be diminished, but when the next generations were born, Solon and his relegators would be outmatched. After his apparent death, the Alliance made a slight change to their document.

As far as the public knew, all plenaries found were killed. The horrible truth about relegators is—is that they are us."

"*What?*" Austin hastily lowered his voice. "Relegators are… are *plenaries*?"

"Indeed they are." Alton inclined his head. "Decades ago, the last descendants of the plenaries were captured and taken to a secret facility. There they were imprisoned, brainwashed, and forced to breed. When their children were old enough, they were manipulated and stripped of their powers, and so the process repeated over and over. The children and their parents *became* the relegators. That is how the relegator population has grown so much over the years.

"Every time a new plenarie begins Post-Genesis, their pendant is broken and an inhibitor is injected into their body. The inhibitors dampen the energy inside them, the same energy giving us supernatural abilities. It prevents the plenaries from developing powers, reincarnating, or even entering the next stages of Post-Genesis. Like Solon's initial relegators, they wear identical armor concealing the truth from the world."

"How did you and the others survive? Were you once relegators?"

"No." Alton shook his head. "As far as I know, we are the last of the pure plenarie race. When they first wrote the Excretion Act, Villhilium, our people's last city, was invaded and then destroyed. A mere handful of us, including myself, escaped and survived. That is when I came here. This place" —he waved around the room—"used to be an abandoned plenarie outpost. After the Macrocosm divided, this chunk of land slipped through the cracks of the dimensions and was somehow tethered to your world. A long time ago, we repurposed these concealed pieces of land and built them into outposts. Here we are hidden, the only way to and from outposts like this is through archways. There are a few more like it, but I'm afraid we're all that truly remains of our people. Any other survivors would have been taken to Hailstone sanatorium, the secret facility where relegators are born."

"That's horrible, Alton, all of it. So where does Maisie fit into all of this?" Austin questioned.

Alton made a rattling sound in his helmet. "Maisie is the last surviving member of the Orchids, one of the oldest plenarie families before the Act. She came to us broken and scarred. I don't know where she was hidden before we met, but wherever it was, it must have been a living hell for her. She will not tell you this, but Maisie blames herself for what happened. She does not think she deserves to be here, so she is always pushing herself to the breaking point to prove her worth. But it takes a toll on her."

Austin jumped up. "But that's not fair," he argued. "It wasn't her fault! It was that Solon guy."

"Austin," Alton's voice sounded somber, "Solon Blak was not his real name. He was an Orchid too—Maisie's older brother."

"Her brother?" Austin startled.

Alton's head bowed, his tone filled with remorse. "She didn't tell me a lot about him, but they were close and much alike. It crushed her when she found out, and now she suffers the ramifications of his actions. It keeps her up at night, and it could potentially send her down a darker path. You see,

Austin, I took each of them in for a reason. I raised Maisie in hopes that she will one day come to accept it and leave the past behind where it belongs, once and for all."

"Nightmares," Austin murmured. "I never would've guessed…"

Alton nodded. "In her own time, she may come to tell you herself, but for now I need you to promise me that you will not tell Maisie what I have told you tonight."

"I promise."

Alton hopped to his feet. "Well, you had better get some sleep. We have a lot to cover tomorrow. I will walk you back to your room."

The truth behind the relegators drove his dream out of his mind as Austin thought of Maisie. When he first met her, he imagined her as a fierce but also friendly girl as far as plenaries probably went. Now, he could only picture her crying out, alone and afraid. Eventually, he returned to his deep slumber filled with cries of terror and flashes of yellow light. He woke up the next morning exhausted, faint memories of the night plaguing his mind. He shook out of his thoughts as a rapid knock pounded on the door.

"Austin, breakfast is ready," Maisie called out.

She sounded so… calm. He couldn't believe she still had the emotional strength to wear a smile on her face after what she'd gone through. Walking into the kitchen, Austin found Braylin and Kate in the middle of a deep conversation as they set the table for five.

"So do plenaries all have the same powers or are they all different?" Kate asked.

"We generally have different powers, but families tend to share the same abilities," Braylin answered, taking a seat at the table.

Aviana brought a steaming plate of sausages to the table. Tossing her apron aside, she sat in her usual spot at the end of the table. Austin flinched when someone touched his shoulder. "Morning, Austin."

Plopping herself next to Braylin, Maisie smiled as she piled her plate with a hearty helping of sausage. She showed no sign of what happened last night. Kate and Braylin sat across from each other, still talking, while Aviana ate at the head of the table, with Maisie on her left. Sitting across from Maisie, Austin helped himself while listening to the ongoing conversation.

"And you can reincarnate? Like, your body changes completely?" Kate asked.

Stifling a yawn, Braylin had dark circles under his eyes from a long night. Answering Kate, he enlightened her, "Depending on the circumstances, but yes. Plenaries can only reincarnate two additional times before they pass on permanently."

She pressed him further. "So have any of you reincarnated before?"

Braylin pointed with his fork at Maisie. "Maisie has. The rest of us have only gone through the next few stages of Post-Genesis."

"Wait, so there are more—stages, was it—after Post-Genesis?"

"Yes," Maisie confirmed. Counting on her fingers, she named. "There's two—no, three additional stages that come after Post-Genesis."

Austin accepted a floating glass from a felera. "So... what happens in each stage?"

"Well," Braylin paused, "it's different for every plenarie depending on what type they are."

Austin forgot about his food and rested his arms on the table. "There are different types of plenaries?"

"Different *velocity types*, to be specific," Maisie clarified. "Besides our powers, we all have some kind of enhanced speed trait. It can be something corporeal, an overall enhancement, cognitive manipulation, a kind of time continuum, or even a different way of transporting."

"So which types do you three have?" Kate questioned with jittery excitement.

Braylin caught Maisie as she tried to steal his biscuit. "Maisie's velocity type mainly affects the way she travels. She can teleport or 'pocket-jump' from one spot to another in a matter of seconds. Her body also has an enhanced metabolism. She can eat a lot, so she's pretty hyp—energetic most of the time."

"Hence the love of food and exultant attitude," Aviana muttered before taking another bite.

"Aviana," continued Braylin, "has the velocity type of corporeal capabilities. It's an elemental ability that allows her to phase her body into pure energy if she concentrates hard enough. She can shift her mass with it and create constructs as well."

Maisie talked with a mouthful of sausage. "And Braylin can touch people and control their body's continuum. He slows them down for a couple minutes, so time appears sluggish to them. He's also super strong and can manipulate light, it's pretty dope."

"What does that make me?" Austin asked.

Braylin folded his hands as he peered at him. "We aren't sure yet. You didn't have a pendant when we found you, but if you are a plenarie, or something like us, you could potentially be like Aviana, just in the early stages of your abilities. But time will tell. After your medical assessment, maybe we can try to test your capabilities."

"Medical assessment?" Austin repeated.

"Meaning we gotta check under your hood to see what makes you tick," said Maisie with a wink.

"What am I supposed to do?" Kate asked.

Maisie wiped her mouth on her sleeve as she spoke. "You can either tag along with us, or I'm sure Alton would *love* to have some assistance in the Athenaeum."

Kate turned to Aviana. "By assistance, she means—"

"Guinea pig." She shrugged.

Kate shuddered. "Guess I'll shadow you guys, then."

Braylin flexed his shoulders as he got to his feet. "Well, you two get dressed, and then Maisie, you can take care of Austin. Just do a basic analysis and run a couple energy tests for us. Kate can meet Aviana and me at the velocity chamber."

The three plenaries materialized into three blurs of blue, silvery-white, and purple that zoomed or teleported out of the room, leaving a small gust of wind blowing in Austin and Kate's faces. Alone together and tussled by the wind created by the plenaries, both friends looked at each other in uncertainty.

Kate spat a lock of hair out of her mouth. "Uh, do you know where or what a velocity chamber is?"

"I don't even know the way back to my bedroom yet," Austin chuckled.

SIXTEEN

REUEL stared at the overturned chair in the interrogation room. Two relegators serving under him stood at attention by the door, shuffling their feet anxiously. The girl might have been a gifted student, but Reuel knew she couldn't have escaped the Tower alone. One of the officers on surveillance duty just showed him footage taken from the garage last night. Austin Bennet had been here, and so had The Orchid. *The Orchid!* Reuel wanted to kick himself. Even with them, it seemed improbable how this girl snuck through the building without assistance.

Someone on the inside, he thought.

The cameras identified the van Kathleen Summers and her friends escaped in. One of their relegator transportation vans was reported stolen this morning. When he watched the footage, Reuel knew immediately someone inside the building had helped them escape. But who? More than a hundred relegators came in and out of the building on a weekly basis.

Even if he was a relegator, Reuel had no clue to the traitor's identity.

He's a relegator. He has *to be,* Reuel repeated to himself.

Four vans chased after the runaways. Two crashed horribly, something to do with a fire extinguisher? The other two followed the stolen vehicle until it crashed into the barriers in front of the highway. Reuel checked the remains of the van. This traitor, relegator, or whatever he was escaped capture. No one had any clue where he'd vanished to or what he looked like, other than the fact he wore black armor. Reuel grabbed the table and flung it across the room. Clenching and unclenching his fists, the hairs on the back of his neck tingled while the lights in the room flickered.

"She escaped then, I take it?"

Reuel avoided Solon's glare; his relegators by the door had also disappeared. "Austin Bennet and The Orchid broke in and helped her escape. They had a man on the inside too, but we have no idea who that might be."

Entering the room, Solon mentioned nothing as he flipped the table upright and drew the chair to its side. With a clawed hand, he offered the seat to Reuel. His face an impassive mask, Reuel took it and resisted tapping his fingers nervously on the table's surface. On the other side, Solon bent over the table, his armor's fingertips digging into the plastic. "The last plenaries are growing restless. It won't be long before they slip up and make a grave mistake. If they crawled back into their hole, we must draw them out. Once you draw them out, *I* will take care of the rest."

"Draw them out?" Reuel repeated. "Don't you get it?

Someone here helped them break the Summers girl out! We have a mole on the inside, Solon. What am I supposed to do about that?"

Solon did not react to Reuel's insubordinate tone. The giant shadow squeezed his hands until the table cracked and crumbled under his touch. "It is time to get creative, Reuel," he insisted with a low growl. "You can use this problem to your advantage. Find the mole, use him to locate the plenaries, and finish the job you were assigned. I would hate to replace you after all the progress we have made."

"And what about the project? The machine—"

"Will be completed on time," Solon hissed as he melted into smoke. "If you cannot find your mole or the plenaries, bait them if you have to. Draw. Them. Out. Do not disappoint me again."

Alone with the broken table and his chair, Reuel dwelled on Solon's words. Turning on his tech-pad, he accessed the database's recent history. Everything appeared normal, but then he noticed something. Anomalies, odd times where someone had overridden commands to certain files and computers. The most recent change had happened last night. One of the elevators was hacked, as was the door to this same interrogation room. After Reuel searched for similar instances, he discovered something about the hacker.

They used a simpler version of the search interface to find and change certain codes and commands. Reuel used a more expensive upgrade for his own tech-pad, which meant his mole couldn't be a high-ranking relegator. Taking that information, he also searched for relegators with access to the Tower's control room and the garage. Next, he narrowed it further by searching for relegators who worked at the Tower long-term. This relegator would've had to plan this thoroughly, so he must be acquainted with the layout of the building. His list of potential moles barely reached seventy profiles. While he headed to the elevator, Reuel brewed over Solon's words.

Draw them out, bait them if you have to.

Reuel smiled to himself. The last shipment of the machine's parts would be on its way to the Tower any day now. One part in particular was very rare, something no rebel or hacker could resist stealing if they knew its purpose. Checking his search again, Reuel had another stroke of potential luck. The hacker had opened the document outlining the shipment's cargo. *So he knew about it too,* Reuel thought as he dialed a call to the office in the garage.

"Yes, I'm calling to see if the final shipment has arrived yet? No? Excellent. I need you to change the delivery address for me," Reuel ordered into his comm. "Yes, change it. I'll send you the new address right now."

A plan slowly took shape in Reuel's mind. After he gave the new location for the shipment to the relegator crew downstairs, he made sure to upload the address onto the database. Within the next two days, the hacker would discover and copy the information Reuel posted. The shipment would only be at the warehouse for a night. It would take another day or more to get it there, but then he'd know where the mole would be next. A trap almost set, and a determined Reuel ready to catch his prey.

Tugging his shirt off, Austin squirmed a little on his bed. Maisie brought a box full of instruments to his room where they worked. Hands on his knees, Austin stretched his neck trying to see what Maisie sorted through. She brought out what looked like a small probe. When the tip of it lit up, Maisie nodded her approval before turning back to Austin. "Keep your arms stretched out, please."

Austin did as she asked. Maisie waved the tool across his chest and then his head. The small device made a rapid beeping sound, making Maisie's eyebrows knit together. Putting the tool away, she dug into her box again. "That's strange, maybe if I use something else…" She strapped a small device to his chest and turned it on. A couple of minutes later, the device started to beep. When Maisie took it off, she didn't look happy. "Okay, so the probe wasn't wrong. It says here that you don't have a polestar."

"I don't have a what?" Austin squinted at the screen with confusion.

"A polestar," Maisie pointed to her chest. "Plenaries have this organ, it's like a second heart. It circulates and distributes the energy inside us and gives us our powers. That must be why you didn't have a pendant on you when we first met. Pendants summon our armor and focus the energy flow of the polestar—we can't use our powers properly without one. If you don't have a polestar, then you can't have a pendant." She reread the scan and bit her bottom lip. "But you have the same energy inside you. I can't read what's producing it, but something other than a polestar is filling your body up with a lot of power. That must be why you have those scars."

Austin looked at the marks across his chest. They grew bigger and more concerning every day. When she was done testing, Maisie cleared away her tools and heaved the box into her arms. Throwing his shirt back on, Austin walked with her down the hall. "Can you get rid of this energy?"

"I don't know yet. Your body is putting up a good fight trying to suppress it, but it's spreading. It's really weird; you seem human, but somehow you're able to generate and harness power like a plenarie. We can do more tests later, but for now we should meet the others at the velocity chamber. I think you'll like this, it's very cool."

"Cool" didn't cut it when it came to describing the velocity chamber. Austin expected something like a simulator or a padded training room, but neither compared to this. The room's arched walls curved into a giant dome. Its flat floor divided down the middle with a long black stripe. The stripe resembled the midnight sky: infinitely dark with twinkling lights shining in the void of its blackness. Aviana, Braylin, and Kate walked over and greeted Austin and Maisie. While the plenaries grouped together, whispering about Austin's test results, Kate showed Austin what the plenaries called "The Track."

"It's sort of like a treadmill," she explained, pointing at the dark stripe. "Braylin told me this part of the floor can also move and morph into any shape, it's between a liquid and a solid-like plastic rock. He called it 'night glass' or—"

"The Track is made out of twilight glass," Braylin corrected as he walked over. "It's harder than diamond, but the substance can easily morph itself into anything the user desires. This part of the floor moves as a walkway would. We use it in training sessions to test and improve our powers and skills."

Kate clapped her hands together and squealed excitedly. "So it's like a superhero training course? Awesome! Are you guys going to train? Can we watch?"

Austin pushed his exuberant friend back down. "Excuse my geeky friend here. So what are we doing here exactly?"

"*We're* here because *we* need to strengthen *our* skills," Aviana interjected icily. She slipped out her pendant and placed it on her chest. Her armor grew all over her body until it covered her completely.

"I thought we could let Austin join us today," Maisie casually mentioned.

Braylin weighed his own pendant in his hands, he gave Austin a quick once-over. "Really? I know you said he could run fast, but The Track isn't something to be taken lightly."

"He would only hurt himself," Aviana added.

Austin's hands clenched into fists. *Challenge accepted, Blu.* "Don't count me out just yet, I want to give it a shot."

Braylin slid him a skeptical glance. "Have it your way, mate. Today is going to be a running trail exercise, we'll try to take it down a notch."

Kate sat on the sidelines while the rest of them stepped

onto the giant track. Roughly eight feet wide and over twenty feet long, it stretched all the way to the walls horizontally. Everyone else wore their armor, but Austin felt vulnerable in his street clothes. *Show them what you can do*, he told himself, *just don't trip or get hurt.* Braylin and Aviana whispered to each other while Austin spoke to Maisie out of the corner of his mouth. "So what am I supposed to do?"

Maisie grinned as her helmet reconstructed itself around her face. She spoke in her augmented voice. "Try to keep up."

Without warning, The Track whirled to life, and the three plenaries kicked off, leaving Austin in the dust. *So that's how they're going to play,* he thought. Pacing himself, he sped off.

At first, everyone clustered together, keeping the same pace as The Track flew under their feet. When they got used to the fast-moving floor, they dispersed. Instead of running, Braylin leaped through the air using his power, his landings sending shockwaves through the floor, almost knocking Austin off the course. Away from everyone in the lead, Aviana burned as a comet of pure blue energy zooming beyond her peers.

Her velocity type makes her pretty powerful, Austin figured. *As pure energy, she can move superfast without breaking a sweat.*

While her friends moved ahead, Maisie stayed close to Austin. In blasts of purple light, she disappeared and reappeared around him. "Come on, you can do better!" she encouraged as she cut across him.

"That's it, I'm done playing around," Austin hissed. The new energy inside him fueled his body as he kicked his legs harder. The pain spreading across his chest hurt, but Austin was determined to push himself further. Superhuman or not, he wouldn't let anyone beat him at a race. Suddenly, he jolted as something cracked inside him, like a dam bursting under the pressure of a flood. His straining muscles relaxed as a new liveliness coursed through them. He picked up more speed and passed a teleporting Maisie and a jumping Braylin.

BOOM!

The ground became uneven as Austin stumbled a little. He skidded left and right as small formations sprouted out of The Track randomly. Up ahead, he saw blue, comet-like tails of energy flying behind Aviana as she ran. Speeding up and dodging past the growing obstacles, Austin could see Aviana was getting larger and larger until he sprinted right beside her. They raced neck and neck on The Track, but Aviana didn't seem to notice his presence.

"Miss me, Blu?" He grinned.

"Not in the slightest," Aviana's voice echoed on either side of him.

Austin blinked in confusion. Not one, but two Aviana girls flew on both of his sides. Somehow, she'd multiplied herself, boxing Austin in as he tried to keep up with them.

Austin, look out!

He hadn't been paying attention as a giant pillar shot up and smashed into him. No longer running, he tumbled down The Track head over heels, crashing into something metal and taking it down with him. Maisie immediately shut the machine off and ran to help Austin up. He had a metallic taste in his mouth as he spat out blood. With a quiver he realized that the metal thing he'd smashed into was Braylin. Tangled together, both guys struggled to free themselves until Maisie and Aviana pulled them apart.

Pulling his helmet off, Braylin plopped onto the ground and groaned. "And that, Austin, is why they invented helmets."

SEVENTEEN

"So, that was a construct?" Austin groaned as he rolled his shoulder.

Braylin winced as Maisie dabbed his scrapes with her special ointment. "Aviana can create constructs, duplicates of herself that shadow her movements. She typically uses them for distractions in a fight or, if concentrated enough, they can serve as a helper, or even as a surrogate of herself."

After their accident, Maisie sat them both down to check for injuries. A large gash cut across Austin's nose, and the scars on his body had grown even more. Now the strain marks appeared on both wrists and ankles. Thanks to his armor, Braylin came out of the crash unscathed—mostly. He bit his tongue during the collision and scratched his arm from the elbow down. After the exercise, Aviana left to run an errand. Kate watched Maisie patch Austin and Braylin up from a distance. Blood always made her queasy. For as long as he knew her, Kate'd had a weak stomach.

"Stop fidgeting, you big baby!" Maisie slapped Braylin.

Working his jaw, Braylin climbed up and checked his arm. "We really need to insulate our armor more efficiently."

Rummaging through a medical kit, Maisie couldn't find what she was looking for and gave Austin an apologetic glance. "I used the last of my healing mixture on Braylin. I'll have to make some more for you, naturally."

"What does that me—ew, what are you doing?"

Maisie grunted and spat into her palm. Her saliva resembled the stuff she used to heal Austin's bruises and cuts from the other day. Coming over to check on Braylin, Kate's eyes bulged as she covered her mouth and gagged at the sight of Maisie's spit. Braylin hurriedly pushed her out of the room before she vomited. Down the hall, his anxious voice echoed, "Not in the hall. Not in the hall!"

"Maisie, was that spit you put on me the other day?" he asked, ignoring the shouts outside.

"Technically those were mostly tears," she corrected, "but I'm not going to cry for you, so stop squirming and let me put some of this on you. Trust me, I can fix that cut on your nose. You'll be aching all day otherwise."

"Nuh-uh, no thanks, I'm good." Austin cringed.

"Look," Maisie explained, "I can heal minor injuries or cuts with my spit, tears, or sweat. It's one of my powers. Are you going to let me use it or not?"

Quickly glancing around, Austin grumbled, "Fine, just get it over with."

Maisie obliged. New skin grew over the bridge of his nose, and the pain in his wrists, chest, and ankles faded. Walking out of the velocity chamber, Austin followed Maisie to the Athenaeum where various screeches and thumps escaped its oak doors, trembling on their hinges. Without bothering to knock, Maisie strode in with Austin in pursuit. They found Alton working behind his desk. He bent over what appeared to be a chest plate of plenarie armor. Maisie walked up to the desk and rapped her knuckles on it. "Alton?"

Not acknowledging her presence, Alton continued to work while making buzzing sounds in his helmet. Austin could only guess the buzzing was really Alton humming.

"Alton?" When he didn't respond the second time, Maisie leaned forward and knocked rapidly on his helmet. "Alton!"

Dropping his hammer, Alton held his helmet until it stopped vibrating. "Gracious child, I heard you perfectly! I said 'hmm'?"

"Sorry, it's difficult to distinguish some of the sounds you make," Maisie apologized. "I came by to tell you that I ran a couple of tests. Austin doesn't have a polestar."

Checking to make sure he hadn't damaged his project, Alton turned his attention back to Austin. "Interesting. If he does not have a polestar or a pendant, then perhaps something else is giving him powers. It must be linked to the plenaries somehow." Alton disappeared under his desk and dug into his pile of parts. "Without a pendant to control the energy inside you, your human body is straining from bottling it up. Until we figure out what is creating the energy inside you"— he jumped back up producing an object resembling a wrist watch—"wear this. It should dampen your powers so you do not injure yourself as much."

Austin wore the device on his right wrist. Cool to the touch, the device gradually warmed up as his body's energy felt drained. As he and Maisie walked out, Alton suddenly jerked. "Oh! I almost forgot. I modified the part you requested, Maisie."

He held out a small, rectangular object wrapped in a green cloth. Maisie's face flushed as she quickly grabbed it from him. "Thank you, Alton. We'll see you later."

Alton looked on the verge of saying something before he nodded and returned to the armor lying beneath him. Maisie led Austin out of the Athenaeum and into the hallway, back to where everyone's rooms were. She walked into her room, leaving the door open. Austin hesitated on entering, standing awkwardly on the threshold. Hiding the piece of wrapped cloth in one of her bedside table drawers, Maisie tucked a strand of her bright hair behind her ear as she smiled meekly at Austin. "Come in, I won't bite."

Strung from one corner of the room to the other, painted relegator helmets had been repurposed into lanterns with shapes and patterns cut into them. A couple more littered the ground, the black helmets etched all over in tally marks. Number of hits perhaps? Similar to Austin's old room, Maisie's embodied controlled chaos. Layers of unkept clothing, discarded books and magazines, and a collection of wrappers buried the floor. She'd covered the lilac-painted walls with pop-culture posters, some of which Austin didn't even recognize.

Hung on the back of one of the uncluttered chairs, a battered green jacket caught Austin's eye. Austin pulled it off and waved at Maisie. "Hey, this is mine!"

Maisie gave him a skeptical glare and made a grab

for the jacket. "That's not *your* jacket, its mine. I found that months ago."

"You found it on the back of my wheelchair," Austin reminded her. He tried to put it on, but he couldn't fit into it anymore. Strange, it had shrunk. Now that he looked at it, he didn't remember having all these colored patches stitched all over it. "Why is it smaller? Did you sew these onto it?"

Maisie snatched the jacket from him. Slipping it on, she pulled her hair up and dropped it over the jacket's back. "Still think this is your jacket?"

Austin raised his hands defensively. "Okay, okay, it's not my jacket. I'm sorry, all right?"

Maisie's eyes flashed at him warily. They had a curious, knowledgeable look full of perpetual energy. Right now, they made her look dubious, even a little defensive. The device on Austin's wrist suddenly beeped. Before he could fuss with it, Maisie pulled his wrist down and examined it. "Alton forgot to set the temporal energy levels to a higher percentage. There, that should make it stop."

Austin looked at her incredulously. *"Temporal energy?"*

Maisie tried to stifle a laugh, her rush of irritation evaporating. "I'm sorry, Austin, I forget how little you know. We can't use normal electricity because of our powers, so we found a way to readapt a new power source. It's called temporal energy."

"You can't use electricity?"

"That's what I said, right? Our bodies' energy can overwhelm electricity-powered objects if in close contact long enough," she explained.

Austin pointed to the television Maisie had on her dresser. "In that case, why hasn't the TV blown up *Mission Impossible*-style yet?"

Maisie smirked with a little pride. "Alton and I replaced the power source with temporal energy so that it wouldn't go haywire."

"So you guys created a new power source... and you use it to power a TV?"

Maisie shrugged. "Plus a couple other things from your world, but yeah. Braylin and Aviana think it's a waste of materials, though."

"That thing Alton gave you, was that another piece of tech you wanted to him convert?"

Maisie bit the corner of her lip as she shuffled her feet. "Yeah."

Sensing her discomfort, Austin hastened to change the subject. "So. You like LEGO?"

"What?"

Austin waved a hand around the room. Maisie had various LEGO kits stacked on every flat surface. Mostly small structures, but a couple reached a few feet. "I had some as a kid, but I know some people still play them when they're older."

All the color drained from Maisie's face. "Oh, um yeah, well, you see—"

"I love the giant Eiffel Tower." Austin pointed next to her door. "You built that yourself? That's pretty impressive. Have you ever been there?"

His reaction took Maisie by surprise. Her cheeks pinked

up a little as she smiled weakly. "I've only seen pictures of it. I've always wanted to go, though. Maybe one day."

Austin noticed another familiar structure. "Big Ben too, huh? Did you use instructions?"

"No, not with most of these," Maisie shyly answered. She chuckled lightly, but her hands trembled a little. "I know, I know, it's kind of silly, but it calms me down whenever I'm anxious or I can't sleep."

Austin remembered the other night. "Because of your b—" He quickly shut himself up and cursed.

"What were you going to say?"

"Maisie, Aviana just came back. She has something she wants to tell us in the Athenaeum," Braylin interrupted as he poked his head into the room.

"Okay, we're coming." Maisie shot Austin another questionable glare before following Braylin out.

EIGHTEEN

BRAYLIN and the others waited for them as they entered Alton's chamber in the Athenaeum. When Kate noticed them walk in, she grinned, nodding at Austin and Maisie and giving her friend a low-key thumbs up. Rolling his eyes, Austin stood beside her and said nothing. While Aviana and Braylin argued by the door, Alton fussed with a pile of spare parts behind his table. The metal plenarie looked at home as he snapped pieces together and hummed a tune.

Walking over to Alton, Austin marveled at the piece he worked on. It looked like one of those plenarie pendants minus the missing initial in the center of the oval. The custom piece glittered silver and blue, a match to Aviana's armor design. Sliding a copper wire into the exposed back of the invention, Alton sealed the back with an oval cover and placed it onto the table. Extending his arm, Alton requested, "Austin, may I borrow your hand for a moment?"

A little skeptical, Austin stretched his hand out. Alton laid the invention onto his open palm. Warm to the touch, it pulsed lively as it sat in his palm. The pendant hummed and grew hotter and hotter. Austin cried out as the device burned his hand. Accidentally dropping it, he dove for it, catching it just an inch from the ground.

Alton sighed as he wiped his metal brow. "My apologies, I did not predict that it would overheat like that."

Austin placed it back on the workbench, cradling his reddening palm. "No worries. Is it a custom pendant or something?"

"An attempt to recreate one, yes. This one has been modeled to store and enhance temporal energy," Alton explained. And with that he disappeared behind a pile of discarded parts, tossing them around while muttering to himself.

"So. What's this all about?" Maisie quizzed Aviana.

Aviana cut off her heated conversation with Braylin and spun around. "I ran into Amari while getting groceries. He mentioned being approached by someone who told him they have some important information for The Orchid, regarding some kind of project the relegators are working on. Amari said the guy wouldn't say his name, but he gave him this as some sort of credential." Aviana opened her fist and held out a shark tooth bracelet.

"Hey, I recognize that!" Kate reached for the bracelet. She waved the band at Austin and Maisie. "It's that relegator's. Y'know, the one who helped us escape?"

"Who?"

Kate slid the bracelet on her wrist. It fitted loosely on her, but she wore it anyway. "When you two came to break me out, I think it was this guy that helped get me out of the interrogation room they locked me in. He must have hacked into one of the Alliance Tower's elevators. I bet he was the driver who rescued us in the garage."

"So what did this guy want?" Braylin questioned Aviana.

"He just said to have The Orchid meet him at some diner in upstate New York." Aviana paused before adding, "Amari did say he looked like a relegator. It's not a lot to go on, it might be a trick."

It didn't convince Braylin either. "It sounds very sketchy to me. Did you get the name of the diner?"

"Yeah, it's called Mojo's. Just some greasy burger joint by the looks of it." Aviana waved. "He wants to meet tomorrow at noon. I said we'd send someone, whether we do or don't is up to us. If it's a trap, it's too risky having all of us go."

"I'll go," Maisie volunteered.

Everyone looked at Maisie. Taken aback from the sudden shift of attention, Maisie cleared her throat. "Look, this relegator's looking for The Orchid, right? If this person really is an ally to us, then we should take advantage of the offer. And if this is some kind of relegator trick, I'll teleport out of there before they can even touch me."

Austin raised a hand. "I'll come with you." He immediately regretted it when Maisie threw him a sharp look. "If you want," he added.

"I'm going too." Kate stepped forward. She glared at anyone who might challenge her. "The relegators still have my parents. I'm not just going to sit around while they're imprisoned. Relegator or not, this guy helped me escape. If he's legit, I want to see if he can help us save them too."

Aviana tapped her foot impatiently. "We can make our decision later, but we have more important matters to discuss right now." Her eyes flickered to Kate and Austin.

With indignation, Braylin shook his head. "Fine then, we'll talk about this more later." He spoke to his mentor, "Alton, can you let Austin and Kate borrow the Plenarie Tome?"

Kate's curiosity got the better of her. "What's the Plenarie Tome?"

"It's a book containing encyclopedias, genealogies, and historical information about plenaries," Alton answered. "I have it around here somewhere…"

"How can you find anything under all this scrap?"

"*Scrap?* This *scrap* is going to revolutionize plenarie armor!" retorted Alton. Rising from the metal heap that blended too well with his armor, he produced a leather-bound book with *Plenarie Tome* written in italicized, silver letters. "Do return it when you've finished. I still need to replicate some notes." Without another word, Alton dove back into the tall pile of metals behind the desk.

Braylin passed the book to Austin. "You two get reading, it'll help to get you up to speed. Tomorrow we will give you our final decision about this relegator business."

"Wait, what are you—"

Austin and Kate got kicked out of the chamber without another word. Weighing the book in his hands, Austin looked to Kate. "*Okay*, I guess we can get started then."

Hopping off the bus, Reuel tightened the strap on his bag and checked his concealed weapon. Relegators may have been the enforcers of justice, but crime still permeated the neighborhood he lived in. Unless promoted to a higher rank, relegators received minimal wages for their services. Reuel worked hard to rise through the ranks, but the expensive rent gutted his paycheck, not including the additional necessities. After he buzzed into the apartment complex, the stairs to the fourth floor creaked and groaned under his feet.

He closed the door behind him and clicked the locks back into place. Safe in room 409, Reuel slung his bag over a chair and flipped the kitchen light on. Dishes toppled out of the sink covered in grime and half-eaten food. The TV had been left on again. Reuel unstrapped his armor and called out, "You were supposed to be asleep an hour ago. And I said no TV after seven."

A scruffy boy with orange hair peeked up from behind the couch. "And you said that you would be back at six. You were supposed to bring dinner!"

"Sorry, Jax." Reuel pulled off a boot. "I had to work late again."

Jackson nodded at his older brother knowingly. "I figured. Emma came by today. We had dinner without you."

"I can see that."

Jackson flopped down onto the cushions again. His brother was examining a scratch on his helmet when he abruptly suggested, "You should ask her out."

"Emma?" Jackson always knew how to catch his brother off guard.

"Then she can babysit me all the time," Jackson added eagerly. "She can cook for us too! If you guys were together, you wouldn't be so lonely."

Reuel set his helmet on his knee. "I'm not lonely." He said it more to himself than to his brother. Working as frequently as he did, relationships slipped away into the back of his mind. When Jackson wouldn't stop giving him the eyebrow, Reuel ruffled his hair. "I got you, don't I?"

"That's what a single person would say." Jackson snorted.

Ouch. Jackson might have only been nine, but he could be savage sometimes. "Did you guys leave anything for me?"

"I left you the vegetables I didn't like."

"Wow, aren't you generous."

With the leftovers heating in the microwave, Reuel decided to wash up after another prolonged day. Changing shirts and washing his face with a damp towel, his reflection glowered back at him in the cracked mirror. Stubble sprouted along the edges of his face again, the rest of his curly hair he'd shaved off. Like Jackson's, it would grow out into a bright reddish-brown, but Reuel preferred a clean cut under his helmet. Small lines framed the sides of his face, traced down his temples, and met at the base of his stubborn chin. The marks the tight relegator helmets created only exaggerated Reuel's hawkish features.

Jackson sat at the counter wearing his helmet when he came out. The microwave neutralized the flavor of his food, but the meal was warm all the same. Neither brother spoke a word for a while, the only sound came from Reuel's fork poking his plate, echoing in the small room like a ticking clock.

"Do you ever get scared going out there?" Jackson drew circles on the table while he glanced at his brother.

"Sometimes," Reuel admitted.

Jackson tugged off the helmet and rolled it across the tabletop. "What do you do when you're scared?"

The question came out in a mixture of anxiety and anticipation. Reuel knew his brother was having nightmares again, and they were becoming more frequent. He shouldn't be left alone, but the outside world was a dangerous place. School didn't fit in the budget and asking for help would only draw attention. After the death of their parents, Reuel trusted no one. Trusting had gotten them killed. So he did the only thing he could: Reuel became a relegator. Being honest with himself, Reuel hated being a relegator. He hated leaving Jackson here alone. Life had a lot of choices, and sometimes the only choices were bad ones.

"What do I do when I'm scared?" Reuel paused, repeating the question to himself. He dropped his fork and reached for his helmet. "Do you know why I wear this?"

Jackson shook his head.

"I wear it because it hides my face. When I go out there, sometimes it can be kind of scary. But I know I have to be brave. I have to be brave because other people need me to be. So I put the helmet on. People can't see my face, so they can't tell when I'm scared. To them, I'm always brave, and it gives them courage. We're all helping each other out there, but deep down we're all scared. It's my job to protect them, even when I'm afraid too, but when I wear my helmet, I feel braver."

"You do?"

Reuel smiled at his brother. "Definitely. It's okay to be scared sometimes, Jax, but that's when we can be brave for those who can't. All right, it's about time we both went to bed."

"Are you going to be gone all day again?"

"I'll try to be back before dinner," Reuel promised, "and maybe—*maybe*—if you're lucky, I'll bring back some ice cream too."

Jackson's eyes lit up. "Mint chocolate chip?"

"Only if you actually eat your broccoli this time." Reuel tossed his helmet to a complaining Jackson.

"Won't you need this for tomorrow?"

"If you need help being brave, just put it on. You can give it back to me when I get home." Reuel drew the curtain that divided the room they shared. Tucked in a corner on a mattress, he wondered if the plenaries would take the bait. They had to, if Reuel was going to succeed for Solon, they had to. For his and Jackson's sake.

Austin dropped the book on Kate's bed as he stared at it. It didn't sound as if they would be called back by the others tonight, so he decided any distraction would be welcome. Written in cursive silver letters, the Plenarie Tome had a worn leather cover fraying around the edges. Flipping past the cover, the table of contents was almost thirty pages.

Turning past the end of the contents page, Austin read aloud, "In the beginning, there was darkness. A place before time itself. And so the universe began. There was light and with it came life. The ancient races predating mankind arose and created the world around us and the beings that dwell in it, and so time began. After the world established itself, a new race of man was born, lesser than its ancestors who first dwelled in the Macrocosm. As time passed, the guardians of the world took sides and rivalries began, causing chaos and death. They divided the Macrocosm, protecting all races from each other and preserving the natural order of the world. Before—"

The sound of Kate snoring cut him off as he glanced at her. Her chest rose and fell slowly. Pulling the covers to her chin, Austin closed the book and quietly left the room. It was getting late, and the plenaries hadn't left the Athenaeum. Returning to his own bedroom, he jumped into bed, dimming the lights a little and continuing where he left off. After the book's genesis chapter, Austin skipped ahead to the chapter after that. At the top of the page it read:

Plenarie Terminology and Classification

Austin's eyes scanned down the page until they stopped at a familiar name: Solon Blak. Alton mentioned Solon when he told Austin the truth about the relegators and their past. Next to the name, Austin read the following text:

Solon Blak—Solon Blak, his true identity unknown, rebelled against his people and desired the Template View for himself. He hoped that with it, he could destroy his enemies and rise as the master of the four realms with his army of rogues. The corrupt plenaries, soon to be named relegators, were the followers of Solon Blak throughout the purge. While Blak still possessed a pendant, he wore his own self-designed armor that could manipulate his aura into a combination of black smoke and electricity. He perished in the last days of the purge, but—

The rest of the page had been torn out after that. Austin looked throughout the remainder of the book, but the second half of the page was missing. Whether it had been intentional or not, Austin wondered why the information was ripped out. And what was this Template View object the passage mentioned? How could he find out more? Though he didn't have a clock or a window in his bedroom, Austin knew it was very late. He could check the Athenaeum to see if anyone was still awake and ask about the missing segment. Then again, the plenaries might not want to share that information. Perhaps one of them had torn it out of the book.

"Where's the missing half?" he asked out loud.

"Hello, do you require my assistance?"

Austin tumbled out of bed. "Who's there?"

At first, he saw no one. Then his eyes adjusted. He could just make out a young woman standing in front of the door. She wore a dress that blended in with the wall behind her. Her curly hair looked blonde, but her overall silhouette faded in and out of view. Smiling, she stepped closer. "My apologies, I did not mean to startle you. My name is Vera. Who might you be?" she asked in a cool voice.

Austin kept his distance from the ghostly woman. She blocked the door, trapping him in the room. Clearing his throat, he tried to sound calm. "Uh, I'm Austin. You're a felera, right? Sorry, I wasn't trying to summon or disturb you."

Vera tilted her head at him. "Of course. I came when you asked a question concerning one of my books."

"Your books?"

"I am the keeper of the library here at the Sacrarium," Vera explained. "I am here to help anyone who has any questions regarding my books."

Austin opened the Tome to the ripped page. "Um, see here where the page is missing? I wanted to know what happened to it, or what was written there." Picking it up, Vera inspected the page back to front. She said nothing while she read. Austin waited another minute before asking for an answer. "Well?"

Closing the book, Vera returned it to him and responded, "The Plenarie Tome is one of our most sacred books here at the Sacrarium. If someone did rip this part of the page out, they must have had their reasons for doing so. While I cannot recall this part you seek, I can, however, suggest books with similar subjects?"

"Sure, that'd be great."

Bowing her head, Vera disappeared. A few minutes later, she returned holding three thick volumes in her arms. Placing them on his bedside table, she turned to face him. "Anything else?"

Austin almost replied when he caught the sound of soft voices traveling down the hall. "Thanks, Vera. Sorry I thought you were a ghost. Er, you'd better get going. Oh wait! Do you mind keeping this between us?"

Vera smiled as she faded away. "Of course."

With the felera gone, Austin switched off the lights and burrowed himself under the blankets on his bed. No one came into the room to check on him and the hall was silent once again. Lying on his back, he closed his eyes and willed himself to fall sleep, wondering what the plenaries had been talking about.

"But why? That doesn't make any sense…"

"Trust me, you'll catch him at it."

Racing down an old staircase, Austin entered a circular room with three doors, each door had a strange symbol above it. The room dissolved into smoke before he could see who stood next to the glowing orb on a pedestal. When everything came into focus, he was in the graveyard back home where he'd first seen the multicolored lightning. Looking up, he watched yellow and dark purple streaks chase each other and collide in a shower of sparks.

Austin, can you hear me?

A flash of yellow light blinded him as multiple voices bombarded his thoughts shouting out, "Wait! Stop! Ryker! Ryker!"

Austin woke up with a throbbing headache. Stepping out of bed, he left his room to get some water. Once he found the kitchen, he opened a few cabinets and discovered an empty glass. After filling it to the brim with cool water, he sat on the edge of the exterior part of the kitchen and rubbed his bare feet on the chilly grass. The sun hadn't risen yet as the moon's pale light shone through the stained-glass dome, illuminating the garden. Setting the empty glass down, his headache gradually subsided as he strolled around the greenery. He came to a stop next to a vast oak tree in one of the far corners of the room. From here, the moonlight shone directly in front of the tree, a perfect reading spot.

Running back to his room and grabbing one of the books Vera gave him, he returned to the spot and sat on the soft grass underneath the shadow of the tree. There he laid the book on his lap and squinted at the book's title: *Dawn of the Darker Element: Vol 1.* The foreword spoke heavily about the chaos in the beginning of the Macrocosm's division. Macrocosm, Austin learned, was another word for the universe. While the subject proved interesting, Austin's attention slipped as his eyelids grew heavy.

"Austin? Austin? Hello! Austin, what are you doing out here?"

Austin woke up as someone smacked his cheek. They blocked out the sun as they stood above him, swimming into focus. Blinking a couple times, Austin groaned. Maisie moved away from him as he sat up, aching. Today she wore denim shorts with a long-sleeved white T-shirt. Thankfully, Austin had slept in his clothes. The last thing he wanted was Maisie seeing him in his boxers. She stood up and extended her hand to help him get to his feet. Taking it, he stretched his back, making popping noises as he did.

"What time is it?"

Maisie tapped an imaginary watch on her wrist. "Seven twenty-two. You shouldn't leave books out in the garden area. Aviana will throw a fit if she catches you with one out here."

"I'll put it back," Austin promised.

Maisie yanked it out of his reach. "I got it. Why don't you walk over and say good morning?"

"Good morning?" Austin shielded his eyes just as Maisie teleported with a crack. Behind the pond, he noticed a giant sunhat bobbing among the plants and giant herbs. Walking over, he trod carefully around flowers and strange plants with thorns and petals. When he caught sight of the yellow hat again, he scooted around a hedge almost twice his height and found the owner. Aviana crouched on the ground working deep in dirt. Dressed in mud-stained overalls, she stabbed the ground with a silver spade.

Under the hat, Aviana had knotted her hair into a tight bun. It amazed Austin how a gorgeous girl could get so dirty and still look amazing. The flattering overalls might have had something to do with it too. While she bent over a potted flower, Austin quickly picked out a flower and stared at it instead. He racked his brain for something funny or clever to say. Should he just go with a good morning? It looked like Aviana didn't want to be bothered. "So. Gardening, am I right?" Austin slapped himself as soon as the words tumbled out.

"Sneak up on me again, and I'll bury you in the ground."

Aviana tossed her tool aside and gently lowered the plant into the fresh soil. "Can I help you?"

"Sorry, I didn't—wait, are those Virginia roses?"

Aviana packed dirt around her new flower and grunted, "Yeah. Recognize them?"

"From my mom's gardening book." Austin squatted in front of the bush next to Aviana. "She loved to show me the pictures of all the plants and flowers. She always talked about planting her own garden."

Finished with her newest seedling, Aviana wiped her dirt-smeared brow and tilted her hat up at him. "And did she?"

"No." Austin plucked at the grass, glancing away. "She died before she got the chance."

Aviana tugged her gloves off and flexed her fingers. In the corner of her eye, she squinted at Austin. His gaze downcast, his shoulders slumped in a hunched position. Flicking dirt at him, Aviana offered the startled Austin her gloves. "Put these on. You can help me trim the rose bushes."

After an hour of back-breaking, sweat-drenching gardening, Aviana rewarded Austin with a bowl of freshly plucked strawberries. Sitting beside her on the edge of the kitchen patio, Austin bit into a strawberry and relished the taste. "You grew these?"

"I grow most of my fruits." Aviana waved a hand over the garden.

Austin wiped his juice-stained mouth and nodded. "What did you guys talk about last night?"

"Nothing you would be interested in," Aviana answered vaguely.

"Did you decide about meeting the mysterious informant or not?"

"We did." Aviana picked at the dirt under her nails. "Even though I voted strictly against it, we decided to go ahead and meet this relegator."

"Do Kate and I get to go?" Austin licked his fingers and wiped them on his jeans.

Aviana's nose wrinkled watching that. "You wanted to tag along, right? Well it looks like you'll be getting your wish."

NINETEEN

In the end, everyone but Alton was going to Mojo's. Braylin and Aviana argued against it, but they ran out of time to argue when noon approached. Teleporting through the arch, they arrived in front of the small diner on the corner of a street. In faded blue letters, that desperately needed to be painted, was the establishment's name.

"Be alert," Braylin warned. "This could be a trap."

A little bell chimed as they pushed through the glass doors. The diner was completely empty except for a group of men in business suits sitting in the corner. With an atmosphere reeking of overcooked meat, it seemed the inside of the diner also needed a facelift. Sitting themselves down in a booth by the window, they picked up laminated menus that were yellowed and sharp enough to cut stone. Staring at the menu, Kate whispered, "How are we going to recognize this guy? Unless he shows up in his relegator onesie, he could be anyone."

When the waitress came over with a notepad, Kate thought

she'd been blinded by a rainbow. Purple ribbons and sunflowers decorated her Dodger-blue hair, and the young woman was dressed in a paint-stained tank top with high-waisted shorts hugging her curves. She wore tinted sunglasses, and the name tag on her top read *Lucena*.

"Can I take your order," she asked roughly in a New York accent.

To avoid suspicion, a few of them ordered burgers from the menu. While Lucena left to put in their order, a new customer walked into the diner. Catching his face, Kate almost slipped out of her seat. Broad-shouldered like Braylin, the man dressed in a leather jacket and ripped jeans. The sides of his head had been shaved, with the rest of his dark hair gelled back stylishly. Kate recognized him by the thin scratches cutting across his face. Scratch, the relegator who interrogated her the first time, spotted them in the booth and walked over.

"So you're the hacker. The relegator who helped me and my friends escape the Tower."

Scratch shushed her while glancing around. "Has anyone ever told you that you're as subtle as a bullhorn? Whatever, I can't stay long. My name's Scratch."

"Hey, Scratch." Maisie reached over the table and shook his hand. "I should have known it was you. I recognized you from the club."

"The club?" Aviana choked on her drink and stared at Maisie.

"I gave your friend here a tip to find Ms. Summers the other day." Scratch returned Maisie's shake with a nod. "I didn't know you were The Orchid. It's an honor meeting you officially."

Pleased with herself, Maisie sat back down. Aviana folded her hands and addressed Scratch. "Amari tells us you have some information regarding the relegators? If you're looking for a reward, don't expect one."

Scratch's smile faded. "You think I'm doing this for money?"

"Well yes." Aviana rubbed her fingers together. "Why else would you betray your fellow relegators and risk getting caught?"

The relegator looked away. His expression was stern, but his hands kept fidgeting with his wristband. "Look, girly, I never volunteered to be a relegator, I got forced into it. My old man was a plenarie, y'know. They killed him and my mom when I was very little. I had no one to go to, then they found me and streamlined me into their service." Scratch's hands froze, and he glanced back up at Aviana. "I don't care about the risk. I'm just making sure the relegators get what they deserve. The Orchid is the only person out there fighting back. I want to help you, but you have to trust me."

"How do we know this isn't a set up?" Braylin questioned him.

"You want proof I'm for real?" Scratch counted off on his fingers. "Let's see, I hacked into the Tower and busted Kate out, I drove you three out of the Alliance Tower, *and* I changed the relegators' password so your friend Amari could get you the info regarding your human friends here. Believe me now?"

For once Aviana did not have a retort. Kate leaned over and touched Scratch's hand. "My parents. Can you help us find them?"

Scratch rubbed his nose. A line appeared between his brows as he spoke. "Last I checked, the relegators moved your parents to another facility. I'm not sure where, the information was redacted."

Kath nodded and stared into her lap. Under the table, Austin took her hand and gave her a comforting squeeze. Swinging her legs and accidentally kicking Braylin, Maisie stopped and then asked Scratch, "So what *do* you have to give us?"

With a pen out of his pocket, Scratch accepted a napkin from Austin and scribbled ferociously. As the relegator wrote, Lucena brought over their meals and whispered something to Scratch. His eyes rounded for a moment before he grunted to her and went back to writing. Lucena kissed him on the cheek and disappeared behind the bar. Dropping his pen, he pushed the napkin to Braylin. "After you guys escaped, the relegators decided to move their last shipment for the project to a different warehouse. I was able to hack in and find the address. It's only going to be there for a night, if you want to intercept it and slow them down, tomorrow night's the only chance."

"Last shipment," Maisie echoed. "What project?"

Scratch tapped his pen against the table. "The relegators are building some kind of machine. I don't know much about it—'cause I'm low-ranking—but they've been working on this thing since the Alliance Tower was built. I've seen a couple of the deliveries; they're making something big. I'm no scientist, but this machine-thing is going to need a lot of power. That's what's in this final shipment. A new power source."

Braylin folded the napkin and tucked it in his pocket. "We'll look into it. How do we reach you if we need to find you again?"

"I come to this place after my morning shift ends on Tuesdays and Thursdays," Scratch informed them as he walked over to the counter, "or you can always leave a message with Lucena." The waitress came around and slipped an arm around Scratch's. Her skin glowed a few shades lighter than Scratch's own deep brown tone. Scratch waved at them before kissing Lucena and walking her out of the diner.

"Well then"—Braylin pushed them out of the booth— "looks like we got ourselves a lead. Time to leave before our luck runs out."

Coming back through the arch, the plenaries made plans for another afternoon of training in the velocity chamber. Austin gulped. Cannonballing into Braylin last time put a damper on his enthusiasm to train. Naturally, Kate had enough enthusiasm for both of them. Before he could protest, she asked them what the plan would be for training today.

"Sparring day." Maisie punched her open palm with a grin.

"We need to talk to Alton first," Aviana reminded her.

Maisie gazed heavenward. "Ugggghhh. Fine, let's make it quick."

"Don't give me that attitude, Maisie Orchid!"

"I'll give you something else when we're in the velocity chamber...."

The two girls bickered all the way to the Athenaeum.

When they continued to argue, Braylin mentioned heading to the library to do some research before they trained. Kate volunteered herself to join him. Sagging his shoulders with a moan, Austin followed the girls. Braylin led Kate down away from the Athenaeum to a different area of the Sacrarium.

Opening the door for her, Braylin walked in after Kate. She stopped dead in her tracks as her jaw dropped. The New York public library had nothing on this! The room was shaped like a tall cylinder with curved walls lined with polished wood shelves packed with books. A large, revolving pillar dominated the center of the vast chamber. The pillar stretched to the towering roof and had a circumference of about fifteen feet. An assortment of books in countless colors and sizes stuffed the wood-furnished column. Surrounding the pillar sat eight tables, each with a jar in their center with flickering lights inside that looked like lightning bugs.

When Kate bent her head back, she saw the books on the higher shelves floating to and from the round walls and pillar, finding new places to sit. Tearing her eyes from above and glancing down, she gasped. Like the rest of the Sacrarium, the floor was a white marble, but the ground of the library pulsed with life as green lines, similar to that of a computer chip, formed intersecting tracks and lines along the ground and connected to the bottom of the column and walls.

Braylin explained that the lines were integrated circuits, processing the library central interface. Computers wouldn't work at the Sacrarium, so the circuits generated a psychic wavelength that was connected to all the data in the room.

"It's quite simple, really," Braylin pointed out. "If you

have a specific book in mind, you just ask Vera to retrieve it for you."

"Who's Vera?"

"Hello, Braylin, do you require my assistance?" replied a voice behind Kate.

Kate yelped as she spun around. She hadn't heard anyone else in the room besides Braylin. A blonde woman materialized out of thin air behind Kate. It was hard to focus on her features, but she smiled at Kate and hovered over to her. "Hello there, who are you?"

"I-I'm Kate," she answered.

"Vera is a felera. She is the heart, and quite literally, the soul of the library," Braylin said.

"Vera helped Alton build the Sacrarium in the early years. When they finished, he made her the ward of the library. Alton was actually the one who named her. Felera usually don't have names."

Countless questions brewed in Kate's mind as she opened her mouth. Smiling, Braylin held up a hand. "I know you must have a million questions to ask, Kate, but I have some research to do in the library. Just ask Vera if you need anything." Briefly inclining his head, Braylin walked away to a nearby shelf, pulling out a rather large volume.

Kate followed him to a table and peeked at the book he read. "Can I help?"

Braylin slid the book he opened over to her. "See this paragraph? I'm trying to find more sections about enhanced power sources in these other books. Grab one of them and check the table of contents. We can find it a lot faster together."

Kate grabbed the book and sat across from Braylin. For a while, no one spoke as they worked in the library. Silence didn't suit Kate as she always buzzed with questions. Talking was also just one of the many things she liked to do. "Braylin? What's the silver metal behind your ears? I noticed them the first night we met."

"Hearing aids." Braylin brushed back his hair so she could get a better look. "Alton made them for me when I first came here. My ears never fully recovered after I escaped relegator custody."

"You were imprisoned by the relegators?" Kate gasped.

"Ages ago. Scientists cracked my skull open and experimented on me. I guess they crossed the wrong wires. They also screwed with my memory. I... I can't remember anything before the operations. Alton stitched me back together and built these special hearing aids so they're compatible with my armor. I can't live without them."

"Oh, Braylin, I'm so sorry." Kate wiped her eyes.

"All in the past," Braylin assured her. "Let's get back to the books, shall we?"

Still looking for a book with energy sources, they continued to organize them into separate piles. Kate's attention slipped as she stared at Braylin. His gaze intent on the work at hand, he hadn't noticed her extended watch on him. Those silver eyes of his had a guarded look, but they also softened whenever he looked at her. Braylin was more muscular than most guys Kate met and had broader shoulders with compact biceps. He stretched at least a foot taller than her. When he smiled, even his teeth glittered a brilliant white. After Kate first met him, her heart somersaulted. He was welcoming and contributive... and really attractive. The thought of plenaries had always frightened her, but now that Kate had actually met one, she wondered if there were any more like Braylin.

"Why do you keep staring at me?"

Kate's face burned as she shook her head. "No, no, I was just—just deep in thought."

Nodding, he pulled a large volume toward him and continued to read. Trying to keep a casual tone, Kate asked, "You and Aviana must train a lot together. Are you two... you know."

"No. Aviana and I aren't dating, if that's what you're asking. Ryker had a girlfriend but—no, there's nothing to say, really."

"Ryker? Who's Ryker?"

Braylin closed his book. "One of the plenaries who used to live here with us. He and his best friend Wade disappeared a few months ago. Are you seeing someone?" he questioned.

Ducking down pretending to grab a book, Kate replied, "Not at the moment. I'm in the market though. Interested?" She slapped her mouth in shock as the words came out. Gradually sitting back up, she tried to look as remote as possible when she looked at Braylin. His face unreadable, he stood silently inert.

Hastily clearing his throat, he gave a nervous chuckle. "Well, we should probably head to the velocity chamber. I'm going to put some of these away before Vera shows up."

Kate watched him get up and walk to one of the shelves on the other side of the room. When his back faced her, she banged her head on the table, cursing at herself repeatedly.

TWENTY

AUSTIN found himself heading to the velocity chamber alone. While Aviana told Alton about their meeting with the relegator Scratch, Maisie suggested Austin should just go ahead to the chamber and wait for them. Two wrong turns later, he found the training room. The Track appeared inoperative, but Austin prodded the surface with his foot just to be safe. Nothing. The floor remained solid as stone. Ten more minutes passed and none of the plenaries had shown up.

Glancing around, Austin practiced throwing punches through the air. He always wanted to try out a martial art, but that dream died after the car crash. Now that he could walk *and* had powers, the dream not only revived, it had grown. He threw a right hook. *Maybe I can find a trainer.* Left upper cut. *Someone to teach me how to fight.* Straight punch. *With my powers and some skill, maybe I can make a difference out there.* Austin yelled out as he jumped and kicked in the air, he missed the landing and fell on his rear.

Standing by the door, Maisie doubled over laughing. "You all right, Chuck Norris?"

Austin sprang up, ears burning. "How long have you been standing there?"

"Long enough to know you've never taken a boxing lesson." Maisie walked over, wiping a tear from her eye. She'd changed into a sports bra and shorts with her hair tied up in a ponytail. When she came closer, Austin noticed scars tracing around her shoulders and neck.

"What's the matter? Never seen a girl show some skin before?"

"What?" Austin stepped back. "No, no, I mean—I would've changed too if I'd known."

"Let's get started. Braylin and the other girl are right behind me," Aviana announced as she strode in.

Oh no, Austin gaped when he spotted her. Aviana dressed in the same style as Maisie; this would be a lot harder than he'd expected. More white spots decorated Aviana's Amazonian-fit body on her exposed stomach and legs. Unlike Maisie, she also wore leather gauntlets with a scabbard strapped to her hip. Encrusted in the hilt, a blue jewel glimmered in the light. While Aviana circled the room, Braylin and Kate arrived together.

Adjusting the strap to her scabbard, Aviana said, "I think we'll go freestyle today. Can you set up the ring, Braylin?"

Braylin grunted and stepped into the center of the room. Raising his hands, his voice boomed in the giant chamber. "Activate standard sparring ring. Default borders."

"Woah!" Austin lifted a foot as the ground under him glowed.

White light ran through the floor in thin lines, forming a giant circle in the middle of the training room. Tempted to touch the light, Austin hopped into the circle. Everyone but Kate stood in the ring where Austin knew the sparring would take place. The thought of going against any of them, including Maisie, made his mouth dry and his legs buckle.

His eyes met Kate's and she mouthed "You got this," giving him a thumbs up. Nodding with a nervous smile, Austin analyzed his would-be opponent. Braylin's stature already gave him the advantage, but Austin remembered he also possessed enhanced strength. Maybe he could outmaneuver him? Speed would be the only advantage for him here. The plenarie whispered something to Aviana who gripped the handle of her weapon nodding.

"Care to join us, Austin?" Braylin waved him over.

Austin shuffled over with his hands in his pockets. If either of the plenaries noticed his unease about the exercise they didn't mention it. When he went over, Braylin folded his arms and tipped his head toward Aviana. "You'll be against Aviana here first. Sound good?"

"Wait, what?" Austin flinched at the razor-like grin Aviana flashed him.

"Well, from what we can tell"—Braylin squinted at him—"you and Aviana have similar abilities. I'm just curious to see how similar. We'll just try it for one round, and then you can sit out if you want."

"Okay." Austin's grunt sounded more like a whimper.

Aviana unsheathed her sword. She swung it gracefully left and right then pointed it at Austin's chest. "Best of luck to you."

Austin retreated toward the edge of the ring. His opponent gave him a once-over before she crouched in a fighting stance. Aviana balanced the flat side of her sword on her gloved wrist, a strange sword position, but her intense glare made it clear she knew what she was doing. On the edge of the circle, Braylin would be refereeing the match and intervene if necessary. Austin was about to ask if he would get a sword but Braylin clapped his hands together. The sound bounced in the chamber like a gong; Austin blocked his ears wincing. That's when the girl with the glowing sword bellowed a war cry and attacked.

CRACK!

"What the—" Austin dropped to the floor as a ball of blue energy shot out of Aviana's sword and flew above his head. Another blast rocketed toward him as he rolled to the right. A sizzling crater smoked where Austin had been lying. The ground trembled as the hole shrank and gradually sealed itself.

"What are you doing? Get off the ground!"

"You failed to mention her sword could shoot freaking energy bolts, Maisie!"

Aviana aimed for a third strike but Austin bolted at her, zigzagging left and right. Adjusting her stance, she raised her sword and turned the blade. "Bold move"—she whacked the sword like a bat and knocked Austin down with the flat side of its blade—"but foolish all the same."

His insides rattling like a maraca, Austin moaned as Aviana pinned him down and kissed his throat with the edge of her sword. Behind the line, Kate bit her nails and Maisie pinched the bridge of her nose. Even Braylin looked disappointed as he walked over to help him up. "Wait." Austin coughed as he smacked Braylin's hand away. "One more round."

Brows raised, Braylin exchanged a glance with Aviana.

"We can go again." She shrugged. "It's his funeral."

Maisie and Kate cheered from the sidelines while Aviana and Austin circled each other for the second time. Aviana had taken him by surprise, but not this time. After Braylin smacked his hands together once more, she repeated the same attack. Austin grinned; he'd hoped she would do that. Tapping into his power, he zoomed around the circle until he resembled nothing but a blur to Aviana. When she couldn't hit him with a blast, she sheathed her weapon and flew after him.

The device on his wrist made him slower, but Austin kept far enough ahead of Aviana. He finished the circle, passing Braylin for the twentieth time while the comet of blue energy soared closer and closer. *Almost there.* Austin kicked into overdrive until Aviana gradually fell behind, then he turned on his heel and streaked directly at Aviana. Just as he'd guessed, his sudden change of direction startled her and she froze. Austin tackled the girl right when she rematerialized and tumbled over her.

By the edge of the ring, Austin slumped next to Aviana. She made a grab for her sword, but he quickly sprawled himself on top of her before she raised it. Pinned by Austin and her own weapon, Aviana's nose almost touched his. Struggling to hold her down, Austin suddenly realized the intimate position they were in. His knees around her hips, he found himself staring at her mouth. Before he lost control of himself, Aviana growled, "Watch the sword, human!"

Blue energy snapped from Aviana's sword and electrocuted Austin. Instead of feeling the rush of pain, his body absorbed the energy and channeled it. A bolt of yellow lightning blasted out of Austin and threw him backwards. "Gah!" His energy outburst threw him into the wall with a crunch and a crackle of yellow electricity.

Kate dropped by his side in an instant. "Austin! Are you all right?"

Dusting himself off, Austin noticed Braylin and Maisie hovering over a giant hole. Smoke rose from where he'd tackled Aviana. He ran over to the plenaries and squatted by the pit he created. "Aviana? Are you okay?"

Braylin and Maisie reached down and heaved out a soot-covered Aviana with scorched clothing. Coughing up a puff of smoke, she wiped the grime from her face and worked her jaw. Before the hole closed, Braylin tugged Aviana's sword out and tossed it beside her.

"Dang, Aviana," Maisie giggled, "your hair!"

"What's wrong with my—*are you kidding me*?" Aviana thundered after she touched her head. Her dark hair had puffed out into a massive cloud of frizzy curls. A flash of yellow snapped her finger when she touched it. "Do you know how long it took to straighten it?" Aviana almost shrieked at Austin.

"Easy, Aviana." Braylin touched her shoulder. "It's just hair. No harm done."

"No harm done?" Aviana spluttered, her finger shook when she pointed it at Austin. "Did you not just see that lightning blast? I haven't seen anything like that since... since..."

The words died on her lips, her tawny eyes budged at some unsaid thought. Grabbing her sword, she placed it back in her scabbard and hurried out of the chamber. "You three practice without me. I… I just remembered… there's something I need to check."

"Wait a sec, Aviana." Austin jogged over to her and reached his hand out. "Good match. You're hard to beat, and that sword of yours is awesome."

For a moment, Aviana only stared at his hand, surprised. When she took it, Austin could have sworn he saw less disdain, maybe even respect, in her eyes when she tipped her head. "You're better than I thought, Austin. Maybe there's hope for you after all."

The rest of the sparring session did not go as well as Austin hoped. Two rounds of getting clubbed by Braylin and three attempts to catch Maisie left his chest aching and his limbs shaking like leaves in the wind. Alton's device worked flawlessly, and Austin got pulverized for it. Some moments he wanted to rip the stupid thing off, but then he remembered his scars. Finally, after another round, the session ended. When they left the velocity chamber, Maisie gave Austin a quick checkup and laughed. "I swear, you hurt yourself more than Wade ever did."

Wade. The name jogged something in Austin's memory. An empty room, an older picture, the bitterness in Aviana's voice when she mentioned his name. "Who's Wade? He was a plenarie who disappeared, right?"

"Yeah, one of the others who survived the Excretion Act," Maisie explained. An old memory brought a smile to her face. "He always broke or injured something whenever we trained. I remember this one time he sparred Aviana—he shocked her so bad, she had smoke coming out of her ears and her hair looked like a burnt cotton ball." She laughed faintly. "She chased him around until he tripped and knocked a tooth out."

When they passed Maisie's door in the bedroom hall, Austin asked her, "You've been searching for him, haven't you? That's how you found me?"

"Yeah." Maisie nodded. "Once we figure out what the relegators are planning with this machine, maybe we'll find the clue we've been looking for. He's out there. I know it."

The hope in her voice touched Austin. He racked his brain trying to think of something encouraging to say, but nothing came to mind. If the plenaries could help him with his powers, maybe he could help them find their friend too.

TWENTY-ONE

SPIDERS. Why did it have to be spiders?

Everyone called it arachnophobia, Reuel preferred the term common sense. The warehouse he stood in crawled with the little monsters. *The one time I leave my helmet at home,* he cursed to himself. Tonight, the plenaries would be coming, and Reuel had the bait waiting for them. As far as warehouses in this area went, the building seemed small. His trusty can of Raid by his side, Reuel personally inspected every inch of the structure. He had every window, every crack and cranny mapped in the back of his mind.

The skylight, the four second-floor windows, and the back door were the only entrances for the plenaries—assuming they didn't magically appear in the middle of the warehouse. Unless they used the front door. No one would be stupid enough to try that. Right? Reuel positioned two guards near the door, just in case. His team of relegators in place, he had the roads in the area ready to be blocked off in case of a getaway car, and he placed the shipment in the storage room. Now all he needed were the shipment's guardians.

Two refrigerator-sized containers rocked back and forth by the protected crate. Their occupants hissing and screeching, Reuel jumped back after one of them almost fell over.

"I hope you're coming, Orchid," he muttered to himself. "I have a couple of pets who are very anxious to meet you."

The locks on the steel cages held, but the monsters inside pounded dents into the frame of their prison. Calling in a special favor, Reuel was able to bring in sharper teeth than meager Rottweilers or Dobermans. They would take care of the plenaries, but Reuel wouldn't trust them to leave his men alone. His plan would be risky, but so were most plans that paid off. After checking his watch for the umpteenth time, Reuel finally gave the signal and bolted to a safer position.

The electronic locks on the cages beeped as they clicked open. When the door unlocked, the shaking and the noises stopped abruptly. Silence. One of the cage doors creaked open. Any spiders scuttling around retreated to the cracks and shadows. From inside the cage, a skeletal hand reached out and touched the concrete floor. Black smoke flooded from both containers as the guardians of the shipment climbed out. Circling the giant box between them, one creature slipped away while the other stayed. It climbed above the prize and perched itself like an arachnid, soundless and poised to leap out at anything caught in its web. Just like the spiders Reuel hated.

Austin couldn't help but sense something inside him had changed—again. The energy still flowed restlessly, but with a new feeling of power, a different surge coursing through him. He had the dream again. Images of the storm and flashes of what felt like memories shook him awake, but slipped away before he could remember them.

Today, Braylin wanted to show Austin a special room in the Sacrarium. All he mentioned about it was something about gateways. Padding down the hall with Braylin and surprisingly Aviana, Austin rubbed his aching head. They walked down the hall, through a heavily locked door, and down a decrepit set of stairs leading to an older part of the Sacrarium. When he entered the room, Austin almost gasped. The circular chamber had three additional doors matching the one they'd just passed through, just like the room in his dreams.

In the center of the room, a single pedestal stood alone, displaying what appeared to be a translucent orb glowing in multiple colors. *The orb!* He walked over to the pedestal with the orb. "I've seen this thing before. What is it?"

"It's called Template View," Aviana enlightened him. "Inside the shell lies the residual energy from the magic the elders used to divide the realms, but its essence also binds all the worlds together. Without it, the realms would collapse on each other and destroy the Macrocosm."

"Realms?"

Waving a hand around the room, Aviana waited for Austin to read the inscriptions above each door. Each gateway had its own inscription on it: *Δωδεκάθεον*, *The Angelic Highlands*, *Maleficus Orbis*, and lastly *Villhilium*, the doorway they walked through.

"The universe is a lot bigger than you think." Braylin grinned at him. "It's not just filled with humans *or* plenaries. Besides humans, there's celestials and seraphim. Seraphim live in the Angelic Highlands. They're actually—"

"Angels? For real?" Austin remarked.

Braylin shook his head. "They are not really angels. Actually, most of them are descendants of—"

"Wait, Seraph? Like the guy in *The Matrix* sequels?"

"Please stop interrupting me," Braylin asked politely.

Austin shut his mouth. When Braylin tried to continue, something shattered up the stairs and down the hall. Muttering something about Alton and Maisie, Braylin asked Aviana to finish the lesson in his place while he checked it out. Austin wasn't sure if he should be really glad or really worried. Lucky for him, Aviana had a passion for the Macrocosm's history.

She explained that when the Macrocosm began, the four realms were united as one world. Over time, rivals emerged from the different species preceding mankind. Unable to maintain the peace, the wisest elders of the races divided the Macrocosm into four parts, hiding the conflicting species from each other. Every realm or world, she told him, is an echo or duplicate of the original, united world. And each species of their own realm has their own unique gifts and abilities. Just like the plenaries.

"Who lives in that realm?" Austin pointed to the door labeled *Maleficus Orbis*.

Aviana shook her head sadly. "The Malefîcî. They were thaumaturgies—magicians, you could say. But the humans of their world feared them and wiped them out. They're extinct now. Sound familiar?"

Turning around, Austin looked at the plenaries' door *Villhilium*. Other beings with powers? Other realms? He thought about his dreams. Did they connect to the other realms or only this one? "When we sparred yesterday, you recognized something, didn't you? I'm not the only person you know who has powers like this, am I?"

Aviana pursed her lips. After the Macrocosm's longest minute, she answered, "No. Wade's energy aura was yellow too."

In his dreams, Austin recognized yellow lightning similar to his. Wade was connected to the accident somehow. Which meant someone else was involved. Someone with purple lightning. A color darker than Maisie's. "Was he the only one who disappeared?"

"No. Wade's best friend vanished too. One day they were here, the next…"

They were not. So two plenaries went missing, and then Austin got blasted by energy after noticing yellow and purple lightning. He'd stumbled upon something, but what? Alton knew something. Could it have anything to do with Solon Blak? Austin remembered his time reading the Plenarie Tome. He was unsure about confessing his discovery of the ripped page to Aviana, as he knew she might blame him for it. Then again, his curiosity of Blak intrigued him more. "And what about Solon Blak? What can you tell me about him?"

"He was the first relegator. We thought he died during the purge, but several years ago, a single relegator attacked the

Sacrarium. Alton worried Blak still lived, but the relegator disappeared after he failed to steal the Template View. Last year, we encountered something similar. We tried to hunt him down and kill him, but we failed—"

"And then your friends disappeared," Austin guessed. "Were they—"

Aviana examined her pendant as she interrupted, "That will have to wait. Braylin's summoning me."

In a blue flash she disappeared. Austin knew something didn't add up because Aviana's pendant hadn't glowed when she checked it.

When he left the gateway chamber, Austin couldn't find the others, so he headed to the Athenaeum. The room unnaturally quiet, he stood outside the double doors and knocked to announce his presence. "Hello? Alton? You there?"

Silence responded as he walked in. All the bridges and spherical rooms stood eerily dormant, unmoving and silent. Austin's footsteps echoed as he walked on the bridge leading to Alton's area. The cleanliness of Alton's workspace came as another anomaly. Walking around, he found Alton reading a book between two rows of shelves. As he walked up to him, Austin noticed Alton wasn't moving at all. "Alton?"

His helmet bent down, he gazed at the book he held, giving no reply. Austin didn't want to be rude, but he had no idea if this was normal or not—at least normal for plenarie ghosts. Knocking on the back of the helmet, he called again. "Alton? Alton!"

Jerking to life, Alton spun around to face Austin. "Austin? Did you say something?"

Suddenly, the Athenaeum creaked and groaned to life as everything moved again. The usual humming and clicking sounds bounced off the walls as Austin marveled at the room. Was it all connected to Alton? After his discussion with Aviana, Austin wanted to know what else they were trying to hide. What didn't they want him to know? He may have had reservations about telling Alton about the ripped page, but now Austin figured it would be best just to ask him about it. Hopefully he would fill in the gaps and ease Austin's burning curiosity.

"Yes, um—" Austin hesitated for a moment. "—I was reading the Plenarie Tome, and I came to a page about Solon Blak. I think someone ripped the bottom half of the page out."

Alton stuffed his book back onto the shelf. "Interesting. I am not sure who would have ripped the page out, but I shall look into it once I finish here."

"Thanks. Actually, I had another question to ask you."

Austin cringed as Alton nodded, the sound of metal being dragged across a rug of needles. "Sorry, my joints are getting stiff again. You were saying?"

"I was just talking to Aviana about Solon. She mentioned him and what you encountered last year. Solon's still alive, isn't he? And then before you found me, some of your friends disappeared, right?" Austin theorized. "And I feel like there's still something no one here will tell me. Like there's something about me that upsets them."

Alton hesitated. Facing Austin again, he spoke carefully,

"After you left the Sacrarium, Braylin came to me and explained your story. We formulated theories as to how and why you got your powers. The day of your accident was the same day the other plenaries here at the Sacrarium vanished." Now Alton's voice became more uneasy, and his armor twitched with anxiety. "That is only part of the story. That afternoon, one of them had tried to steal the Template View."

"What?" Austin startled.

Alton nodded nervously. "Braylin confirmed that Ryker Darkthistle, one of our closest friends, was caught trying to steal the View from the gateway chambers that day in June. He said that Wade Chiffon, another dear friend, stopped him from taking it, but both plenaries vanished right after that. It is still a mystery as to what exactly happened, but neither of them returned or have been spotted in this realm since. Some of us suspect Ryker might have been in league with the relegators. But we cannot be certain, and we do not know what happened to Wade."

Austin suddenly remembered a glimpse of his strange dream. He'd heard Chiffon's and Ryker's names before in his visions, but how could he have known that? How did it all connect?

"We don't have any solid evidence against Wade or Ryker besides a story, but Braylin and Aviana provided some facts that support Ryker's betrayal," Alton added.

"But what does that have to do with me?" Austin questioned. "Why wouldn't anyone tell me this before?"

"Because," Alton explained slowly, "you might not be human after all. You might be one of the missing plenaries."

"What?" Austin gasped. His voice echoed over and over in the giant chamber.

"Listen to me, Austin," Alton begged. "Two plenaries vanished on the ninth of June. The same day strange energy struck you. You survived this with only a couple of scars. What you experienced, what actually might have happened, was Wade might have been fatally wounded. When plenaries die, they can reincarnate into a new body. The reincarnated plenarie does not remember his or her past life, but sometimes they experience memory flashes or remember their past lives over time."

"No way," Austin rejected. "I wasn't—I'm not a reincarnated plenarie!"

"Perhaps not, but Aviana told me about what happened in the velocity chamber," Alton continued. "You are changing more and now you have an energy aura. That is what the yellow electricity coming off you is. Now do you understand why we did not want to say anything?"

Austin's brain hurt. His stomach turned, and nothing made any sense. Taking long gasps of breath, he whispered, "So I might actually be Wade? Will I turn into a different person?"

"We cannot be certain about anything," Alton replied. "There are other facts contradicting this theory. Personally, I do not believe you are Wade or even Ryker. That is why we are trying to understand you better."

Is that all they saw him as? A mistake or an echo of someone they used to know? Austin had no choice but to take Alton's word for it. "You'll keep me updated if you find that missing page?"

Alton went silent as he looked past Austin. "Aviana? What are you doing here?"

Sure enough, Aviana walked up with a combination of amusement and inquiry etched on her face. "I was looking for Austin, actually," she replied. "Braylin and I are going to scout out the address Scratch gave us. I need him to babysit Maisie while we're gone."

Alton's shoulders slumped. "You know I am right here, right?"

Aviana offered him an apologetic glance. "Sorry, Papa, you can get a little—er—distracted from time to time. I need a professional."

Alton tilted his head. "You make a valid point. I will be here if you need me. Be safe, you two. After you check it out, come right back."

Nodding, Aviana turned to leave. Austin ran after her. "Hey, what do you mean by babysit?"

Austin bumped into her as she came to a sudden stop. Turning around, she explained, "I doubt Maisie will listen to me and stay here. She rarely does. She'll try to sneak out again, so you'll need to be the voice of reason and keep an eye on her in the velocity chamber. Got it?"

"Yeah sure, but when—"

In a burst of aura light, Aviana vanished.

"Thanks for the input," Austin grumbled.

Wandering around the Sacrarium, he found Kate in the sanctuary's library. The rooms here never ceased to amaze him. Kate read at one of the tables stacked with columns of books. Plopping into a chair beside her, Austin grabbed one of the books she'd been reading. "Interested in Rune Robotics now, are we?"

Groaning, Kate dropped her head on the table. "I told Braylin I would help him with his research."

Austin reached over and rubbed her back sympathetically. "Let's take a break and find something to eat. I bet Maisie's hungry too."

Kate's eyes widened. "Wait, she didn't go with them?"

"Nah. She's stuck with us. Aviana told me to keep an eye on her while they were gone."

Kate face-palmed herself. "And you left her alone?"

"She's in the velocity chamber. She wouldn't—oh."

Sure enough, they found the velocity chamber empty when they checked it. Rushing to Maisie's room, they caught her dashing around looking for something. Tossing a backpack on her bed, Maisie glanced over her shoulder. "Oh, hey, guys. Need something?"

Austin shook his head. "Look, Maisie, Aviana told me to watch you and keep you here. And that's what I'm going to do."

Maisie pouted her lips and planted her hands on her hips. "Then you're definitely gonna get fired from babysitting. Unless…"

"Unless what?" Kate said slowly, like she already knew the answer.

Maisie formed air quotes with her index fingers. "You can come with me and 'watch' me. Technically you're still doing what Aviana wanted, right?"

"That's true." Austin shrugged.

Kate thumped him on the chest. "Oh, come on. If you're going to go with 'technicalities,' you're supposed to watch Maisie *here*!"

Folding his arms, Austin smirked. "*Technically*, I just have to watch her and be her voice of reason. Besides, it's better to stick together, right?"

Maisie flashed a mischievous grin. "Exactly! We'll go sneak out, break into the warehouse, grab this power source thingy, and then sneak back in before Braylin or Aviana even know we're gone."

"Do you even know where you're going?"

Maisie waved the wrinkled napkin at him. "Braylin is one of the easiest guys to pickpocket, plus I got the fingers for the trade." She grinned. Shouldering her backpack, she walked past Kate while Austin followed. They walked into the entrance chamber when Kate called after them. "Hey! Wait up!"

"What happened to staying put?"

Kate glared at her friend. "Where you go, I go. You can't make me stay here, Austin."

"Fine." Austin sighed in defeat. "You should get your jacket too. We'll wait for you by the arch."

Kate ran to her room and slipped on her jacket. Zipping it up and bolting back to the entrance chamber, she watched the white light in the archway flicker off.

"Son of a…. You two are so dead when you get back!"

TWENTY-TWO

In a brief flash of blinding white light, Maisie and Austin arrived on an empty street, concealed in the darkness of night. Their breaths puffed out like cigarette smoke in the cold air as they exhaled. The warehouse stood alone on its own block. By the looks of it, they were just outside New Jersey. If they were still here, Aviana and Braylin would only be scouting, but Maisie and Austin didn't want to be seen by anyone, so they walked in the shadows.

"Wait"—Maisie grabbed Austin's arm—"we have to wait a minute. Jay's gonna meet us."

Austin pulled his arm away. "What? You invited *Jay* to tag along?"

"I did. We could use the extra muscle. Got a problem with that?"

"No." Austin shoved his hands into his jacket pockets.

The girl of the hour walked out of an alley and strutted up to the duo. Jay wore a T-shirt with an angry teddy bear's face wearing an eye patch. Around the picture, purple letters spelled out *Tuff Stuff*. She wore an oversized army jacket over the shirt with combat boots and distressed jeans. In her smaller stature, she stuck her chin out and looked up at Austin. "Well, well, well. What are you doing here, shorty?"

Austin didn't take the bait. "Same reason as you, Jay. *Now* can we go?"

He expected the warehouse to be larger. The site looked abandoned with a deserted street. No sign of life, no lights glimmering through the wrecked windows. Giving the front door a wide berth, Maisie walked around back with Jay and Austin on her heels. The back bore no windows or signs. With the exception of a dumpster bursting to the rim with old trash, nothing sat in the empty parking lot.

Danger, a voice whispered in Austin's head.

Looking at the rusty bin pushed against the wall, he noticed scratch marks on the concrete beside it. The dumpster had been moved recently to this spot by the looks of it.

"I think there's something behind this," he whispered to the girls.

The container almost completely hid the door sticking out behind it. Jay, growing as she did, pushed it aside. The door's handle, rusted with age, would not turn. Digging into her backpack, Maisie pulled out a small, rectangular device and planted it on the handle of the door. Pushing a red button on it, she quickly ran back with Austin and Jay. With a quiet bang, a small hole replaced the handle and the lock on the door. It opened after Austin gave it a rough push. Walking into the damp, dark entrails of the building, they entered a smaller section in the back of the warehouse.

"What was that thing you used on the door?" Jay hissed gruffly.

"An automatic tape measurer," Maisie replied.

"What? So plenarie tape measurers explode?" Austin blanched in the dark.

Maisie shook her head. "No, I swiped it from Alton's lab. He made it himself, so I figured we could use it."

Sneaking into the larger part of the building, they looked around but found nothing out of the ordinary. Just an empty warehouse. Walking next to Maisie, Austin whispered, "Not that I'm complaining, but shouldn't there be a bunch of relegators guarding this place?"

Maisie's nose wrinkled. "That's what I was thinking. I'm starting to worry that Aviana was right. This is getting fishy."

They were silent as they continued to check the rest of the warehouse. Spiders roamed the floors and scattered around their feet. Maisie walked along the walls, trying to find any boxes, only to find barrels of old gasoline. Not exactly a revolutionary power source. They almost gave up when Jay swore in the dark. When Austin and Maisie found her, she pointed to a steel cage while rubbing her nose. "Bumped into this stupid thing! Who leaves a couple of cages lying around?"

Jay had a point; two empty cages sat upright in this corner. Between them, a wooden crate rested untouched. Peeking through the cracks in the wood, they glimpsed a faint light pulsing in the darkness. Austin ripped the top of the crate off and gently lowered it to the floor. The origin of the light came from a medium-sized camping lantern. It looked ordinary except for the source of the light. A small orb resembling the Template View. The light burned bright orange, and electricity pulsed from it like static.

Austin reached down when Maisie grabbed his arm. Looking at her, he followed her gaze looking up diagonally. Just above them on the ceiling resided its guardian. It was difficult to tell in the dim lighting, but the creature had to be at least six feet tall. It had a stout, skeletal body with long, spindly arms and legs the color of rust. Its face embodied a horrific nightmare; empty eye sockets and a mangled build, like a tortured corpse, with black mist leaking out of its exposed cavities. Its jaw sagged open, revealing a gaping hole with black, razor-sharp teeth riddled along the peeling gums.

The monster perched like a spider on its web ready to strike any prey that fell in its deadly trap. If it detected their presence it did not show it. Taut as a trampoline, its knife-like fingers gripped the steel support beams around it. Backing away, they crept behind the metal barrels glancing back at the ceiling.

"What in the name of Tolkien is that?" Austin gasped.

Maisie's hand instinctively touched her neck. Austin noticed the scars, standing out like faint red veins against her pale skin. "That's—that's a blindcrawler," she shuddered. "One shouldn't be a problem but—"

Austin held his breath. "But what?"

Maisie's eyes, wide in fear, locked with his. "But blindcrawlers always travel in pairs."

Austin forgot to breathe. His knees weakened as the hairs on the back of his neck sprang up, goosebumps sprouting all over his skin. Feeling lightheaded, he inhaled the musty air, trying to calm himself. Exhaling slowly, he asked Maisie, "How do we kill it?"

Maisie shook her head. "We can't. At least not here. Even if we draw out this one, we have no idea where the other one is so—"

"Guys." Jay pointed.

"—we need to find it and somehow draw them both out and grab the lantern and take it back to Alton," Maisie continued.

"Guys."

Austin ignored Jay. "So where could the other one be? Plus, when we get them out in the open how do we kill them?"

"*Guys!*" Jay screamed.

Dreading what she pointed to, Austin bent his head back, his nausea instantly returning. Identical to the first, the second blindcrawler crept along the wall, looking down at them. It made no sound as it landed a few feet away, stretching to a staggering six-and-a-half feet. Sizing up the three of them, it shrieked out a cry, like nails being dragged across a chalkboard.

"*Run!*" yelled Maisie.

Jay didn't need to be told twice. She bolted out the door before Austin or Maisie could even blink. Lights blinded them as voices boomed in the suddenly alive room. Surrounded by relegators, Austin and Maisie met each other's eyes.

They'd walked into a trap.

One relegator, the leader, Austin figured, stepped into the room and clapped his hands together slowly. His face exposed without a mask, the relegator had a shaved head with pointed features like a bird's. The blindcrawlers didn't attack, they circled Austin and Maisie as predators.

"Austin Bennet." The relegator's voice brimmed with satisfaction. "I was hoping I'd get to meet you. Now, I didn't think I'd find you here, but a bonus nonetheless." He looked at Maisie and tilted his head. Maisie wore her armor but she'd taken off her helmet. "The Orchid, I presume? Not what I expected, but we were sure you would take the bait."

The blindcrawlers hissed again. Around them, the other relegators shuffled around nervously. Only the one in charge seemed unafraid of the monsters. Instead of an adze, he wielded what must have been a relegator silencer. The gun strapped to his hip, his hand hovered over it guardedly.

"Maisie," Austin hissed to her, "what do we do?"

"The building is surrounded. All means for escape have been cut off. This doesn't have to get ugly; surrender and come quietly. Or, if you want, we can let the blindcrawlers take you down for us," the relegator in charge addressed Maisie.

Austin watched as one of the blindcrawlers limped toward one of the relegators. Shaking in his armor, the relegator fumbled with his adze and aimed it at the creature. His superior noticed and his confident grin melted into a panicked expression. "Dustin, stop! Don't provoke it! They can sense your—"

BANG!

His shot missed the blindcrawler and ricocheted in the warehouse. The blindcrawler pounced on the relegator and ripped his armor apart like cardboard. Its partner attacked as well while the other relegators exploded into panic and

187

retreated out of the warehouse. The leader opened fire on the monster, but his weapon only pissed it off. Sailing through the air and trailing black smoke, the two blindcrawlers circled around them, screaming as they closed in. Words failed him as Austin's feet glued themselves to the concrete.

"We need to bail! Now!" he yelled. *"Maisie!"*

Maisie didn't respond. Hyperventilating, she stood frozen on the spot, pale as a sheet.

Austin shook her by the shoulders. "Maisie? Maisie! Snap out of it!"

"It's—I can't—I don't know what to do!" Maisie panicked.

He tackled her to the floor as a blindcrawler soared above them. Maisie's panic attack worsened as Austin shielded her from the monsters. Scooping her up, he tried to dodge the blindcrawlers, but he wasn't powerful enough to take them on alone. Alton's device slowed him down too much. A couple more scars instead of dying sounded pretty reasonable to Austin right then. He yanked the device off, the energy inside him exploding as it flowed everywhere.

One of the barrels of gasoline ruptured, triggering a chain of blasts unsettling the steel supports of the building. A blindcrawler flew through the fire, its claws stretched toward Austin as it leapt at him. Two gunshots boomed as the monster crashed into the fire, thrashing and burning in front of them. With his gun raised, the relegator looked at Austin with Maisie in his arms. Instead of aiming at them, he shook his head and tossed his weapon aside. He ran to another fallen relegator who cradled his left leg.

"Look out!" Austin yelled out a warning to the relegator.

The leader noticed the steel beam coming down and shoved his friend out of the way. Austin watched the injured relegator limp out of the crumbling warehouse without a backward glance at his rescuer. Austin ran out the exit and dropped Maisie away from the danger zone. "I'll be right back!"

"You're not going back for him." Maisie grabbed Austin by his jacket. "We need to get out of here. Austin, wait!"

Austin dove back into the warehouse. Remembering the burning apartment building, he covered his mouth and glanced around. The crate splintered into embers with the lantern lying in its ashes. In the corner past it, Austin noticed a figure trapped under a steel support beam.

"I can't get out!" the relegator shouted as he tried to lift the column.

Austin looked back at the lantern. A blindcrawler shrieked in the chaos close by. Running over to the remains of the crate, Austin grabbed the lantern. The exit was open behind him. He could just run out and leave the relegator to his demise.

The relegator noticed Austin and reached out. "P-please," he begged.

Pieces of the roof rained down and piled on the floor. The air blackened with smoke and gasoline as the inferno grew hotter and hotter. Eyeing the prize in his hand, Austin had a choice to make.

Under the beam, Reuel's right arm was crushed and burned. The metal scorched his skin as he tried to shove it off him. Burning his hand, he screamed and searched for Austin Bennet.

He was gone.

Smoke blinded Reuel as he coughed and tried again. The skin on his left hand stung and reddened from the spreading burn. Wiping the ash from his face, he dropped his hand and let his head thud on the pavement. Of all the deaths he could've had as a relegator, it figured he'd be burned alive or crushed. What would happen to Jackson? Who would take care of him? He was supposed to be bringing back ice cream for them tonight. Reuel cursed as he sweated in the oven-like building. Catching The Orchid seemed like a pointless hobby now. Regrets piled on Reuel as the nerves in his arm slowly died.

Just make it quick, he pleaded to anyone. Dying slowly had always been a fear of his.

That's when the second blindcrawler caught him. It prowled through the fire, sniffing him out. Reuel froze, his throat protesting to cough again. The beam pushed against his arm harder, forcing a scream from Reuel. And the blindcrawler heard it. As it approached him, Reuel's head flew around, searching for his discarded weapon. A few feet away, its black color glistened in the shimmering heat. Too far. Reuel couldn't reach it.

Stretching above him, the blindcrawler crouched down and reached out. His legs flailing around defensively, Reuel shouted as the monster extended its claws near his throat.

"Over here!" someone yelled in the warehouse.

The blindcrawler hissed and flew away. Reuel sighed, but he had no time to rejoice. Closing his eyes, he braced himself for the black void to consume him. Suddenly, the steel beam shook. Reuel opened his eyes. Next to him, Austin Bennet crouched, covered in soot and burns. While he tried to lift it, Reuel used his free hand to push as well. Even together, they couldn't move it enough to pull him out.

"Just go," Reuel wheezed. "Leave me."

Austin ignored him. The beam wouldn't budge, but the teen wouldn't give up. Yelling as the metal seared his palms, Austin gritted his teeth as he strained his muscles. Above them, the remains of the ceiling caved in.

"Move over, shorty!"

A muscled girl jumped next to Austin and raised the bar like a plank made of foam. Together they tossed it aside and pulled him out. Coughing from inhaling more ash, Reuel couldn't keep his eyes open. The last thing he saw before blacking out was the building collapsing over them in a rain of fire and ash.

"Time to go!" Austin yelled to Jay.

The warehouse toppled like a tower of cards and dissolved into flames. They dragged Reuel out to the street and lowered him down next to a curled-up Maisie. Dropping next to her and gasping for clean air, Austin craned his head up at Jay. "You came back?"

"That's two you owe me now," she grumbled as she wiped her arms.

Austin glanced at the relegator. Unconscious, he looked pretty banged up. His right arm had been crushed by the beam and burns covered half his body. Austin probably looked terrible himself. Behind them, the fire that had consumed the warehouse spread further. Sirens screamed louder as Austin crawled to his feet. "We got to go. Jay?"

Jay threw one of the relegator's arms around Austin's shoulders. "You two can teleport back. I've got a car waiting for me down the block." When Austin tried to thank her, she shrank down to her normal size and rolled her eyes. "You can keep your thanks, I want something else in return for sticking my neck out for you."

"Like high heels?"

"Oh, I should've let you burn." Jay glowered at him. "I'll be cashing in my favors soon, shorty. Now get outta here."

She disappeared around the block without another insult. Austin spotted two firetrucks and a squad of relegator vans streaming down the road at them. He grabbed Maisie's pendant and threw it on the ground. Carrying the relegator fireman style, Austin grabbed Maisie's hand and they jumped through the white portal just before the relegators flooded the area. Traveling through the dimension, they fell through the arch and landed on the cool floor of the Sacrarium. His face pressed against the marble floor, Austin let go of Maisie and the relegator. The relegator groaned beside him and rolled over. Shaking, Maisie breathed in short bursts.

"Where the bloody hell have you been?"

Austin waved a hand on the floor. "Hey, Braylin, just give me a minute—"

"Give you a minute." Braylin hauled Austin off the ground and shook him. "You two—oh no, Maisie, you didn't—" He spotted the relegator and knelt by his side. His eyes closed, Braylin's voice sounded grave. "You brought a relegator to the Sacrarium?"

"He's hurt." Austin grimaced at his own hands, the skin all but charred. "They left him to die. We couldn't leave him."

Braylin said nothing as he scooped up the relegator and ran him out of the entrance chamber. When he came back, Kate followed him, looking just as livid. Slapping Austin on the cheek, Kate almost screamed at him, but she croaked and hugged him instead. "Idiot! Why did you go?"

Braylin stood across from them with his usual folded-arms stance. A dark storm churned in his gray eyes with a frown, unsettling his handsome features. "I put the relegator in one of the spare bedrooms. Is everyone okay?"

"When did you find out we were gone?" Maisie asked.

Braylin's eyes lost the hostile look in them, morphing into an apologetic glance as he waved his hand. The lights in the room activated as they illuminated the entire chamber. With the lights on, Aviana stood in the corner dressed in a navy-blue robe. Austin wasn't sure how long she'd been there, but he gulped and wished he could just teleport away. Anywhere from here. Stepping out of her corner, Aviana stood beside Braylin as she ground out, "You two. Explain. Now."

TWENTY-THREE

ALL at once, everyone talked and argued in a chaotic rhythm. Already in a rage, Aviana's voice couldn't be any more deafening. "One at a time," she ordered. Austin winced as Aviana's hazel eyes glowed with fire, burning through him. "Now, *you* tell me everything that happened."

As best as he could, Austin retold the events of the night, trying to make it sound less dangerous and wild. After mentioning the strange lantern they'd seen, Austin opened Maisie's backpack and handed the mysterious lantern to Braylin.

Examining it, Braylin's eyes rounded in surprise. "You actually got it?"

"Take it to Alton," Aviana ordered. Braylin nodded as he sped away. Aviana groaned, pinching the bridge of her nose. "You both disobeyed direct orders and could've gotten yourselves seriously hurt, or worse, killed. As for you, Maisie, I'm officially banning you from leaving the Sacrarium."

Maisie's head snapped up instantly. "You're *banning* me from leaving the Sacrarium? That is so unfair!"

Aviana shouted again, her words hitting Maisie like piercing darts. "Don't talk to me about being unfair. I can't even trust you to obey the simplest of orders. You're such a child, Maisie. You always screw things up, and I have to be the one who fixes them! Can't you do *anything* right?"

Maisie flinched at every word, every syllable a bullet. She looked so small and frail as she made a choking noise in her throat. Eyes welling up with tears, her face flushed scarlet as she ran off. Tapping him on the shoulder, Kate's eyes darted to the hall and then to Austin. Austin nodded as he watched Aviana storm off in an angry huff. He followed Kate down the hall and knocked on Maisie's door. "Maisie? You there?"

No one answered as he tried a couple more times. He could hear someone sniffling in there, but he decided to leave her in peace. When he glanced at his hands, the burns were gone. His skin had healed itself but was still red from irritation. Weird. After a quick shower, Austin changed into clean clothes and climbed into bed. Physically, he felt exhausted, but his mind was racing. The trap with the relegators, the weird lantern, and Aviana and Maisie's fight kept him up. Eventually drifting off, his dreams resurfaced with the strange lights, indistinct yelling, and the blindcrawlers they faced earlier.

In his dream, Austin ran on clouds with a major thunderstorm raging around him. Austin was running, faster than he ever had. He wasn't sure why, but he felt an impulse to chase the

light ahead of him. It was purple. Not bright like Maisie's but darker and more foreboding. Catching up to it, he noticed it was another plenarie in armor running beside him.

"Ryker!"

The plenarie sped ahead of him, disappearing into the flickers of lightning. He pushed his body harder until they flew side by side. The other runner slammed into him and they fell to the earth, crashing in a graveyard. Pinned to the ground, Austin's cries sounded distant and unclear as the plenarie stabbed him.

Austin gasped as he awoke. Clutching his chest, he rubbed it until the dream's pain evaporated. Outside his room, someone swore, making him jump. When he poked his head out, the door to Maisie's bedroom was opened a crack. He quietly approached the door and glanced into the room.

Maisie sat on the floor by her bed, the torso part of her armor balanced on her lap. Parts scattered around her, she worked on the back of the suit, the metal plates wrenched apart and scratched. Austin noticed more damage under the coverings as Maisie picked at the broken plates with a small tool. After prodding at something, Maisie cried out and yanked her hand back. Sucking on her finger, she wiped her sweaty brow and kicked the armor aside.

Austin turned to leave, but then Maisie drew her knees to her chest and curled up. With her arms wrapped around herself, her quiet sniffles stopped when he gently rapped his knuckle against the wall. "Having trouble with your armor?"

Maisie's puffy red eyes spotted Austin and widened. Closing the door in his face, she told him to go away. Dejected, Austin leaned his arm against the door. "Hey, I'm sorry about what happened. I should've tried harder to keep you here. I guess I'm a lousy babysitter."

No answer.

He tried again, "I know you're upset, but if you ever want to talk about what happened back there, I—"

The door flew open and Austin jumped away. Maisie leaned against the doorframe, her nose scrunched up and her lips pressed. "Are you done yet? I'm trying to fix my armor and mope in here, and you're apologizing to *me*?"

"Oh, you were fixing something? I thought you were just cussing and hitting something with a screwdriver." Austin grinned.

Maisie tried to hide her smirk. "You are *so* annoying. Come here, I could use your hands for this."

"I bet you could."

Maisie had Austin hold the metal plates of her armor open while she slipped her nimble fingers inside. With a couple of pins in her mouth, she rearranged some parts under the layers of metal and used a pin or two to maneuver what appeared to be wiring. She told Austin to push the plates back together when she was finished.

With a grimy brow and black-tipped fingers, Maisie put her project aside. Streaks of grease and oil were smeared in her hair after she tied it up into a messy bun. When he asked her what she was trying to fix, she explained, "I got into a fight some time ago with some blindcrawlers. They damaged the part where my armor's spine would be. If I don't keep putting it back together, my armor locks up and I can't move as fast."

"That's what your scars are from"—Austin pointed—"aren't they?"

Maisie moved her tank top strap and showed him her shoulder. "They never heal, not completely. Something in those mutants' claws keeps opening the skin." She pressed her face into her knees, her voice cracking like shattered glass. "I see them every time I sleep. Then I hear his voice…. There's no rest, only nightmares."

Austin opened his mouth and closed it. In times like this, Kate was better at comforting people, he usually just made it awkward. With his back against the bed, Austin admired Maisie's relegator lanterns. "Why did you become The Orchid?"

Maisie picked up a battered relegator helmet off the floor and squinted at it. "Isn't it obvious? Look around, Austin. Relegators are taking over the world. They're killing the only people who even have a chance of beating them. No one's fighting back, and nobody stands up for the plenaries. That's why I'm rebelling, that's why I became The Orchid."

"I bet a lot of the relegators feel the same. Maybe some would even side with you."

Maisie snorted. "Where have you been for the last two decades? Relegators aren't good, Austin. End of story. There's us and then there's them."

Austin frowned at her. "But they're plenaries. Like you."

"They are *nothing* like us." Maisie threw the helmet across the room. She glared at Austin, her fists clenching.

"They're just like the blindcrawlers. Monsters engineered for the United Alliance's dirty work. It doesn't matter what they were! Forget it, I don't expect *you* to understand."

Gritting his teeth, Austin blew out his anger in a hot breath and shook his head. "Look, I get it. You don't like relegators. I'm just saying that maybe they deserve a second chance. Don't be so hard on them—or yourself."

"A second chance?" Maisie laughed bitterly. "Trust me, they don't. Neither do I."

"Why? Because it was all your brother's fault? Is that it?" Austin slapped a hand over his mouth, his eyes wide.

Maisie blanched. Bewilderment morphed into panic, which ignited into anger. "I never mentioned anything—you couldn't have." Realization blossomed on her hardening face. "Alton. Did Alton tell you that?"

"Yes—well it was—I mean—"

"What else did he say?" Maisie glowered while advancing on Austin. "Is that what you've been doing? Talking behind my back? Did they put you up to this?"

"No," he protested. "I—"

"Nobody trusts me!" Maisie yelled with angry tears. "Aviana makes you watch me, then I can't leave the Sacrarium, and now they're telling you about my past?"

"Maisie, wait!" Austin toppled into the hall as she shoved him out and he banged his head on the floor. Maisie's door slammed shut with a loud hiss and *thunk!* Behind the door, he could hear her kick something and swear venomously.

His head pounding from crazy dreams, lack of sleep, and arguments, Austin returned to his room. First Aviana and

Braylin, now Maisie? *All I have to do is piss Alton off and then it'd be everyone,* he thought, slapping himself for good measure. Besides Kate, the only other friend he had at the Sacrarium probably hated him now. No matter how hard he tried, Austin couldn't go back to sleep, he just kept thinking about his argument with Maisie.

Everything was black.

For a moment, Reuel thought he'd died. None of his limbs could move, his body felt embalmed like a mummy. Then he gasped in air and choked. Coughing, he struggled to kick away the blanket wrapped around him. His legs free, he still couldn't see a thing and realized someone had blindfolded him. After trying to touch his face, Reuel felt his left wrist cuffed to the bedpost above him. For some reason, he couldn't get his right arm to move. Trapped. On the bright side, this bed had a comfier mattress than the one he usually slept on. Goose bumps tingled his skin as a screeching sound echoed across from him.

"Where am I?"

The screeching sound stopped. "You're recovering in a bedroom. You won't get any more information than that, relegator."

A female's voice, pleasant-sounding if you ignored the scorn in the tone. *Relegator.* The way she pronounced it made Reuel shift on the bed. He turned his head where he guessed his hand was restrained. If he was being restrained, then his captors were probably the plenaries he'd tried to catch.

Accomplices of The Orchid? "Is it too much to ask you to remove the blindfold?"

Footsteps came closer and he felt a presence near him. The cloth was tugged off and after blinking a couple of times, Reuel glanced up. The skin on his wrist was raw from the tight cuff, the metal jingled as he tried to shake it. Out of the corner of his eye, something made him cease struggling. Reuel's breathing accelerated. He couldn't move his right arm, because there was nothing to move. His right arm was gone. Staring at the bandaged stump of his shoulder, he started to hyperventilate. "What… what happened to me?"

"A lot of your body is covered with third degree burns. My friend did the best she could, but she had to remove your arm. The nerve damage was too severe."

No, no, no. Reuel yanked his cuffed hand, demanding, "Uncuff me. Uncuff me right—"

The girl jabbed a medicine shot into his arm, clamping a hand over Reuel's mouth. Relaxing, his struggles subsided as the sleeping drug's effects kicked in. When he woke up, Reuel gasped and glanced at his arm. Still gone. The sluggish aftereffects of the drug replaced the shock he'd felt earlier. Reuel blinked hard, trying to rationalize. There was always prosthetics, if he could afford it.

"If you freak out again, I'll give you a stronger dose," the girl warned.

Reuel watched as she walked back and sank gracefully down in her chair across from the bed. On her lap she laid a sword, a beautiful piece without a speck of dust. The screeching noise returned as she continued to sharpen it. Looking up at

Reuel, she pursed her lips, on the verge of saying something before changing her mind and returning to her work.

Tall and dark-skinned, the girl had spots of vitiligo dotting her body with a large one around her left eye. Her hair puffed into a thick fluff of black-brown curls with an off-center part. Shapely, he noticed how she had a little muscle too. A warrior and a goddess wrapped in a blue dress. If she was trying to ignore him, she succeeded spectacularly. Reuel rattled his cuff again. The room had no windows or any signs giving away where they imprisoned him. Quietly swinging himself around, he edged his feet toward the floor.

The sounds of the girl sharpening her sword stopped immediately.

Reuel froze and looked at her, a silent challenge sitting between them. When he eased himself back into bed, she resumed her task without a second glance. Reuel shook his cuff again and repeated the annoying sound over and over. At first, the girl ignored the noise, but he spotted her wincing every time he did it.

"Will you quit that already?" she snapped after another minute. The rattling stopped, and Reuel raised a brow at her. "You're only alive because the human saved you. If I'd known he was going to bring you here, I would have intervened. So please, try not to be annoying, okay?"

Reuel rolled his eyes. "You can drop the act, I'm not stupid. I know Austin's one of you."

"No act, you're just stupid. Austin's a human, just like you."

Reuel paled, he wasn't feeling so sluggish now. Nobody, minus Solon, knew the truth of his identity. He knew the truth about the relegators; the newer generations said nothing about their true heritage. When his parents died, Reuel was only sixteen. A boy with no money and no way to provide for a younger brother. It wasn't until he turned eighteen that Reuel found his stepsister, Sonia.

A respected relegator, she forged his documents and redacted his last name to avoid suspicion and enlisted him to work under her using her own plenarie surname. Working through the ranks, Reuel convinced everyone he was a true relegator. And it worked, until Solon discovered him. Instead of turning him in, Solon took Reuel under his wing. With his guidance, Reuel would make his way to the top. But all that was lost now.

The trap had failed. Once again, The Orchid slipped through his fingers along with Austin Bennet and his friend. Most of his relegators escaped the warehouse, as far as he knew. To them, he died in the fire. What would happen now? Would the plenaries torture him for information? Hold him for ransom? Would Solon even care? Maybe he would just move on with the plan without a second thought. Reuel was replaceable, but the plenaries didn't know that yet. Who would take care of Jackson?

Jackson. Reuel bowed his head. Last night he was supposed to be home, bringing ice cream and taking care of his little brother. Reuel quickly blinked and turned his head. "How did you know? That I'm human?"

"We couldn't detect any sign of an inhibitor inside you," the girl explained. "All relegators have one." She opened the door and walked out. Halting, she turned to look at Reuel before leaving. Those searching eyes of hers reminded him of an owl's, bright and probing. An old instinct inside Reuel itched for a pencil. The light from the hall touched her face just right, giving it a warm, brown glow. Her picturesque appearance would make a beautiful portrait. She finally replied, "I'll be back with some breakfast. Don't go anywhere."

The door closed. Sighing, Reuel frowned at the thought of drawing. A memory flickered inside him like a dying candle. His mother had been an artist; she'd told him he had the gift as well. Before they died, that's all Reuel ever wanted to be. An artist, just like his mother. *Art school.* He laughed sadly at the old dream. It seemed like a lifetime ago when he'd painted cities and sketched figures in their old home. Reuel looked at where his right arm should have been. Lost. Just like the dream, just like his parents.

TWENTY-FOUR

HOLDING the gauntlet cautiously, Alton inspected it for any faults. Literally blowing through four failed prototypes, he prayed as he clamped a jumper cable to the rim of it. Flipping the power switch on the portable battery, he backed away with his hands clasped together. The gauntlet twitched with plenarie energy as currents passed through the enchanted metal. Waiting another minute, he switched the battery off and removed the cable from the glove. Teeming with excitement, he hastily grabbed a blank piece of parchment and traced a pendant emblem onto it.

"Testing, testing. Entry log one hundred fifty-seven."

Without a pen, the sheet of paper wrote on itself:

Alton Malachite, Entry log #157

Reassured with the functionality of his special paper, Alton continued to speak. "The gauntlet has a positive response to temporal energy. If I can calculate the proportion of metal to energy, I believe I can perfect the armor to properly conduct—"

Alton screeched as the glove exploded. Moaning, he climbed back up using his table as a lift. Nothing remained of the glove other than a black crater. Picking up the slightly singed piece of parchment off the floor, he glanced at the words scrawled across it:

The gauntlet has a positive response to temporal energy. If I can calculate the proportion of metal to energy, I believe I can perfect the armor to properly conduct screaming noise.

"Very funny," he grumbled.

Crumbling the paper up and discarding it, Alton sat back while rubbing the sides of his helmet. It could be odd at times. He didn't get tired as normal men did, but all the same his spirit grew weary inside the armor. It didn't bother him, the life in his mangled suit. His only regret about it might be the absence for the need of sustenance. The distraction of his work often helped divert this loss. A soft tapping rang on the doorway. Alton knew who knocked without turning. "Come in," he beckoned.

Walking into the lab, Aviana approached Alton's bench. "I thought I heard you screaming in here."

"I was not screaming," Alton murmured.

Aviana snatched the ball of paper off the floor and flattened it out. Smirking, she turned it around, revealing the proof of her assumption. Found out, Alton sighed. "Okay, I did *shout out,* but I was *so* close to finishing the armor."

Aviana raised a dark eyebrow as she glanced at the smoking hole. "What did you blow up this time? A foot?"

"A hand," Alton corrected.

Aviana would never see it, but Alton smiled to himself. The expressionless helmet he used as a head showed no emotion, both a convenience and a tragedy. Before his final incarnation, Alton dreamed of having children. Raising Aviana had been an answer to his prayers. Watching her grow up and teaching her the way of their people was the best time of his life. After his death, he'd chosen to remain behind to protect his daughter. To his delight, he gained five more children to look after. Fathers shouldn't have favorites, but Aviana couldn't be more precious to him.

"You look beautiful today," Alton complimented.

The edges of her lips touched her cheeks as Aviana ran her hands down her dress. A midnight-blue silk, fitted for her specifically. Folding her hands behind her back and swaying a little, she confessed, "Well, you have yourself to thank for that. Your tailoring skills would make you a fortune."

Alton threw a rag over his bench's new hole. "I find fortune in you six. A man cannot ask for a better life—well, afterlife." While he continued to work on his latest project, Aviana updated him on the relegator, explaining that she would interrogate him after breakfast. Rambling to himself, Alton inspected a part and chucked it behind him. "Have you seen my metal tongs any—ah, thank you."

Setting his tools aside, Alton laid the metal plate pieces

he'd shaped onto his workbench. Next to them, the lantern Austin and Maisie had stolen glowed like a rising sun.

"So. Do you know what it is?"

Alton's hands trembled slightly as he looked at the lantern. Aviana recognized his excitement as he channeled it through his armor. "It is just a theory, but I believe what we are looking at is a sample of contained plenarie aura energy," he explained.

Aviana shook her head. "Impossible. Our pendants are the only devices that can harness our energy. How could the relegators strip a plenarie's powers and contain it? Even with their inhibitors, they don't have the skill to manipulate it like that."

"Impossible for a device perhaps, but not for a plenarie." Alton titled his head as his mind wandered. "For someone to create something like this is dangerous. It would seem that the relegators *are* building a machine." Alton stowed the lantern under his desk. Standing back up, he revealed more parts to his project and lined them up with the newer ones. Taking a step back to admire his work, he gestured for Aviana to inspect it herself. His voice teemed with excitement as he asked for feedback. "What do you think?"

It was definitely a work of art. Aviana marveled at Alton's craftsmanship and revised concept for plenarie armor. It was thinner, more form-fitting than their current design. The suit gleamed a dazzling silver with hand-painted blue details running along the front and sides of it. Brushing her hand against the arm, Aviana's long fingers ran down the smooth, tepid metal. Her eyes stopped at the hand. Checking both to see if she was right, her mouth twitched. "Your suit has two right hands," she pointed out.

"What?"

Sure enough, the hands to the suit were identical. Both thumbs stuck out on the left side with the pinky on the right. Alton's curses sounded more like squeaks and creaks as he slapped his helmet. The impact created a new crack in his visor as he dropped his forged hand. "Brilliant. Now I'll have to take it apart and refit it...."

Aviana gave Alton an affectionate peck on the cheek before taking her cue to leave. Walking down the hallway, she thought about Alton's words. What kind of machine would the relegators be building with this kind of power? Did it connect with Wade's disappearance or Austin's accident? If Solon was behind all this, she was going to find out.

With a plate of food for the relegator, she stood in front of the sealed guest room door. Checking herself one last time, Aviana sucked in a quick breath and walked in. The lights blinked on as her eyes adjusted to the dimmer room. His back facing her, the relegator sat on the edge of the bed, his left arm awkwardly raised to the bedpost where it cuffed him. Aviana noticed his bare shoulders tense, detecting her presence, but he did not turn around.

Across his lean body, the impressions from his armor reminded Aviana of scars. Burns blotched his shoulders and lower back, resembling crude paint spots. Copper-colored fuzz sprouted from his shaved head. He looked young, maybe a little older than Aviana herself.

A human, pretending to be a relegator? Why?

Aviana set the plate next to him on the bed. "I have some questions for you, relegator. But first I have to be sure I can trust you to tell the truth."

"Trust me"—the relegator yanked at his chain—"I don't trust you, plenarie."

"Let me make this very clear." Aviana pulled the plate away. "Your life is in our hands. We haven't killed you, we could have left you for dead, like your relegator buddies did, but we didn't. All we want is information. If you're smart, you will give us what we need. When we get what we want, we can discuss letting you go—on certain conditions. Deal?"

Aviana watched him think it over. Finally, he nodded his agreement.

"Good. I'll be right back. Just need to grab a couple of things."

She was about to close the door and leave when he turned around. "What's your name?"

With her eyes meeting his, Aviana said nothing as she sealed the door. Walking back down the hall, she made her way to the entrance chamber. The archway lighting up, Aviana suited up as she zoomed into the white light. Before she interrogated him, she needed someone to help her learn more about her relegator. Another relegator's help, to be specific.

TWENTY-FIVE

THE darkness has returned. He's regaining his strength and his plans are slowly falling into place. You must stop him! You must learn how to control and use your powers and help the plenaries. Find the lost one, Austin. Know your allies and know your foes. There are darker things at work here. Terrible trails lie on the road ahead, but you must persevere. Trust them, trust her. Things will never be the same for you. It's difficult, I'm here but I'm not. I don't think I'm dead. I will help you... guide you. Wake up, Austin Bennet! Don't give in to the darkness. You must be strong. Your path will only become harder from this point on.

"I'm up!" Austin snapped awake and sat up.

The quiet library was empty. At one of the tables, Austin wiped the drool from his mouth and glanced down at his book. He must have dozed off while reading again. Closing the Plenarie Tome and pushing it aside, Austin tried to remember the dream. A warning? That voice, it sounded familiar. Austin looked at his chest, the marks had spread more again. Without Alton's device, they would only get worse.

Crack!

Austin screamed and tumbled backward. In a flash of purple sparks, Maisie sat in the chair opposite him. "There you are. I've been looking for you."

"Well, you found me," Austin grumbled as he climbed up.

Maisie's voice was as energetic as a senior citizen home. "Alton's curious about what kind of abilities you might have. Aviana's out and Braylin's busy with Kate, so he asked me to bring you to the velocity chamber so we can see what else you can do."

Following Maisie to the velocity chamber, Austin tried to talk to her, but he choked every time. Was his brain short-circuiting? Did his tongue swell up? Maybe he was just terrible at apologizing. Finally, as they entered the chamber, Austin cleared his throat, his words rushing out like an untamable stream. "I just wanted to say—last night—I wasn't trying to—y'know. I guess—"

"There you two are!"

Alton was waiting for them, holding a pen and a clipboard. Unlike Austin and Maisie, the metal plenarie twitched with excitement and anticipation. If he detected the tension between the two of them, Alton did not express it. Walking to the middle of the room, Maisie summoned her armor without the helmet. "Shall we?"

Alton was already scribbling notes on his clipboard as he watched them earnestly. Turning away, Maisie lifted her hands as two walls rose from the floor. Both appeared on opposite sides of the room about twenty feet away from each other. Spinning around to face Austin, she stretched her right palm out as purple electricity sparked from it. "Pocket-jumping allows me to jump between spaces in a matter of seconds. I can teleport, but as you already know, it's very limited. Now, with enough concentration, I can also do this."

As the ball of energy glowed in her hand, she threw it at the wall to her left. When it made contact, it blew a hole in the wall with the rim of it illuminating purple. Energy flew from her hand once more as she tossed it to the wall on her right. Identical to the first, a hole grew in the center of the wall with purple edging around the rim. Maisie summoned her helmet before running straight into the hole in the wall on her left and appearing out of the hole on the right. The portals vanished with a small *snap* as she removed her helmet. "Pocket-jumping. Quicker ways of travel. As long as you can create a second portal, you can travel anywhere."

"Thank you for that demonstration, Maisie." Alton added another note to his paper. "Now try it for yourself, Austin. I want to see if you can do it."

Standing beside Maisie, Austin stared at the wall on his right. Raising his right hand, he willed himself to generate electricity. His hand remained empty as he tried again. Nothing. After trying a few more times, Austin's shoulders sagged as he dropped his arm. "I can't do it."

Alton tried to hide his disappointment. "Oh. Well perhaps—"

"Concentrate on the portal, not the energy," Maisie said to him gently. The sudden change in her tone took Austin by surprise. She held his hand up, lifting it a little higher. "Try to picture where you want to go. Don't worry how you're gonna get there, just picture a window in your mind you want to run through."

Inhaling deeply, Austin imagined a portal opening in the wall while holding his hand up. A flicker of yellow appeared in his palm as he gasped. Concentrating harder, he cheered excitedly as his hand pulsed with yellow bolts of energy. With a loud crackle, the lightning vanished, leaving his hand bare. "Wait, what happened? I had it for a moment."

Alton dropped his stationery and clapped his hands together excitedly. "Extraordinary! You almost generated enough energy to create a portal. If you can phase *and* pocket-jump, you may have some kind of power replication ability. Given some time, you could manipulate light, create constructs, or even bend energy to your will. Wait until Avi hears about this!" Alton clanked out of the velocity chamber, his sheets of paper flying behind him as he ran down the hall.

"He seems to be enjoying this," Maisie remarked.

"I'm sorry," Austin blurted. Maisie's smile slipped as she looked at him. When she said nothing, he continued, "About last night. I didn't mean to upset you about—y'know."

Folding her hands behind her back, Maisie nodded and then jerked her head at one of the walls. "Okay. Why don't you try it again?"

An hour past two, Aviana returned to the Sacrarium through the archway. Removing her helmet, she was headed to her room when she bumped into Braylin.

"I see your errand was successful." He nodded to the envelope she carried. "So, what's on the menu for lunch?"

Thrusting her helmet at his chest, Aviana strutted past him with her nose in the air. "Hmph! I deserve more credit than you give me. I'll think about cooking after I'm finished with the relegator."

Braylin's mouth twitched as he walked away. Tossing Aviana's helmet over his shoulder, it vanished in a small burst of blue light. Aviana removed the rest of her armor as she entered her room. Opening the sealed envelope Scratch gave her, she read through the details about their newest guest. His name was Reuel. No last name, it had been redacted from the relegator database. *Makes sense, if he isn't a plenarie then he wouldn't want anyone knowing his real last name*, Aviana thought.

Age twenty-two, he'd served as a relegator since the age of eighteen. The status line labeled him as deceased. Rolling up the papers and tucking them under her arm, Aviana tied her hair back, ready to embark on her interrogation with Reuel the relegator. He lay sprawled across the bed when she walked in. Noticing her, he sat up, eyes narrowed.

"Ready to talk, Reuel?" she questioned. Hearing his name, Reuel paled, then nodded dejectedly. "Okay." Aviana folded her papers and walked back and forth. "Last night, you set a trap to catch The Orchid with a shipment as bait, correct?"

Reuel looked away, his small mouth a thin line across his pointed face.

"Reuel, I asked you a question," Aviana reminded in a

honeyed tone. "Tell me why."

"It's my job to bring The Orchid in," Reuel gritted. "As you can tell, it didn't work out for me."

"That shipment contained a power source. An orange orb of energy?"

Reuel tried to slip under the covers of the bed again. "You tell me. My orders were to bring The Orchid in. I used a classified shipment to lure him—her—in. End of story."

"Reuel, if you want to get out of here you can't lie to me."

Reuel knew that but telling the truth would get him killed. The project was a highly classified development. Besides the few details Solon shared with him, he only understood the design and potential capabilities of the machine. Even if he didn't enjoy working as a relegator, Reuel despised snitches. But Jackson was counting on him. He'd been gone too long already. Without him, his little brother was in danger, and he wasn't referring to the crazy neighbor down the hall.

He had no choice, Jackson needed him. "You have my file, so you know I have a little brother."

Aviana checked her papers. "Jackson?"

"If I tell you what I know, the relegators will find him and kill him." Reuel jerked his chin at the pile of damaged armor in the corner. "I don't enjoy my job, but it provides for me and my brother—I'm all he has."

Brushing her hair away from her eye, Aviana glided over and sat on the edge of Reuel's bed. "I understand your concerns, but you have to trust us."

"Trust you?" Reuel pulled at the chain that bound to him. "You have me shackled up. I've been locked in this stupid room for hours, and you use my life to barter for information. Why in the world should I trust you?"

"Hey, who's the relegator here? *You.* Remember? If anyone shouldn't be trusted, it's you. Look at what you've done to the plenaries!"

"The plenaries took *everything* from me!" Reuel shouted back. His outburst silencing her, Aviana watched him with folded arms and her jaw clenched. Reuel's eyes watered, but he didn't care. "My parents supported your people. After the Alliance wrote the Excretion Act, they helped them sneak out of the state. We used to hide refugees in our house. My parents risked everything to protect your people."

Aviana waited for him to continue, her eyes hard as amber.

"We were having dinner when they broke in." Reuel closed his eyes, the memory haunting him like a phantom. "My dad told me to hide with my brother and the two plenaries staying with us. They came for the plenaries, but my parents wouldn't give them up. So the relegators dragged my mom out screaming. I *watched* them murder my dad trying to protect her. The next day I snuck out to find food for us, then I came back and found my baby brother crying alone. The plenaries *we protected* abandoned him! They stole every penny we'd scraped together over the years and hit the road."

Blood trickled from Reuel's wrist. As it dripped on the bed, he locked eyes with the girl. "I hate the relegators, but I have no choice but to work for them because that's the only way I can take care of my brother. My family is dead because we helped you. Why should I trust you now?"

When the girl stood up, Reuel watched as she yanked her sword out of the scabbard. When she swung it at him, Reuel shut his eyes, waiting for the killing blow.

SNAP!

Reuel's hand sagged on the bed, free at last. The chain cut, he flexed his arm and looked up at the plenarie standing before him. After she put her weapon away, she took his arm and ripped the cuff off like paper. "I never knew my real parents, they died when I was a baby," she confessed as she wrapped his wrist with a piece of cloth. "I know what it's like to lose people close to you. Why should you trust us? Austin Bennet saved your life. You kidnapped his friend and hunted him down. He could've left you to die, but he didn't. If you can't trust us, trust him."

"Where are you going now?" Reuel questioned as she opened the door.

"Come on"—she waved to him—"you need to take another shower. You smell like piss and smelly feet."

Skeptical, Reuel followed her into the hall. The bright light forced him to squint as he asked her, "I still don't know your name."

"Aviana," she replied, leading him down the hallway.

Aviana. The name repeated itself in Reuel's head over and over as he hobbled after her. She was strong; Reuel confessed she was attractive too. Under all that indifference, a soft side resided, but could Reuel really trust her? It had been years since Reuel trusted anyone. Why should he? People, even plenaries, eventually let you down. Why would now be any different? Maybe it was because she was willing to trust him, or because something told him he could really like her, so Reuel decided to take the chance. He would trust this plenarie. He would trust Aviana.

TWENTY-SIX

ΠUSTIN'S next few attempts to summon the energy to pocket-jump were less than successful to say the least. Never would he have guessed that having powers would be so draining. And frustrating. After pushing him to try again and again, Maisie finally took pity on him and suggested they take a break. They bumped into Kate when they left the velocity chamber, then Maisie's eyes lit up as she remembered something she wanted to show them.

Austin and Kate followed Maisie through the Sacrarium toward the hall to the bedrooms. Stopping in front of a blank wall, Maisie drew a symbol on it. A purple letter appeared for a moment as the wall opened inward to a dark room. Kate and Austin followed Maisie into the new room as the lights activated. Kate gagged as she walked into a giant spiderweb. "Ugh, when's the last time you cleaned this place?" She coughed.

"No one's been in here for years," Maisie explained.

Looking around, Austin marveled how similar the room resembled an antique shop. Chipped tables, moldy shelves, and dusty chests full of countless foreign objects glittered in the light. "What is this?"

Maisie waved a hand around. "It used to be Alton's collection room. He sealed it off when we were younger but then forgot about it. Now it's just used for extra storage and hiding unwanted objects." She snorted an involuntary sneeze as she buried her face in her arm. "Great. I think I'm allergic to the dust in here."

Kate coughed again when Austin disturbed the dust by stepping past her. Waving her hand to clear the air, something in the room caught her eye. On a chipped wood table, a small cube with weird runes and carvings engraved all over it stood out without a single cobweb or speck of dust disturbing it. Gingerly picking it up, Kate turned the cube in her hands. It weighed more than it looked. Shaking it, she noticed something bounced around inside. No matter how hard she pulled, Kate couldn't get the box to open.

"Maisie! Are you in there?"

"Yes!" Maisie tripped over a three-legged stool and flopped onto the floor. Dusting herself off, she ran up to Braylin, who was now inside the cluttered room with them. "What's up?"

"Have you seen Aviana? Alton wants us to meet him in the entrance hall." Braylin's voice tightened with concern. "It's the High Sultana."

"Come on." Maisie grabbed Austin's arm and pulled him out as she dashed after Braylin.

"Hey." Kate stumbled as she tried to follow. "Wait for me!"

The hidden door shut itself before she could get out. Pounding on the door, she yelled, "Guys! Come back. I can't get out. *Guys!*"

The door remained sealed. Kate swore as she kicked the door and bashed her toes. Eyes watering, she slid down and leaned against the wall, still holding the strange cube. She tried to open it, but it remained stiff, frustrating Kate, so she threw it at the wall.

Clunk!

She winced, then sighed in relief that it didn't mark the wall. When she picked it up and eyed it, she noticed the side had cracked, leaving a hole. Kate brought the cube to her eye to squint inside and see if anything had fallen out. She cried out as a dazzling light blinded her. Throwing it again, she rubbed her eye until her vision cleared. The box cracked in two, yet nothing was inside. She picked up the two pieces, sighed and then chucked it away. It shouted. Kate screamed again, hearing the voice coming from behind a statue.

She spotted something glowing in the corner behind the stone. Holding her breath, Kate grabbed an old umbrella and tried to poke whatever was behind the statue. A bright light pulsed in the darkness and she jumped back. When the light faded, she slowly peeked behind the statue again and came face-to-face with a creature the size of a baseball. Nowhere near as bright as the sun, it still hurt her eyes to glance at it.

Scooting back, Kate braced herself, but nothing happened. When she peeked out of one eye, she spotted the light-ball-thingy—she'd have to come up with a better name— had rolled out from behind the statue and now hovered in front of her face. Stretching out a shaking finger, Kate gave it a tiny poke. It floated back a little but still remained in the air as it watched her. Watched. Was that even the right word? It had no eyes or marks on its yellow surface, its only prominent feature was how it glowed like a light bulb.

"Hi?" she whispered.

"Hello," it greeted.

Kate screamed as she swatted it, knocking it out of the air and into the corner. It made an effort to get airborne again but fell to the ground. Once it hovered again, it swayed a little as it floated back in front of Kate.

"Sorry," Kate apologized. "What are you?"

The orb grew a little brighter as it spoke. "Apology accepted. To answer your question, you named me Orion after the constellation."

Kate pointed to her chest. "I named you?"

Orion bobbed up and down in a nodding gesture. "You did, Wade. Though it has been a while since I saw you last." The orb whirled around Kate, examining her up and down. "You have changed a lot since I was last active. Did you reincarnate?"

Kate tried to hit the orb again but it quickly moved. "No, I didn't *reincarnate*. I'm not Wade. I'm Kate."

Orion said nothing for a moment as he stared at her. "You are not a plenarie. You are a female human," he concluded.

"Oh, really?" Kate snorted. "What gave it away?"

"The female's build is different from the male's," Orion enlightened. "You have—"

"Okay, okay. You don't need to continue."

Orion continued to fly around her as Kate followed it with her eyes. "I have been in low power mode for too long. I will need to absorb temporal energy to recharge." Without warning, Orion opened the door and flew out of the room.

"Hey!"

He headed to the Athenaeum and squeezed through the open crack in the doors. Barging in, Kate watched as Orion whizzed around looking for a power source. He flew above the bridges and chasm below as he rocketed into Alton's lab. He was hovering over Alton's desk when Kate jumped up and tackled him out of the air.

"Kate? Are you in here?"

Kate quickly shoved Orion in her back pocket. "Braylin! I got stuck in that room, where's Alton?"

"He's with everyone else in the entrance hall," Braylin explained, walking up. "Come on, now's not the time to wander around."

Orion vibrated against Kate's butt as he pushed her toward Braylin. "Okay, thanks. I'll be with you in a moment," she promised. When Braylin left, she bolted out before Orion could escape her clutches. Thankfully, no one noticed her running into the kitchen. Pulling Orion out of her pocket, Kate held on to him tightly. "What do you think you're doing?"

"I have been in low power mode for too long. I need to absorb some temporal energy to recharge," Orion answered.

Orion whirled under Kate's hands as she struggled to hold him down. "Okay, truce. I'll let you go, but you can't fly off without my permission. Deal?"

Orion's light flickered a moment as he fell motionless. "I

will agree to your terms. You are a very contentious human, Kate." Removing her hands, Kate waited for Orion to bolt. He remained in the air hovering but did not fly away. "I may be required to agree with you, but I still require energy to function," Orion pointed out.

"Can you just plug in or something?"

Orion dropped into Kate's open hand as he replied, "I do not 'plug in.' Humans give off their own energy from their bodies. I can convert my systems to adapt to this energy instead of temporal energy."

"Okay then, do it."

Orion's yellow light vanished, leaving a blank, white orb in Kate's hand. The orb flickered to life a minute later, illuminating to a faint, bluish-gray color. Voices echoing down the hall grew louder. Holding onto an angry Orion, Kate snuck down to the entrance hall and poked her head around the corner. Braylin, standing next to Alton, spotted her and smiled with a slight nod.

"Your heart rate has increased," Orion reported.

"Shut up." Kate shoved the orb back into her pocket. Walking over to Austin and Maisie, she nudged her friend. "What's going on?"

Austin looked sideways at her. "I think we're about to have a visitor."

After Kate walked in, Austin watched with the others as the archway's light blossomed and then blinked out. Everyone held their breath. A silhouette began to take shape as the figure fully materialized. When the woman no longer appeared transparent, Austin recognized her features and gasped.

Lada had returned.

Dressed in an olive-green dress that popped out against her fair skin, Lada wore no shoes. Golden rings wrapped around three of her toes on each foot, with silver bands decorating her bare arms from her wrists to her shoulders like sterling vines. Lada towered above everyone, forcing even Braylin to look up just so he could look her in the eye.

"Dang, that's a big woman," Kate whispered.

Maisie hissed out of the side of her mouth, "That's a lucrean. Her name's Lada, and she's the High Sultana of her people."

Austin kept his gaze slightly downcast, but he could sense the lady's eyes locked on to him. Alton's armor made involuntary creaking noises, a sign of his unease in the moment. "High Sultana, what a privilege it is to see you again. How can I help you, my lady?" he squeaked.

Lada smiled, looking down at Alton. "You never visit, you never write. Must I always be the one to reach out?" Her head turned toward Kate and Austin. "Aren't you going to introduce me to your guests?"

Alton's expressionless mask left his face unreadable, but the High Sultana looked amused if not a little exhilarated. "This is Austin Bennet and his friend Kate Summers."

Lada glided soundlessly toward Austin, soaring above him. He bent his head back, so he could meet her eyes. She seemed to be looking through him rather than at him. "Aren't you just adorable! You must be the human I have heard rumors about."

Maisie grew impatient. "What are you really doing here, Lada?"

The High Sultana removed herself from Austin and found Maisie standing by Braylin and Kate. Maisie barely reached Lada's abdomen. "Maisie Orchid. You have not changed much since I saw you last. Very well, I came because I wished to speak with Alton. I also wanted to deliver the invitation myself."

"Invitation?"

"Yes." Lada beamed, poking Maisie on the nose. "I am hosting a private dinner in my palace this evening. Austin is to be my guest, of course. There is so much I would love to learn from him. It is only for one evening, I promise you. As soon as dinner is over, I will bring him back to you promptly."

Pulling at his collar, Austin smiled weakly. "Well, I—"

"If my hospitality is not enough, I can offer you something else." Lada twirled a hand, conjuring an oval ornament out of thin air. "What about one evening in exchange for this?"

"A plenarie pendant!" Alton looked as if he might jump out of his armor. "How did you get that?"

Lada turned the pendant over in her hand. "This old thing? I *made* it, Alton. Completely compatible with plenarie energy, armor, and... *other things.*" As Alton reached for it, Lada snapped her fingers and the pendant disappeared. "You will get the pendant *after* Austin shares a meal with me in Lucreet."

She knows I don't have one, Austin realized. And if this pendant actually worked, it might prevent more scarring and damage to his body. Nodding, he faced Lada. "I'll do it, but on one condition. I... I don't want to go alone."

Silent, the lucrean's hair danced around her while she peered at Austin. Finally, she dipped her head. "Very well. I will grant you this request." Both Maisie and Kate stepped forward, but the High Sultana shook her head. "Only one will join our company. You may speak amongst yourselves, but I must return to my duties as High Sultana. I will be expecting you at seven, Austin Bennet. Do not be late. Goodbye, Alton." The woman faded until she completely vanished, leaving a glimmer of white light.

"Wait, where'd she go?" Austin gawked.

"Lada never leaves her queendom," Alton explained. "What you saw was a projection of her through your mind. Lucreans like Lada are telepathic. Most of the time they communicate with each other through their minds."

"That's so cool! What's a lucrean?"

"Lucreans are ancient elemental beings," Maisie told her. "Probably the greatest architects and smiths in the Macrocosm. They helped the first generation of plenaries forge the first pendants and create the armor that harnesses our powers. After the Excretion Act when the United Alliance discovered them, the remaining lucreans retreated to Lucreet, a pocket dimension."

"Which is where I'll be going," Austin said as he glanced back at the arch.

TWENTY-SEVEN

REUEL had never been anywhere like the Sacrarium before. The building's architecture was old-fashioned, but the structure surprised him with its advanced technology. After his shower and much needed bathroom break, Aviana let him join her in the library. Reuel had a little trouble focusing on the books. Following Aviana to one of the tables, he reached for a book, almost expecting her to snatch it away from him. When she didn't, he frowned at the text. None of it was in English. Then he realized he was reading it upside down.

"Tell me about the machine, Reuel. The relegators' latest project?"

Reuel found her hazel eyes looking into him thoroughly. The way they penetrated him, he wouldn't be surprised if she could read minds. His heart started pounding when Aviana touched his hand. "Reuel?"

Closing the book, Reuel quickly pulled his hand away. "The relegators want to create their own power plant.

They're building a prototype in Alliance Tower. Once they get it to work, they want to build one in every state across the country. That way, everyone will have to depend on relegators for clean energy."

"No, no that can't be all." Aviana shook her head. "There's got to be more behind it."

Looking back at the relegator, she tried to keep her voice even. "You were in charge of bringing The Orchid in. Have you ever come across any other plenaries in the last few months? Anyone with blond hair or short black hair?"

Reuel thought about it for a moment. "No. Just The Orchid and Austin Bennet—who isn't a plenarie apparently. He's got blond hair."

"Not him, someone else."

The way she said that intrigued Reuel. *She's looking for someone,* he thought with a twinge of jealousy. "I'm sorry, I haven't seen anyone else. There's the plenaries impri—er— kept in the Hailstone facility; the ones who are born and raised to be relegators. But as far as the rest of the world knows, the plenaries are either all dead or caught, minus The Orchid."

Not all of them, Aviana wanted to say. But there was one question she had to ask him, something deep down she wanted to know. She leaned over the table, causing Reuel to edge away in his seat. "Who's in charge of the project? What's the name of your superior?"

"It's the same person," Reuel drawled slowly.

"Give me a name."

"Aviana, I—"

Aviana grabbed him by the shirt and pulled him out of

the chair, practically holding him mid-air. "I said give me a name!"

"Solon." Reuel winced. "Solon Blak."

Aviana's grip on him slipped, Reuel banged his head on the table and fell over. When she ran around and pulled him up, her skin had paled. "I'm sorry," she apologized absently. "I just remembered something."

"You know him? Solon?"

"I… I know the name." Aviana sat back down and covered her face with her hands. "Reuel, what can you tell me about him?"

"Why do I have to wear this?" Austin groaned.

Braylin handed Austin a black silk jacket to wear over his white collared shirt. "You'll be in the court of the High Sultana. You have to look presentable."

"But we're still in August. I'll have a heat stroke in this thing," Austin complained.

"The weather won't be as humid there," Braylin reassured. "Lucreans don't tolerate humans in general, so to look your best may ease their intolerance."

"I hate dressing up. Everything's itchy and stiff."

Braylin shook his head as he chuckled. "You sound like Maisie. Kate and I had to hold her down so we could get her to dress in something more appealing than a tank top."

Despite Austin's protests, Kate forced him to comb and gel his unruly hair back to look neater. Ready to go, Austin sat in the entrance hall, fidgeting in his Sunday best and pulling at the straining collar. Maisie ended up being the one who would accompany him to Lucreet, but as soon as Kate tried to dress her up she'd revolted. With a pair of high heels in her hands, Kate chased Maisie into the entrance hall where Austin waited. Sitting next to him, Maisie folded her arms with a repulsed look on her face. "We're going to the kingdom of the lucreans, this isn't a stupid prom!"

"I just want to give you shoes and a little makeup," Kate pleaded.

Maisie's jaw dropped as she jumped up. *"Makeup?* No way! You got me to wear the dress, but hell will freeze over before I wear high heels or makeup."

Even with her powers, Maisie was no match for Kate's persistence. Within the next half hour, she stood alongside Austin in front of the archway, hissing with total loathing in a colorful choice of vocabulary. They would be heading to Mojo's where one of Lada's people would take them to her. Braylin activated the archway as they prepared to leave.

"Good luck, Austin." Kate beamed. "Looking babelicious in that dress, Maisie."

"You're lucky I can't kick in these shoes," Maisie muttered.

Austin whizzed through the arch, dashing after Maisie. They teleported to the street across from Mojo's. Braylin didn't tell them how long they would have to wait, but Austin was dying in his jacket. Equally displeased in her outfit, Maisie kept slipping on her heels. Losing balance for a moment, she cursed a word Mrs. Summers would have grounded Austin for life for if she'd ever caught him saying it. A lady walking with her daughter covered her child's ears, glaring at Maisie with disgust.

"You try wearing these!" Maisie yelled at her fleeing back.

Austin tried to stifle a laugh, but it came out as a loud snort instead.

"Laugh at me again and I will shove these right up your crack," Maisie cautioned.

Austin stretched his mouth thin to force back the laugh coming on. "Sorry. It's just funny seeing you get frustrated about something most girls *love* to wear. Plus, your nose twitches like a rabbit's when you're angry."

"*Most* girls," Maisie growled. "I hate dresses and makeup. And my nose doesn't twitch!"

"You just did it," Austin pointed out while chuckling.

Covering her nose, Maisie grumbled to herself. Dropping the subject, Austin looked left and right. "So how much longer do we have to wait?"

"Oh, it's you two." A curvy girl with light brown skin and blue hair walked out of the restaurant. Adjusting her shades, Lucena placed her hands on her hips. "I have to take you to the High Sultana's before I go home."

"You're a lucrean?" Austin blurted.

Lucena bared her teeth, sharp and silver, at Austin with a hiss. "Say that any louder, I dare you. Hurry up, I don't want to hang around long. Give me your hands."

The lucrean's cold hands matched her tone. The world around them erupted into a white light, blinding Austin. More or less, the lucrean teleported them the same way they traveled to and from the Sacrarium. When everything cleared up, Austin's retracted pupils widened as his mouth shaped into a giant O. The buildings, towering into the clouds like upside down icicles, glimmered a transparent blue with different colors like the northern lights. Soft, angelic music filled the fragrant air, making Austin drowsy and his eyelids heavy.

"You've been teleported just outside the palace of the High Sultana herself. Follow the path and it will lead you inside," Lucena explained. "I'll be back to take you home later."

Without another word, the girl disappeared. The glass path she indicated glowed like the architecture around them. Leading the way, Maisie stumbled a little in her shoes but pressed on. The path cut through a garden with white-colored grass and trees with crimson-red bark with blue leaves. The large estate they stood before mirrored the structure of a cathedral. The doors opened by themselves, beckoning the visitors to enter.

A wall in front of them split open into two doors. Out of it, two lucrean guards armed with javelins escorted the High Sultana herself. In the chamber, her hypnotizing voice boomed like a sportscaster's. "Welcome to Lucreet, Austin Bennet! So glad you could join us! Please, follow me."

Glancing nervously at Maisie, Austin walked behind the Sultana and her intimating guards.

Rubbing his nose, Reuel groaned as he dropped back into his chair. After Aviana had dropped him, she calmed down a little. "Solon keeps a low profile, he's one of the higher ranking relegators. One of the few to work on the machine project for the United Alliance."

"What else?" Aviana demanded. "What does he look like?"

"Well… he doesn't wear normal relegator armor. Big, kind of scary, if I'm being honest. His armor's got claws on the fingers and toes too. I've never seen his face, he's always wearing that skeleton mask of his."

Aviana's eyes widened like camera lenses. She sprinted out of the library and flew down the hall. Stitches growing in his sides, Reuel managed to catch up with her when she stopped in front of two giant wooden doors. Calling after her, he pushed through the doors and froze in his tracks. The room he entered had floating spheres made of glass attached to moving bridges. While Aviana ran down the bridge connected to the doorway, Reuel treaded carefully after her.

By the time he caught up with her again, Aviana was in one of the giant spheres, which turned out to be some kind of laboratory. She spoke frantically to a rusty suit of armor. Reuel almost screamed when the armor actually talked back.

"This is worse than I imagined," the suit creaked, then it jumped after noticing Reuel. "Intruder! Wait, is that the relegator?"

"Alton this is Reuel. Reuel, this is my father, Alton," Aviana introduced them.

Reuel approached them cautiously. "Your father is a suit of armor?"

Aviana spoke on, "If Solon's working inside the United Alliance again, then he's probably hijacked this 'project.' Whatever his scheme is, it has something to do with that power source."

Reuel coughed into his fist. "*Ahem.* Does anyone want to

explain to me what is going on?"

"Come with me, we need to find Braylin." Aviana dragged him out of the lab and across the bridge.

"Aviana, wait!" Reuel planted his feet and yanked his arm back.

Aviana stopped and looked at him. They stood alone in the hall connecting to the library close by. A little taller than her, it surprised Reuel how easily she could pull him around. She *did* have the unfair advantage of two arms, though. And she was pretty strong. Before he got the words out of his mouth, Aviana swept over and pushed him against the wall. Eyes narrowed, Reuel could see the vulnerability buried in her alluring eyes. In that moment he thought she was going to kiss him, but his chest deflated when she backed away and sighed.

"This is serious, Reuel. Now's not the time to play both sides. I-I need to know that I can trust you. If Solon gets the power source, clean energy is going to be the least of our worries. I just want to know that you'll side with us. I need you to tell me right now."

In his head, Reuel knew he belonged with the relegators— with Solon. For years he'd served as a relegator, why would he change now? Everything he held dear would be at risk. His life, his job, and Jackson. *Jackson*. How could he sabotage everything he'd worked so hard for? Losing his healthcare plan wouldn't be the worst, but without a job he would be sending him and his brother to the streets, penniless and hungry. It was a lost cause, siding with the plenaries. Both his parents were dead because they'd helped them. Only a fool would make that mistake twice.

Reuel looked into Aviana's expectant eyes. In that moment she wasn't glaring at him like he was some kind of monster or waiting for him to attack her. No, she was panicked. Something about Solon scared her. Had he overlooked some hidden scheme or agenda? What could Solon have done, besides any relegator, to hurt these people? Reuel never liked being a relegator. If there was any way to make them pay for his parents, he would do it in a heartbeat. But he didn't, because they were all he had. A single thread tying him to the only security he had left.

And yet...

Aviana risked trusting him. She'd even shown him their library here in their hidden sanctuary. A spark rekindled inside Reuel. In his short time here, he'd been shown mercy and kindness. Mercy and kindness he didn't deserve. His own relegators abandoned him, but the plenaries had saved him and patched him back up. *They chained and interrogated you,* a voice reminded him. *How do you know they won't kill you when they don't need you anymore?*

True, but it still conflicted Reuel. Maybe because he was beginning to like Aviana, or because it's what his parents would have done. Reuel took a long breath and came to a decision. He just hoped he wouldn't live to regret it.

"I'm with you, Aviana," Reuel exhaled. "I trust you in return for trusting me."

When she beamed at him, Reuel thought he would melt into jelly, then she hugged him. Now he thought he would combust altogether.

Aviana pulled away. "Let's introduce you to Braylin."

Reuel didn't want to let go of her. "After that, we can make arrangements to get you a better room and some of your own clothes."

"A better room?" Reuel raised an eyebrow at her.

"If you're going to stay here, you'll want a bigger room, trust me."

A bigger room? It took all Reuel's willpower not to kiss her right there. "Thank you, but I can't settle here just yet. We need to grab my brother before the relegators figure out I didn't burn to a crisp in that warehouse."

"After we find Braylin and tell him about Solon," Aviana promised.

Following her down the hall, Reuel couldn't remember the last time he'd smiled this much. It was going to be dangerous, there would definitely be hard times ahead, but right now, Reuel just wanted to be with Aviana. For the first time in years, Reuel believed in a plenarie.

TWENTY-EIGHT

BRAYLIN was right. Instead of sweating in his suit, Austin shivered head to toe instead. The only source of warmth in the palace came off the High Sultana herself, and Austin politely kept his distance as best as he could. Maisie, though, had better reasons to be freezing. The brilliant green dress she wore was sleeveless and made out of a thinner material.

Lada seemed to relish seeing subordinates exploited. Having changed from the dress she'd worn as a projection back at the Sacrarium, Lada wore a revealing ballgown. A silver crown of branches rested on her white locks of hair, matching the bands on her arms. She looked very much like an elf queen. Lada and her guards stopped in front of a giant door made of what looked like sparkling diamond. As the door swung open, the lucrean guards stood at attention by the sides of the open doorway. With light shining into the room, Austin's body twitched from the heat seeping through.

"This way, Austin. I must speak with you before we dine."

Gulping in a steadying breath, Austin stepped out of the room after the High Sultana. Maisie tried to follow, but Lada's guards crossed their javelins into an X, blocking the doorway.

"You want to tell your guards to let me pass?" Maisie called after Lada.

The High Sultana turned around and smiled at Maisie. "This is a private discussion, Maisie Orchid. Do not worry, my guards will take good care of you until we come out."

Before Maisie could protest, the door slammed itself shut. Alone with the High Sultana, Austin's palms slicked with sweat. Without a second glance, Lada beckoned him to follow her. At first, Austin assumed they walked outside, but the ceiling above them arched into a dome with golden branches spreading out as support beams. Budding from the branches, glowing flowers bloomed above them. The light illuminated the entire garden like the sun on a quiet summer's evening.

Lada stood on a bridge in the middle of the garden waiting for him. Resting her arms on the stone-carved rails, she looked over the little steam trickling through the polished rocks. When he stood beside her, Austin could barely stretch his arms over the chiseled rail.

"Beautiful, is it not?"

Austin sneaked a glance at Lada from the corner of his eye. Her hair floated around her like she was swimming underwater. A lock of it tickled Austin as she brushed it away from her pointed ear. It was hard to tell what she was looking at, with no pupils and all, but Austin guessed her mind drifted elsewhere, beyond the garden.

"You didn't tell the plenaries we'd met before. Why?" he

asked her.

Lada walked away from the edge. Down the path, she led Austin to a bench beside a bed of ruby-encrusted roses. When she sat down, she patted the seat next to her. Austin plopped himself beside her, waiting for a reply. Finally, the High Sultana spoke as she plucked one of the gem flowers from the ground. "Why does anyone do anything? Truthfully, I do not trust the plenaries, and the feeling is mutual, I am certain. Tell me, Austin, did you trust them with information of us being acquainted with one other?"

"It must have slipped my mind. That's all. Is this about what you said on that airplane? You said you saw potential in me or something?"

Lada brushed a strand of Austin's hair away from his face. "Ever since June, something has been growing inside you. Something powerful… and dangerous. I watched as the relegators and plenaries discovered you and raced each other to find you. You are not an ordinary human, are you, Austin Bennet?"

"Something tells me you already know the answer to that."

"Of course." Lada flattened the front of her skirt. "I know about your accident, and I know about the scars. Can you show them to me?"

Unbuttoning the top of his shirt, Austin displayed the marks on his chest to the lady. She glanced at it for less than a second before looking past his eyes.

Consigned reincarnation.

"What?" Austin gasped. Lada's voice in his head sounded uncertain, even fearful. Slowly leaning back, the High Sultana looked away, pinching her bottom lip. Shaking out of her disturbed thoughts, she turned back to Austin. "I want you to listen to me very carefully, Austin. This power inside you cannot be contained. Forces like the relegators or even the plenaries will try to take it from you. You are a danger to yourself and to the rest of us in this realm."

"What are you trying to say?"

Lada grabbed Austin by the shoulders, her face etched with concern. "I am saying you are not safe. My scouts warn me that an old enemy of the plenaries is rising. He will stop at nothing until you are out of the picture. You cannot trust the plenaries—they will see your abilities grow and fear you. None of them have the power to protect or help you. That is why I think you are ready to hear my proposition."

"What kind of proposition are we talking about?"

With a flick of the wrist, Lada produced the pendant from earlier. When Austin reached for it, she lifted it away. "When plenaries were first born, all they had were their polestars. The energy inside them was unstable and did more harm than good. My people watched them suffer and took pity on them. We helped them forge pendants, devices that harnessed the energy inside them and even summoned their own armor to protect them. Ever since then, they have used the pendants to control their powers."

The pendant vanished from Lada's palm, and stroking a curtain of her animated hair, she continued. "That was ages ago. Pendants no longer have to be forged. Plenaries go through a process called Post-Genesis and come out with their own device. After the process they can make armor magically appear like that." She snapped her fingers. "But you, Austin, are not a plenarie. You do not have a pendant. Your human body cannot cope with the strain of these gifts you have. I can give this pendant to you, and you can use it to help control your powers."

"There's an 'or' statement following, isn't there?"

Some of Lada's hair draped around Austin's shoulders like an arm. Lada cupped the side of his face and smiled at him. "You have a choice, Austin. You can stay with the plenaries and probably die, *or* you can come and live here with me and be safe."

"Say what now?"

"Think about it," Lada insisted. "A pendant is only a temporary solution, and even with it, you are in danger from the relegators. Here in Lucreet, my powers are all but limitless. I can protect you *and* help you control your powers without hurting your body anymore. You could live peacefully here with me at the palace."

Tempting, but Austin wasn't born yesterday. "What are you looking for in return?"

"Life is not just a big party, Austin." The High Sultana giggled. "You would have responsibilities, of course. There is always the chance someone may try to overrule me. Every High Sultana has her insurgent subjects. My guards are strong, but I have kept my eyes open for someone with the right capabilities to protect his ruler."

"You want *me* to be your bodyguard?" Austin snorted at her.

"You could be so much more than that, Austin." Lada promised. "A friend of the High Sultana to say the least, but together we could protect and restore the lucrean people. There is so much room to grow in this realm, and it takes a strong leader to oversee such progress. Any thoughts, dearie? You are doing that thing with your eyebrows when you are confused."

Austin moved away from the bench. Remaining seated, Lada looked at him with eager anticipation. "I'm honored, Lada—I mean, High Sultana, but I need to think about it."

"Of course." Lada rose up, her skirts piling around her. "We have all night to discuss our plans. Time to have some dinner. I hope we haven't kept your friend waiting too long."

Maisie was busy arm wrestling one of the guards when they walked in. Before she pinned his arm, the guard jumped up and took his place beside the High Sultana. His fellow guard doing the same, they marched the High Sultana and her guests to the banquet hall.

"Do excuse me," Lada apologized to them. "Before dinner, I must speak with some of my councilors. Wait here in the hallway until I send someone to usher you in."

The three lucreans disappeared into the banquet hall, leaving Austin and Maisie alone in the giant between-room. Flexing her arm, Maisie grunted at Austin. "What'd the Sultana say?"

Austin kept his eyes on the carpet. "She just asked about the accident, that's all."

If Maisie didn't believe him, she didn't say it. It was warmer in the garden. Unstrapping and discarding her heels,

Maisie wrapped her arms around herself as she sat on the floor, wiggling her toes. After he dropped beside her, Austin threw his jacket around her bare shoulders. Pulling it close around herself, Maisie smiled. "Thanks."

Buttoning his shirt back up, Austin bent forward a little to get a better look at her. Maisie's makeup made her look older, enhancing her pretty features. Her eyes shone like green sapphires with the gentle shade of eye shadow around them. The plum lipstick she wore made her lips pop out against her light skin, emphasizing their plush texture. As she turned to glance around the room, Austin noticed freckles decorated her nose and cheeks like speckles of caramel, matching the color of her hair, which stood out like a sunset against the blue and white colors of the walls around them.

Austin couldn't find his voice for a moment. Was it starting to get hot in here? He discarded the thought as he asked Maisie, "What's consigned reincarnation?"

Maisie played with her hands, averting her eyes. "Supposedly, when a plenarie dies they can bestow their powers to a human. The human reincarnates in their place, sort of, but there's no one around who can prove it's possible. Why—"

A small voice interrupted Maisie as it squeaked behind them. Austin and Maisie twisted around to see a small child, a lucrean child, standing above them. She looked about seven—maybe eight—years old, with white hair in a long braid, and wore a simple baby-blue gown, barefoot. Like all lucreans, she had no pupils and angled teeth. She had a few freckles on her nose with a slight gap between her front teeth.

Maisie greeted the girl warmly, "Hi there. What's your name?"

"*Lil-eh-more*," the girl slowly pronounced. Waving to Austin and Maisie, she pushed through the doors, running into the banquet hall.

Jumping up and kicking her heels away, Maisie pulled Austin up. "Come on, no one can be in the High Sultana's presence unless formally arranged. We'd better get Lillemor out of there and take her outside or something."

Pushing through the doors slowly, Austin and Maisie gazed over the elaborate dining table and found Lillemor sitting in Lada's lap.

"I see you have met my youngest, Lillemor," she smiled. "You are just in time for dinner."

TWENTY-NINE

IT turned out Lada had three children. Lucian, her only son and the middle child, wouldn't be joining them and her oldest daughter had run off a few weeks prior. Lada gently ran her long fingers through her youngest child's hair while buoyantly talking about her family. "My son was just promoted to the head of the royal guard. I am so proud of him. My oldest *would* be replacing me as High Sultana within the next decade, but she has run off with her lover, a *relegator* of all things. Ugh! It seems little Lillie here will be my heir instead, won't you, sweetie?"

The child giggled as she wiggled one of her loose incisors. Lada brushed her lips on Lillemor's small head. Austin still couldn't wrap his head around Lada being a mother. With her looks, the High Sultana's age shifted between twenty or a glowing forty.

"Will you have children?" Lada asked Maisie.

Maisie squirmed uncomfortably in her seat. "I don't know.

I've never really thought about it."

Lada whispered something in her daughter's ear. The child hopped down from her mother's lap and skipped off and out the door. Dinner was served, but Lada paid more attention to Maisie, her eyes brushing over Austin, who sat between them.

"You have had the time to, certainly," the High Sultana mused.

Maisie uncharacteristically avoided her food. Her hands lay motionless at her sides with agitation jittering through them. To Austin's distaste, Lada seemed to appease herself more with Maisie's interrogation rather than her food. Taking a swift drink out of her goblet, Lada relaxed back against her chair, resting her chin on her elevated hand. "You cannot hide it from me, child. Your remorse betrays you. I have lived long enough to recognize survivor's guilt when I see it."

Maisie blanched even more as her eyes glistened. Noticing her shaking, Lada sighed and ceased her probing. "Forgive me, I forget some old wounds never heal."

"Excuse me, I need to get some air." Maisie almost knocked her chair over running out of the room.

Jumping to his feet, Austin moved to bolt after her.

"Austin, where do you think you're going?"

"Back in a moment," he promised as he left the banquet hall. Going down the hallway looking around for Maisie, Austin found himself standing on the steps to Lada's garden. A breeze blew through his clothes, sending shivers throughout his body. Sitting on the lowest steps with her head bowed on her folded arms, Maisie's back faced Austin. Her shoulders heaved a little as she sniffled softly. When he kneeled in front of her, Austin tried to find her eyes under the yellow-copper curls shrouding them. "Maisie?"

She uttered nothing, but her heavy breathing became very still. Austin gently reached out, parting her hair to view her face. The makeup Kate had applied earlier smeared around her cheeks and under her eyes, the natural green mixed with a puffy red from the tears she'd cried. Her freckles stood out like blemishes on a fruit against her salt-white skin. Unfocused and distant, her eyes drooped down, droplets of water trickling down her face. Holding her face gently, Austin brushed a tear away and tilted her head up a little. Eventually she looked at him, her eyes drowning in suppressed tears.

She's trying to hold them back in front of me, he realized.

Sniffling loudly, Maisie raked her hair back and wiped her nose. "Sorry. I shouldn't have let her get to me."

"Hey, don't say that," Austin scolded as he dropped his hand.

Maisie weakly chuckled, shaking her head. "She's right though. Everything my brother did, all that pain he caused, I feel *horrible* about it. He killed Aviana's dad and countless other innocent plenaries. Alton should never have let me stay at the Sacrarium. All I do is cause trouble, that's all we Orchids are good for, I guess."

"Maybe," Austin admitted as he dropped beside her, "but you know what I think?"

Maisie glanced at him but said nothing.

"I think you care a lot about Alton and the others. You push yourself to try harder, and you're not afraid to throw yourself in harm's way if it means saving someone's life—like mine or Kate's. You joke a lot, but you're also pretty smart. I can easily say you're one of the nicest people I've met, and you've helped me so much with my powers. If you're good for anything, it's being a friend to others," Austin insisted. "That's what I think anyway."

Maisie hugged him and then punched him in the arm. "Thanks, Austin. I needed that."

"Sure thing. Shall we wrap this up?" He pointed behind him.

"As soon as possible, please. I want to get some ice cream before we hike it back to the Sacrarium."

Lada was still reclining in her chair at the end of the table when they returned. The meal was cleared away, but the High Sultana smiled as they sat down. "Better now, are we?"

"If you don't have any more questions for us, High Sultana, we wish to leave with the pendant you promised Alton," Maisie replied.

The High Sultana climbed out of her chair. With a promise of giving them the pendant after, there was one more thing she wanted to show them. Through the hallways and down a spiral staircase, she led them to a hidden chamber that opened at the High Sultana's touch. Following Lada and Maisie into the chamber, the empty room confused Austin. Lada indicated the room around her. "This is the cogitari chamber. A room that allows the occupant to enter and rematch memories of their past."

"I'll pass on that," Maisie insisted as she edged toward the exit.

"It is not for you. I want Austin to try it for himself."

"Wait, what?" Austin gaped at Lada.

Touching his forehead, Lada explained, "I have looked into your mind, there is something dwelling in your subconsciousness. You only remember fragments of the night you were stuck by that energy, yes? This chamber can help you understand what really happened to you that night in June." She gestured for him to stand in the middle of the chamber. "Close your eyes, think about that night. When you do, you will know the truth you have been searching for."

Austin walked into the center of the room. Maisie and Lada stood by the door, watching him intently. Closing his eyes, he thought about that night in June. For a moment, Austin thought he'd fallen asleep, but he opened his eyes and gasped. Stranded in the middle of a desert, he looked around for any sign of Lada or Maisie. "Okay, now what?"

A stone door answered his question as if conjured out of thin air. Opening it skeptically, Austin peered through the doorframe and into another room. After he stepped inside, the door slammed itself shut and vanished behind him. Austin took a deep breath. Blind in the dark, he tried to reach for the walls of the mysterious chamber. His palms touched cold, damp bricks, and he followed by sense of touch. Feeling the edges of another doorway, he walked through into an even darker room. Austin almost shouted again when a single light illuminated the room in the center.

The Template View.

Glancing around for any more signs, he found none and touched it. Austin yelled as countless voices screamed inside his head.

"Catch him at it!"

"Ryker! Ryker!"

"Stop!" Austin shouted as he clutched his ears. Collapsing on the floor, he willed his eyes to open and spotted the memory. He wasn't viewing an image, he actually stood *in* the memory. Gray coloring shrouded the world around him. Everything smoked and blurred, but he remembered this place clearly. He noticed himself in the graveyard, sitting in his wheelchair by his mom's grave.

High above where Austin stood in the memory, a dark, swirling funnel formed. Crackling around it, yellow and purple lightning streaked back and forth inside the tornado. The funnel hit the ground with a deafening *crack* as the sounds of the storm escalated, trapping the other Austin in its chaos. Austin watched as he got thrown out of the wheelchair.

Looking at the memory, he clearly saw what the lightning really was. Just like in his dream, two plenaries in armor chased and fought each other. Masked by exploding arcs of their own colored lightning, they collided, creating a shower of sparks and obscuring Austin's view of the fight. They crashed on the ground right when the tornado died around memory-Austin.

Shoving the other person off him, Austin recognized the knife sticking in the fallen plenarie's torso. Austin could feel the wound in his own chest as the man with the yellow lightning pulled it out of himself. As he cried out, a giant pulse of energy threw his returning attacker off him. Crawling to his feet, the plenarie with the darker purple electricity vanished, leaving the wounded plenarie alone.

His eyes watering from the pain in his chest, Austin

squinted at the man as he shouted, "*Ryker! Ryker!*"

Then the plenarie spotted memory-Austin lying on the ground close by. Yellow light cracked throughout his armor as the blade in his hands disintegrated. Dissolving into pure energy, he collided with memory-Austin, who flew into the air and crashed back onto the ground.

Austin? Can you hear me? You need to wake up!

Do not touch him, Maisie, Lada's voice echoed.

The world around Austin vanished as it morphed into a city being blown apart. Relegators murdered plenaries in the streets as a giant figure roamed through the chaos, giving the order to kill them all. Strange, Austin had never seen this vision before. Looking around at the ongoing carnage surrounding him, he tried to run away from the violence. A monster in black armor constantly reappeared, cutting down any plenaries standing in his path. That's when Austin realized who he was looking at: Solon Blak.

This was Maisie's memory of watching her brother betray their people.

Solon was chasing after a plenarie carrying a small box when Austin woke up in the cogitari chamber. He lay on the ground, drenched in sweat and breathing in gasps. Maisie knelt beside him, eyes wide with fear. "Austin! Are you hurt? You were screaming."

The pain in Austin's body melted away. Taking deep breaths, he groaned, "I'm fine. That was weird. I'd never seen that before."

Maisie eyed him nervously. "What did you see?"

Austin rubbed his temples. "I-I saw two plenaries

fighting… the night I got my powers. I think one of them killed the other. But it was weird, after that I saw a city being destroyed. Solon—"

"That's it, I'm taking you back to the Sacrarium." Maisie helped him up and wrapped one of his arms around her shoulders. Glaring accusingly at Lada, she reminded, "We only came here because you had something for Alton. Give it to me now while I can still hold my temper."

Lada summoned the pendant and held it out, offering it to Maisie. Snatching it from her hand, Maisie heaved Austin up the stairs and walked him out of Lada's palace. The High Sultana hiked up her skirts and ran after them. "I did not think it would overwhelm him like that. Come now, there is no need to leave just yet."

"You got your dinner, now it's time for us to go," Maisie snapped back.

"Austin," Lada pleaded with him. "You do not blame me for that incident back there, do you? There is still our discussion to be finished."

Letting go of Maisie, Austin wobbled a little on his feet. When he looked at Lada, he almost puked. "I'm sorry, Lada. I don't think I have an answer yet. I… I just want to go home."

"Take this." Lada offered him a small crystal. "When you want to reach me, give it a squeeze and think of me, then I will come to you. I hope this does not put a damper on our friendship."

"Bye, Lada." Maisie shooed her away.

Picking up her skirts again, Lada stormed back into her palace, letting the doors slam behind her. After he pocketed the crystal, Austin eased himself down onto the steps. Maisie laid the back of her hand across his forehead. "You're a little warm. When we get back to the Sacrarium, you should get some rest. Now where is that waitress?"

Popping in front of them in a white flash, Lucena dusted herself off and walked up to them. "You called me? Let's hurry up and—woah, what happened to you?"

Dressed in casual clothes, Lucena had taken off her shades, revealing her colorless eyes. Her bold eyeliner matched her blue hair with its turquoise-dyed tips. She eyed them curiously as her hair twitched with excitement. Maisie crossed her arms and narrowed her eyes at the lucrean. "Your High Sultana almost turned my friend's brain into mush. I would recommend taking us back before I bust in there and punch her lights out."

Wincing at her statement, Austin looked apprehensively at Lucena. Eyes wide, her hair actually froze in the air as she pressed her lips together. She suddenly burst into shaking fits of laughter as her hair waved around with new energy. Wiping tears from her colorless eyes, she nodded. "By all means, punch her lights out. She knows how to screw with your head, my mom."

"Wait, you're her other daughter?" Austin marveled.

Lucena shrugged. "Not by choice. We should leave now, I gotta close up shop at Mojo's. You can say hi to Scratch before you go home."

THIRTY

The night sky above them darkened as they teleported in front of the closed diner. The other employees had left, but the lights still flickered on inside. Sitting in a booth drinking a milkshake, Scratch watched them enter and clicked his teeth. "So, I assume the warehouse burned down because of you guys?"

"It was a rough night." Maisie waved as she slid into the booth.

Scratch grunted. "Well, I hope you found what you were looking for. All the relegators in the Tower are going ballistic. They told the press it was faulty wiring or whatever. No one wants to admit that The Orchid burned down one of their warehouses."

When Austin told Scratch about the power source, the relegator reached into his jacket and handed him a thick folder labeled *Restricted Access*. After the warehouse fiasco, Scratch managed to hack into the relegators' database after Reuel's supposed death. The relegator was anything but pleased with his discovery of more bad news.

Flipping through the folder, Austin eyes bulged. "What is this thing?"

The pages and photos in the folder depicted a machine. A large one with specifications and notes taken from restricted data on plenaries and their powers. Austin frowned. Why did it look so familiar? The project was labeled as a "Genesis Engine." According to its description, the machine was built to target anything standing on two legs and blast them with a dangerous amount of energy. *Plenarie* energy.

The relegator took a deep breath. "I dug up more redacted files on the plenaries last night. Turns out the Alliance has been secretly experimenting on them. They're trying to understand their powers and see if they can replicate or even enhance them. Most of the experiments failed, but a handful of projects are still running as certain subjects demonstrated positive results. The Genesis Engine is one of those projects."

Austin glanced back at the folder. The Engine could harness plenarie energy and manipulate it. By generating a storm of energy, it would blast the world's population in the process and mutate them into plenarie-like beings with dangerous power. "They're going to create their own worldwide Post-Genesis," he realized with a tremor.

"If humans even survive the process." Scratch shook his head.

Maisie slammed her hands on the table. "After decades of turning us into weak relegators, the Alliance wants to make the rest of the world into effing plenaries?"

"I don't know what to make of it." Scratch shrugged glumly. "The point is, if someone doesn't stop the Alliance, this machine is going to blast the whole world in a storm of energy. But this kind of power is just too much for humans. They're more likely to burn up rather than survive a transformation like this."

Maybe not, Austin thought of his scars. If plenarie energy had done this to him, could the same be said about the rest of the world? Probably not. He thought about his dreams, the vision that had plagued him since that night in June. Remembering the tall dark shape in one of them, Austin realized why the Genesis Engine looked familiar. He'd seen it before. Relegators had been marching out of a tall dark tower, a tower Austin had been inside only once before.

"Reuel? Reuel, wake up. Don't make me shove you off the bed."

Half-awake in his bed, Reuel blinked. "Wha—Ow! What was that for?"

Sprawled on the floor tangled in his own blanket, he glared at Aviana who stood above him. Dazzling in one of her blue dresses, Reuel was a little disappointed to see she'd straightened her hair again. He liked it natural and curly. After a hasty breakfast, Aviana informed him they were picking up his brother. Reuel was still wobbling from teleporting when they arrived on the street. During the day, his neighborhood wasn't as dangerous, but he wouldn't risk the chance.

Where's my...

Reuel suddenly remembered he'd lost his gun during the warehouse fire. Then again, nobody would come near them spotting Aviana with her sword. As they approached the door to the apartment building, Aviana froze and grabbed the hilt of her weapon.

"What's wrong?"

The tall girl glanced around. After summoning her armor, she walked down the steps. "Go inside and get your brother. I'm going to search the perimeter."

"Trust me, the neighborhood always looks this trashy."

Aviana flicked her wrist at him. "Go on in, I'll come up in a second."

Buzzing in, Reuel sprinted up the stairs and knocked on the apartment door. "Jax? You in there? I forgot the k—" The door creaked open, unlocked. Reuel's pulse throbbed faster. He treaded quietly as he entered the room. The lights still brightened the room, Jackson left a huge mess in the kitchen. After turning the TV off, Reuel checked the bedroom and the bathroom.

No Jackson.

Reuel ran back into the kitchen. No note, no sign of where his brother had vanished. He bolted toward the door when a familiar voice growled, "Back from the dead, Reuel?"

From the corner of his eye, Reuel watched a shadow materialize behind him. Solon Blak stood in the living room, admiring Jackson's drawings taped to the wall. When Reuel approached him, the relegator's skeleton mask grinned at him. Answering the unspoken question, Solon looked down at him. "Your brother is out getting ice cream with your friend,

Emma. I think we have some catching up to do before they return. Don't you agree?"

"My condolences for your arm. Aside from that, you look well for a dead man."

Reuel struggled to find his voice. "I... I barely made it out alive. I don't remember much about that night. They... um... let me out of the... hospital this morning."

"I see." The relegator dragged one of his claws across the counter. "You lost the shipment. Did you manage to burn any of the plenaries with the building?"

"Well... no. No, it was Austin and The Orchid. They got away."

Solon tilted his head at Reuel. His silence only terrified him more. After a moment, he spoke again, "We can discuss your failure another time. Right now, we must focus on the final stages of our project. The Genesis Engine is almost ready."

"Genesis Engine? I thought we were designing an energy plant prototype."

"Don't be naïve," Solon chided as he circled Reuel. "The United Alliance is careless. Without the relegators, they would have dissolved years ago. Now they sit back and leave the world to its own ruination. It is time for us to take control for ourselves."

"Take control," Reuel repeated. "What are you talking about?"

Solon waved his giant clawed hand. "I am talking about the endgame. Now that the number of relegators has grown beyond their control, the United Alliance is vulnerable. Our forces combined with the power of the Engine will overthrow the world government once and for all. Tonight, the Engine will go online as planned. I expect you to join me at the Tower."

"Of course." Reuel bowed his head, goose bumps sprouting on his arm as Solon's dark shape passed him. "I won't disappoint you again."

"No. You won't." Solon faded away into shadow, his words still echoing in the room.

Did he suspect him? The relegator seemed to know everything, like a dark, omniscient being. *If this Engine goes online tonight…* There was hardly any time to think of that now. Reuel spun around as the door creaked open. With her sword in hand, Aviana inspected the room before approaching him. "Is everything all right? Where's your brother?"

"No, we've got a problem, Aviana." Reuel pushed her out the door and slammed it behind him.

"Problem? What are you talking about?"

Jumping down the stairs, Reuel flew out of the building. "I'll explain in a second, but you need to call your friends and have them meet us someplace. Austin and his friend should come too."

"Reuel, tell me what happened in there. Is this about your brother?"

"Solon's making his move." Reuel threw a side glance at Aviana. "I know what his machine really is, and it's going online tonight."

Aviana called the other plenaries, minus Alton to meet her and Reuel at Mojo's diner. Reuel relayed the meeting with Solon and everything they'd discussed about the machine. After he spoke, Austin and Maisie put a giant folder with the details of the Genesis Engine on the center of the table. All eyes turned to Reuel.

"How do we destroy it?" Austin questioned him.

Reuel's shoulders sagged as his head bowed. "That's just it. The Genesis Engine *is* Alliance Tower. Solon planned this from the beginning. The structure, the location, every design and detail are a part of the machine. I thought maybe without the power source, Solon would give up, but he's relentless. I should have known he'd have a backup plan."

"Even with the orb, it'll take a lot of juice to power this thing," Braylin said. "Even just to cover the United States, you need something extremely powerful."

While everyone argued back and forth about the machine, Austin remembered another object from his dreams. Alton mentioned someone wanted to steal it, but for what? Now he knew why. "Something powerful like the Template View?"

All the plenaries regarded Austin as if he'd grown a second head. Reuel raised his head from his hand and glanced around. "The what?"

"Someone's tried to steal it before, am I right?" Austin quizzed Aviana.

Aviana had no reply. She was biting her lip when the thought dawned on her. "We need to leave. Right now."

Setting the last joint in place, Alton clapped his hands together as he admired his work. After fixing the hand, touching up the helmet and legs, he was finally done. He laid the parts out to resemble a body, then examined the armor for any defects. Finding none, he threw a blanket over it and took out Austin's new pendant. It was a work of art; Alton envied the lucrean craftsmanship. Lada left the device without a plenarie emblem, but instead circled intertwining strings of gold at the edge of the piece.

Alton polished the pendant, humming while he worked. Beside his covered project, the orange orb glowed and flickered energy inside the lantern shell. Alton was curious to see if Lada's pendant could absorb the energy from the orb, but he hadn't tested it yet. Solon would be searching for it; Alton was well aware of his old foe's determination. Not even a sword in the chest had been enough to stop Solon from dying.

More than a year had passed since his children encountered the first relegator. They fought him and barely escaped with their lives. Ever since then, Alton dreaded the day when they would be forced to face him again. As he rubbed the metal with a rag fiercely, it slipped out of his hands and tumbled under his workbench. Cursing as he got on his hands and knees, Alton banged his helmet under the table as he searched for the metal piece. Across the bridge, one of the doors to the Athenaeum slowly opened. The carrying clicking noises of the chamber masked the sounds of heavy footsteps echoing toward the lab. Alton found the pendant and climbed back up. He finished polishing it and then set it aside.

"Alton Malachite."

Alton didn't need to turn around to know who stood behind him. "You may wear his mask, but you are not the Solon Blak I ended that day."

As he stepped into the lab, Solon Blak faced the old plenarie in his own distinct armor. Blocking the table, Alton realized the lantern still sat on the workbench. Instead of reaching for it, Solon walked up to Alton and gazed down at him. For a moment, no one moved a muscle. Alton thrust his sword out from his gauntlet, aiming for Solon's throat.

Solon reflexively caught the blade with his hand. Grabbing him by the neck, Solon raised Alton off the ground until he dangled in the air. He uttered nothing as he ripped Alton's sword arm off. When Alton tried to swing his other arm, Solon thrust the sword-tipped limb through his chest just below Alton's pendant. Alton gasped as green smoke gushed out of his chest and arm.

"Now I will take what is rightfully mine." Solon threw the plenarie over the workbench. After he examined the lantern, he smashed it on the floor and scooped up the orange orb. When he noticed the pendant sitting on the table, he knocked it onto the floor and crushed it under his foot. As Solon walked out of the room, he glanced over his shoulder. "You don't mind if I take the Template View as well? No? I didn't think so. Good bye, Malachite."

THIRTY-ONE

WHEN Austin and the others returned to the Sacrarium, a petrified Vera greeted them. Immediately, they knew something was wrong when they saw her. She phased in and out of focus, leaving gaps in her sentences. "Alton… attacked… Template View… stolen… imbalance… must stop him!" she wailed.

Throwing off her helmet, Aviana gasped at the felera. "Vera, what happened?"

Vera vanished completely and didn't return. Without another word, Aviana zoomed out of the room heading to the Athenaeum.

Austin turned to Maisie. "What happened to Vera?"

Anxiety radiated off Maisie as she answered. "Felera spirits are tied to the Template View. If something happened to it…."

Maisie and Austin raced down the hall to the stairs as they bolted into the gateway chamber. Jumping down the worn staircase, they found the pillar where the Template View once rested in ruins. The gateway doors were thrown open as the vacuum of the portals sucked the contents of the room into them. As she struggled to push against one of the swinging doors, Maisie shouted at Austin, "Help me close them!"

Austin ran up to the door labeled *The Angelic Highlands*. The door opened to a swirling vortex, its vacuum pulling him into it. Holding onto the door for dear life, he heard a phrase being repeated over and over as images of a sword and people with wings flashed into his mind. *With wings of flight and the mind's might, old forces shall reunite to reclaim what was lost. With wings of flight and the mind's might, old forces shall reunite to reclaim what was lost. With wings of flight...*

"Austin! Grab my hand!" Braylin yelled.

As he did, Braylin tugged him out of the void just as Maisie slammed the door shut. The voices died out as the images faded from his mind. Maisie and Braylin sealed the other doors, but no one knew how long the doors to the other realms had been left open.

"Alton!" Maisie ran up the stairs with Braylin and Austin right behind her.

When they made it to the Athenaeum, Aviana knelt next to Alton on the floor by his workbench. Alton had been impaled by his own right arm through the chest. Small puffs of green smoke bled from the wound as he groaned. On the floor next to him, Austin noticed pieces of what must have been Lada's pendant.

"Solon took the lantern and the Template View," Alton creaked.

Aviana's head snapped up. When her eyes found Reuel, she

marched over to him and grabbed him by the shirt, bringing her sword to his throat. "You did this! You wanted us all out of here so your boss could grab what he wanted. Traitor, I should slice your throat right now!"

"Let go of me." Reuel squirmed. "I never told Solon about this place. I would never betray you, Aviana!"

"Lock him in his room," Aviana ordered after she shoved Reuel toward Braylin. "Make sure he doesn't try to escape. We'll deal with him later."

Reuel dragged his feet as he fought Braylin, but the plenarie pinned his arm down and hauled him away. "Aviana! You've got it all wrong! *Listen to me!*"

The relegator continued to shout and scream until he was out of earshot outside the Athenaeum. Helping Alton to his feet, Aviana checked the injury. "Maisie, can you take a look at this?"

Maisie touched the arm and peered closely at the bigger hole in Alton's armor. After she dove behind Alton's workbench, she ran back to him with a roll of duck-tape. "I can pull it out, but we have to be quick. Austin, help me with this. We have to wrap it around him fast. Aviana, get ready to pull his arm out."

After the count of three, Aviana freed Alton's arm and Maisie and Austin wrapped his chest in silver tape. He looked like a robot-mummy art piece made out of scrap. Sitting by his table, Alton instructed Maisie while she reattached his broken limb. Aviana paced the room, seething. "How could I be so stupid. I fell for that relegator's stupid trap and now Solon's out there with the orb *and* the Template View. You should never have saved him," she yelled at Austin.

"Blame me all you want, but we've got bigger problems to deal with, Aviana," Austin snapped back at her. "We have to stop Solon from activating the Genesis Engine and destroy it before he can use it to expose the world to plenarie energies! I was exposed to some back in June, and I barely survived. The rest of the world won't be as lucky."

Aviana narrowed her eyes at him. "Can you guys give us a minute? Take Alton to his quarters to rest. I need to talk with Austin. Alone."

Kate began to protest until Aviana gave her an unsettling glare to rival her own. Following a slow-moving Alton, Maisie and Kate left Austin alone with Aviana. Aside from the noises coming from the Athenaeum's bridges, Alton's lab fell silent. Sitting on the edge of Alton's workbench, Aviana crossed her arms and glared at Austin. "You know something. Don't you?"

"Can you be more specific? I—"

"Wade and Ryker vanished the same day you were blasted by that energy," Aviana reminded him in a clipped tone. "You know what happened to at least one of them, don't you?"

Austin nodded. "I think I do. When Maisie and I were in Lucreet, Lada showed me my memory of that night. It was the first time I could remember the whole thing."

"I want to see it for myself."

"Um"—Austin scratched his head—"can't I just tell you?"

Aviana ignored him as she searched Alton's shelves for something. Tossing parts and tools over her shoulder, she pulled out what looked like a projector tied to a metal cap. "Alton made this. It's called a memory cap," Aviana explained as she placed it on Austin's head. "It hasn't been used for years, but it should be able to play the memory."

"I know this is important to you, Aviana, but we don't have time. Solon's out there with the Engine!" Austin exclaimed.

"I know!" Aviana whipped around to face him. Austin's heart melted, seeing the raw, unchecked emotion and pain in Aviana's eyes as they watered. "You don't know what we're up against. I do. There's something I have to know before—" She choked as she flipped a switch on the memory cap and turned Austin's head to face the back of one of the shelves. As the invention flickered to life, a black and white image appeared on the surface. Eventually it changed to color, then the sound caught up with the rolling film.

"What is it you want to see?" Austin asked as he watched the memory begin to play.

Placing her hands on the sides of his head, Aviana adjusted the cap and stared at the projection. "The truth. What really happened in June."

THIRTY-TWO

AUSTIN *was in the graveyard, sitting in his wheelchair by his mom's grave. The lightning storm was starting to form above him. It was the plenaries. They moved so fast they looked like bolts of lightning bouncing off each other in the air. As they continued to fight, their collisions exploded in a shower of yellow and dark purple light. Some of the lightning from their fight rained down, striking past the trees by Austin.*

While he wheeled over to the trees, the two figures were zigzagging around each other, their pulsing energy crackling loudly in the sky. Austin was thrown out of his chair as the storm surrounded him. He was trapped in the middle of it, sprawled on the ground when the two plenaries crashed down close to where Austin lay...

Now Austin recognized them both. It took him some time to figure it out, but now everything fell into place. The plenarie with the purple lightning was Ryker, and the other one had to be—

"Wade."

Austin turned as Aviana whispered the name. Her eyes glistened as she watched the projected memory. Together they watched Wade shove Ryker off him. There, in the middle of Wade's chest, a knife glittered.

"No!" Aviana screamed as she dropped to the floor.

"Ryker!" Wade shouted as he and Ryker were blown away from each other in a blast of yellow light. Stumbling a little, Ryker got to his feet and he sped off, leaving Wade dying on the grass. Wade's body began to glow as he crawled to his knees. Ripping the blade out of his chest, he tossed it aside as it disintegrated into nothing. Yellow lightning spurted out of him as his body dissolved into pure energy. "Ryker?" he called weakly.

On the ground, Austin groaned as he turned over and noticed the glowing Wade. Hearing the sound, Wade spotted him. He erupted into raw energy and collided with Austin. Flying through the air and falling to the ground in a crumpled heap, yellow electricity ran down Austin's sizzling body until it settled inside him.

The projection fuzzed until it died out. When Austin looked down, Aviana was sobbing on the ground as she pounded the floor with her fist. "No! No, no, no."

He touched her shoulder gently. "Aviana?"

The projector on his head sparked back to life with a new memory he didn't understand, until he suddenly realized it was one of Aviana's.

The memory was in the Sacrarium. Aviana was shorter, her hair shoulder-length and straightened. Brushing some of her hair to hide her left eye, she crossed her arms. She looked around her mid-teens. Next to her, a cleaner, less damaged Alton stood with a younger Braylin and Maisie. They waited in the entrance chamber staring at the archway.

"Any minute now," Alton kept repeating to himself.

"I'm bored, can I go back to bed?" Maisie whined.

Aviana and Braylin exchanged a glance as they sighed. The arch suddenly came to life as it filled the room with white light. Two figures ran out of the portal, dropping into the room. Wade looked around Austin's age, identical to himself in the picture gathering dust in his room. His expression held a hint of a devilish smile. Behind him, a paler teenager with black hair avoided everyone's eyes. A younger Ryker.

Unlike the old picture, Ryker's mouth curved downward and his jaw tightened. Unaware of his friend's discomfort, Wade gave the plenaries an impish smile as he greeted them. "Waz up? Or should I say how do you do? Do people still say that? Whatever." Wade threw his arms open wide for a welcome hug as he grinned broadly.

Maisie was nodding off and starting to snore. Braylin wasn't amused by Wade's entrance, and Alton seemed at a loss for words. Dropping his arms, Wade's confident smile wavered, though he continued without skipping a beat. "I'm Wade Chiffon and this little wallflower here is my best friend, Ryker Darkthistle. We apologize for being late. We had a little trouble leaving the country to get here. Anyway, I just wanted to say thank you for offering us sanctuary. I'm sure we'll all be good friends in no time."

Aviana elbowed Maisie who jerked awake. "It wasn't me!

Oh sorry... Oh. You're here. Hi! I'm Maisie, Maisie Orchid. I can't believe we're meeting new plenaries. Sweeeeet!" Shaking their hands vigorously, Maisie stepped aside for the others to introduce themselves. Braylin shook their hands, giving them a polite hello.

After shaking Alton's hand, Wade walked up to Aviana, extending his own. Blushing slightly, Aviana gave him a breathless hello. Ryker, who had been silent the whole time, greeted them all with a quiet hello as he tightened his grip on his bag.

"Is it only you two?" Maisie asked. She stood on the tips of her toes, craning her head to see if anyone was coming in behind Wade and Ryker.

Wade nodded as he wrapped an arm around Ryker. "Yep, just the two of us, right, Ryker?"

Ryker's shoulders hunched as Wade ruffled his hair. "Yeah... just us."

For a moment, Wade fell silent, communicating something reassuring to his friend through his eyes. Nodding, Ryker relaxed a little and brushed down his untidy hair.

"We'll show you to your rooms, then," Alton said as he led them out of the room.

His gaze downcast, Ryker walked past his friend without another word. As he followed, Wade's bag split a seam, dumping some of its contents out. Unnoticed by the others, he quickly shoved it all back in as Aviana knelt beside him. When she bent over to pick up a camera, the hair covering her spot moved away. Right when Wade noticed it, Aviana quickly tried to hide it again.

When Wade asked her why she covered it, Aviana's face flushed and she mumbled something incoherent. He reached out and tucked her hair behind her ear. "There. That's better."

"I hate showing my spots," Aviana confessed to him. She rolled up the sleeve of the sweater she wore, revealing more white patches on her elbow and forearm.

"Why, because it makes you look different?"

Aviana bit her lip, pushed her sleeve back down, and pulled some of her hair over her eye. They finished repacking Wade's bag and walked after the others.

"Y'know"—Wade tilted his head at her—"I've never met a plenarie with leucoderma before." When Aviana said nothing, he continued. "If you don't want to talk about it, that's cool. I just figured you should know that you don't have to hide it."

"Why not?"

Wade grinned at her. After a moment, Aviana shyly smiled back. "I think God made each and every one of us to be beautiful and unique. Spots like yours shouldn't be covered, they make you who you are. I guess what I'm trying to say is, I think your spots are beautiful, because that's how you were made to be."

Aviana swallowed and then nodded. She was still quiet, but her smile never faded.

"I didn't catch your name." Wade stopped next to her.

Aviana's face reddened as she stuttered, "Oh, I—I'm Aviana. Aviana Blu."

"Pleased to meet you, Aviana." Wade grinned.

When the memory was over, another one started to play right after it.

Aviana was reading in the library alone with a small stack of books beside her. Voices grew louder outside the library. The door opened and two people in the middle of a conversation barged in. An older, more at ease Ryker was followed by a girl Austin didn't recognize. And yet, there was something oddly familiar about her. She was slim and graceful like a ballerina, with straight brown hair draping down her back. When she talked, she had a slight European accent.

"I didn't mean to. I tried to say sorry, but she won't listen to me," she moaned.

"Just give her time to heal, Emily," Ryker calmed her.

Aviana smirked as she watched them walk up to her. The girl named Emily lagged behind, folding her arms crossly. Knocking lightly on the table, Ryker greeted Aviana. "Hey, Aviana, Wade wanted me to ask you to meet him in his room."

"Why?"

Ryker shrugged as he picked up one of the books next to her. "He said it was private." Curiosity glistened from Aviana's eyes as she jumped up. Running to Wade's room, she quickly composed herself by taking a deep breath. After she knocked on the door, she entered when Wade called her in. He sat on his bed crisscrossed, holding something behind his back. Aviana plopped beside him as he handed her a picture frame. Austin couldn't get a good look at it through the memory projection, but he guessed what it was.

"It looks great," Aviana whispered.

Wade gave her a lopsided grin. "Duh! I light up every picture I'm in. Oh yeah, I guess you do too."

Laughing, Aviana shoved him playfully. "Watch it, Chiffon, you'll fall over with that big head of yours."

"I'll fall over?" Wade raised his brows. "I'll push you off the bed right now, Avi-Navy."

"Don't call me that. Your nicknames are horrible."

"Sorry, Avi, gotta make me." Wade grinned at her.

Aviana stood up beside Austin, reached up and tried to touch memory-Wade's face. Her hand blocked the light from the projector as she sniffed quietly. Everything darkened as the memory cap played one more recording.

An older Aviana walked down a hall with her hands knotted together anxiously. Taking a turn, she bumped into Braylin, knocking the Plenarie Tome out of his hands.

"Sorry, Braylin!" Aviana apologized.

Dashing down the hall, she caught up with Wade who was heading to the gateway chamber. Stopping beside him, she gave him a warm smile he did not return. The carefree smirk he usually wore was missing and instead replaced with a stern expression as he walked swiftly past Aviana. Wade didn't seem to even register her as he moved past her.

Twisting around, she jogged beside him with wide eyes and slightly parted lips. "Wade, is something wrong?" Her fear was more evident as her face grew fretful.

Wade stopped abruptly as he faced her. There was a pleading look in his eyes when he spoke. "Yes, but I need you to stay here."

"But—"

"Stay here," he repeated as he ran with yellow lightning trailing behind him. Alone in the hall, Aviana hugged herself as she stood rooted to the spot.

The memory cap powered down after the memory froze. Austin pulled the helmet off, then glanced around the room. Aviana was gone. Rushing out of the Athenaeum calling out her name, he found her just outside the doors. She stood with her tight fists whitening. Her head bowed as her shoulders continued to shake. "Did you know?"

"Know what?"

Aviana spun around and poked him harshly in the chest. Her eyes were swollen red and her lip quivered slightly as she talked. "I saw your memory. Did you know it was Wade?"

Austin sighed. "When I started to remember more I put it together. But I didn't really know for sure until now."

Fresh tears streaked down Aviana's cheeks as she nodded.

Austin couldn't meet her eyes. "We can morn him later, but we need to find Solon. He's got everything he needs to power the Genesis Engine. Before he makes another move, we need to take him down."

"No."

"What?" Austin gawked at her, throwing his hands up impatiently. "Aviana, we don't have time for this! We need to get going!"

"No!" Aviana's bitter voice pushed forward. "There is no *we*. I should never have trusted you. You have no place among us."

"What?" Austin was shocked. "I can help!" he roared.

Aviana shoved him back as she screamed, "*You wouldn't even have powers if Wade hadn't died! He could have reincarnated. Come back and things would have been the same! What do you think you are, some kind of hero? You're not even a real plenarie! You're just a stupid human that got in the way!"*

She vanished, leaving a spark of blue light and Austin ashen-faced and speechless.

The sad truth was Austin knew she was right. Who was he kidding? He wasn't supposed to have powers; he shouldn't have been able to walk again. It was all just a huge mistake. Walking around aimlessly, he found himself in the bedroom hall. Kate was sitting in front of her door, then climbed up and ran up to him. "Austin? What happened? What's wrong?"

Austin waved her away. "Where is everyone, Kate?"

"They're in the library. Reuel's been pounding on his door for the last twenty minutes." Kate's face was still concerned. She tried to brush his hair away from his face, but Austin pushed her hand away.

"I need to talk to them. All of them."

THIRTY-THREE

AUSTIN and Kate found the plenaries in the middle of a heated conversation in the library. Books littered the floor in the dim and dormant room. Without Vera, the library was lifeless. Braylin stacked the fallen books while Aviana spoke to the rest of them. She'd already told them about the fate of their friends and the origin of Austin's powers. Braylin's bronze complexion had paled while Maisie teared up silently.

Aviana ignored Austin and Kate's arrival as she continued to argue with Alton. At the mention of abandoning the Sacrarium, Alton refused indignantly. "For almost twenty years I have guarded this place. I do not know if there is anywhere safer for us out there. I am sorry, my children, I do not know what to do."

"You can fight."

Everybody except Aviana turned toward Austin. With their attention, he continued, "I'm not asking you to forgive humanity or forget about the last few decades, but we need to take Solon down once and for all. He's going to wipe out the human race with his machine, and he won't just stop there. He'll come back to finish the job here. If you let him win, you won't just lose your home. You'll lose everything you've tried to save."

"Do you think defeating Solon will suddenly change everything?" Aviana berated him. "The Alliance will just stop hunting us down and it'll all be sunshine and rainbows?"

Austin forced himself to face her. "Maybe not, but Solon is the one who turned the world against you. Plenaries are powerful beings, and that scares us. But if you took a stand, you could show the world why it shouldn't be afraid of you. You can inspire them to make a change, to see the plenaries in a new kind of light. All it takes is for one person to start it."

Austin waited for someone to say something, anything. When Aviana approached him, she pushed past him and walked out of the room. After she left, Braylin and then Maisie followed without a reply. When Maisie stood in the doorway, she opened her mouth to speak but changed her mind and disappeared with a flicker of purple sparks.

"Austin"—Alton touched his pendant, tilting his head up at Austin—"in my lifetimes, I have seen many wars. Whenever plenaries were involved, the outcomes always ended with desolation. We tried detaching ourselves from humanity, and then we were slaughtered. If we fought back, we would face the same dilemma."

Patting Austin sadly on the shoulder, the door closed behind Alton as he exited the chamber. Now it was only Kate and Austin in the library. Walking back to the table, Austin slammed his fists against the wood. A hand gently squeezed his shoulder.

"Austin?" Kate's face also paled. "Don't be so hard on them, they're just scared."

Austin was scared too. If Solon's machine didn't change everyone, it would kill them all instead. Somebody had to do something. Remembering the burning apartment building, he came to a realization. No one had come to those people's aid. Instead, Austin had thrown himself into danger and saved that family. He hadn't been thinking, he'd just run in without hesitation. "We're not going to let Solon win," he began. "I wasn't sure what to do with my powers before, but now I do. I'm going to use them to kill that relegator and destroy his machine."

"How do you unlock a door that doesn't have a lock?" Austin scratched his head, standing in front of the blank white door trapping Reuel. "Any ideas, Kate?"

"Have you tried 'open sesame'?"

After pushing and touching every inch of the door, Austin knocked three times on the surface. Somewhere inside, Reuel had given up. Raising his hand, yellow sparks twitched around Austin's fingers. With a deep breath, he closed his eyes and concentrated.

Crack!

Austin opened his eyes, he was standing on the other side of the door. On the floor, Reuel lay there, gaping at him in astonishment. After he teleported them both out of the room,

Austin dragged Reuel into his room with Kate and sealed the door.

"Time to repay a debt, relegator." Austin squatted in front of the hunched-up prisoner. "With or without the plenaries, I'm going to take Solon down. You need to tell me everything you know about his plans and anything that might help us get into the Tower. I'm only going to say this once. If you're—"

Reuel snapped back at him, "What good would lying do me now? My brother is out there somewhere, alone. If I help you, I won't be doing this for *them*. This is to save my brother."

Austin nodded. If Reuel could get them into Alliance Tower, they could sneak in and steal the Template View back. Once they disabled the Engine, it would be up to Austin to find and kill Solon Blak. After he explained his plan to Kate and Reuel, the relegator reminded him that they would need someone to hack into the Tower's mainframe in order to shut the machine down. Maisie or even Alton might have been up for the task, but it didn't seem like either would be changing their minds now.

While Austin tried to figure out another solution to their hacker problem, Kate slipped out of the room and disappeared. When she came back, a floating orb glowing a faint blue followed her. It turned out that the orb had a name for itself. Kate explained how she was trapped in the storage room and discovered Orion. She played with a lock of her hair, something she did whenever she was anxious. "Orion is like an artificial intelligence. He can help us break into the Tower and shut down the Genesis Engine."

Austin high-fived his best friend. "Great, now we have our

hacker, but before we go through with this, there's someone I need to talk to first."

When Kate asked him who, he wouldn't say. Stepping out of the bedroom, Austin sped to the entrance chamber and stood in front of the archway. In the palm of his hand, a small crystal glimmered like a pale stone. As soon as he squeezed it, the piece glowed and projected the silhouette of a colossal figure in front of him.

"Have you come to a decision, dearie?"

Lada grinned down at Austin greedily like a child eyeing a bowl of candy. Folding his arms, Austin stuck his chin out at her. "I'm ready to make a deal, but I need to borrow something. And I have to use your cogitari chamber again."

Austin teleported to Lucreet with Lada's help via the archway. When he arrived at Lada's palace, she guided him down toward the chamber and presented him with another pendant. Examining it in the light, Austin asked her, "How many of these did you make?"

"Enough." Lada smiled.

After she opened the doors to the empty room, Austin walked in behind her. The cogitari chamber looked exactly the same: glowing white walls and ceilings with no furniture or decorations. In her white dress, Lada almost blended in with the light completely. Only the pink strands of her hair popped out against the colorless room. The last time Austin was in Lucreet, Lada told him she'd seen something hidden in the back of his mind.

If it was what Austin suspected, he needed to find it and

communicate with it. When he explained to her what he wanted to do, Lada lifted a finger to his forehead with pursed lips. "It is not easy to read thoughts, some people are simple, others are more complex. As I weave through your thoughts, it might sting a little. If I find the source, you will have to hold onto it until I can make the connection."

Austin didn't know what to expect. Would he be inside his mind again? Closing his eyes, there was nothing to see except darkness. Then he spotted it. A tiny light flickered in the back of his mind. Reaching out for it, Austin winced as Lada continued to probe him. Without opening his mouth, Austin spoke in his mind. *I need your help. I know you're there. You've been helping me with my powers, whispering to me. How can I defeat Solon Blak?*

Nothing replied as he waited. Doubt creeped into his mind as he sighed. *Please…*

Not today.

"What?"

I said not today. Solon Blak will be defeated, but not here, not now.

"Then what am I supposed to do?"

The Genesis Engine needs the energy inside the Template View to function. You have to remove the View from the heart of the machine and destroy the Alliance Tower. Solon will try to stop you, so you must be ready to fight.

"I know, but how can I fight Solon if I can't even match a plenarie?"

You won't be alone, Austin. That's how you'll beat Solon. Humans and plenaries must work together if there'll ever be a chance of winning. Find the View, destroy the Tower, and watch out for Solon. He's not who you think he is.

"I know that now. We'll bring him to justice for everything he's done, I promise. Who are you? How are you inside my head?"

A friend, but you must hurry. Time's running out, Austin.

Austin begged the voice to tell him more, but the light and voice vanished. When he opened his eyes, Lada wobbled on her feet, the strain of keeping the connection had been too much for her. Even her skin looked paler than usual as she breathed deeply. "I… I have been more than patient with you, Austin. It is time you kept your end of the bargain."

Austin offered her an arm to steady her. "You'll get what you want, Lada. Just give me a little more time."

"We both know you have little of that," Lada huffed as she walked with him out of the chamber.

THIRTY-FOUR

"Austin? Where have you been? Hey, where are you going now?" Kate jogged after Austin as he rushed to the Athenaeum. Her orb whizzed beside her as she bumped into Austin just outside Alton's lab. Resting on his workbench, a giant blanket cloaked the shape of a figure.

"I'll try to return this, Alton. I hope it doesn't blow up." Austin yanked off the blanket, unveiling Alton's prototype armor. *Awesome.* He grinned as he admired the details. The armor glittered silver with blue details painted around the plates and joints. On the helmet, two jagged lines forming a divided T served as eyeholes with tinted glass. Pulling Lada's pendant out of his pocket, Austin snapped it into the heart of the chest plate and stepped back. Yellow light shone throughout the grooves of the suit, just like the energy in plenarie armor.

While Austin donned Alton's new armor, Reuel found what remained of his damaged relegator armor. The four of them—Kate still counted Orion as a person—headed to the entrance chamber where they found the archway blocked. Dressed in her own armor, Maisie unmasked herself and whistled at Austin. "Someone looks ready to kick ass. Huh, I should have known Orion was gathering dust somewhere. He's like a nanny-cam with anger issues."

"I do not have anger issues!" Orion shrilled.

Austin took a step closer toward Maisie. "You changed your mind?"

In a few strides, Maisie came face-to-face with Austin. She had to look up at him, but her nose twitched and her eyes narrowed to slits. "Nobody makes Maisie Orchid look like a coward. Especially not some arrogant, self-righteous blondie with zero-percent chance of winning."

"We're glad to have The Orchid with us." Austin grinned down at her.

Running around the corner and stumbling into the room, Braylin found the group activating the archway. He tried convincing them to stay, but no one listened. "The four of you are bloody thick, you know that? Fine. But Kate stays here!"

"Well tough," Kate snorted. "Never send a plenarie to do a woman's job. You won't even help us!"

Braylin blanched at that. Mumbling something like bloody clods, he convinced Kate to let him take her place instead. Before she stormed out of the room, Kate jabbed a finger at a startled Braylin. "If Austin doesn't come back in one piece, I'll knock those pretty teeth right out of your mouth. *Comprende?*"

"Agreed." Braylin pulled out his pendant and placed it on his chest.

As the archway activated, Austin glanced behind him one last time. Kate stood in the doorway, looking at him with anxious eyes. He wished she could see him smiling at her, but all she saw was the helmet staring at her blankly. After he waved to her one last time, Austin ran after Maisie and Braylin while holding on to Reuel.

Winston Gilman sipped his coffee, admiring the view from his office window. From here, he could admire the Alliance Tower standing proudly in the heart of New Jersey. As the United States representative of the Alliance, he loved pretending he was the president of the country. After the United Alliance formed, the role of president had been decommissioned, but Winston imagined he was one anyway. He had the power, and he certainly had the money to do whatever he wanted.

For the last seven years, he sat in this chair, overlooking the relegators' progress and the Alliance's changes to America's government. Other countries had other directors, sure, but Winston Gilman controlled the rest with an iron fist. His staff monitored every project, and every enterprise sat within his reach. Tonight would be the crowning achievement of his career. One of the Alliance Tower's newest projects had been to create the first clean energy plant in the States. There would be a party of course; Winston picked out his favorite suit to wear for the event. Sitting at a smaller desk across from him, his secretary read through his letters and documents.

Winston had handpicked Dominic Harrison, a young prodigy in the works, as his assistant. The young man had potential, but he also posed as a threat to Winston's position. Which was exactly why he wanted Dominic under his thumb. Dominic wouldn't be going to the party tonight; he would be too busy filing reports and trying to catch up with all the paperwork Winston left for him. When he spun his chair around and gazed out the glass once more, Winston frowned as the lights in his office flickered.

"Call up the electrician, Harrison." He nodded to his secretary.

When Dominic dialed the number on his mobile, the door creaked open. Stepping through the frame, a giant figure hidden in smoke and darkness approached Winston's desk.

"How did you get in here?" *Probably just one of the relegators from downstairs, trying to rattle me*, Winston reassured himself. When the intruder uttered nothing, he wiped his brow nervously. "This is a restricted area, relegator. As your superior, I command you to return to your post at once." The intruder's breathing sounded like the bloodcurdling rattle of a dead man. Winston yanked drawers open, searching for his pocket pistol. Before he found the weapon, the monster in black armor grabbed him by the throat and raised him out of his chair. Winston flailed and kicked as he gasped for air. "Whatever you want, take it! Please! Let… me—"

Solon Blak dropped Winston's still body back into the chair. Trembling under his desk, Dominic covered his head as his desk tumbled aside.

"I'm just the secretary," he screamed.

As he hung into the air by the neck of his suit, he expected a metal gauntlet to crush his throat. When nothing hurt, Dominic peeked out of one of his eyes. The terrifying stranger lowered him to the ground, dusting his jacket off and straightening his askew glasses. Dominic dropped to his knees and raised his hands above his head, shaking.

"You look like an intelligent individual," Solon rumbled in a bone-chilling voice. "How would you like a job? We need a replacement for the Head Director of the United Alliance..."

The archway transported them right in front of the Alliance Tower. Curtesy of Reuel, Austin and the plenaries bypassed the security of the garage without a hitch. Once they got Orion to a computer, he displayed a hologram of the building's schematics. "I am detecting a significant amount of energy coming from this floor. There is a direct connection from the power source to an isolated control room five floors beneath it."

"We can split up," Austin suggested. "Two of us will go and steal the Template View while the other two go with Orion and see if there's a way to permanently shut down or cripple the Engine."

Reuel pointed to the control room. "There's just one problem. The system will automatically shut down if the alarm is triggered. All doors are electronically locked. That big door right there won't open again once it's closed."

Braylin volunteered to hold the garage door open. With his increased strength, he would lift the door, promising to guard it long enough so that Austin and the others could make it out. Reuel, Maisie, and Orion walked into the elevator and waited for Austin. Before he joined them, he walked back across the garage. Braylin stood with his arms crossed in front of the steel door waiting to be dropped, guarding their only escape route.

"Braylin?"

The plenarie swung around, facing Austin. "Yes?"

Austin ran up to the big guy. It was impossible to tell what his expression was under that helmet, but Austin knew he was probably raising those caterpillar eyebrows of his. "Kate has a crush on you." *Well* somebody *has to say it.* "If—I mean— *when* we get back, you should ask her out."

Braylin remained silent. Finally, he jerked his chin at the elevator. "You need to get moving. I'll see you guys soon."

Once Austin jumped into the elevator, Maisie pushed the button on the wall and they went up. When the doors opened again, the trio expected to find the floor swarming with relegators. The floor looked to be deserted as Orion led the group down the hall to a giant sealed door. It matched the steel door in the garage, only smaller. When Reuel entered a code on the access panel beside it, the screen displayed an angry red X.

"Child's play," Orion huffed as he floated in front of the panel.

The orb projected a beam of light over the screen. Austin and the others watched as he scanned the tech and hacked into the software of the Tower. When Orion finished, the panel blinked green and opened the vault-like door. Living up to the name, hundreds of buttons and switches lined the control room's walls. A giant monitor displayed the blueprints of the

Tower, outlining the electrical controls of the multiple floors.

Sitting in one of the chairs, Reuel started flicking switches and turning knobs. "You two go find that power source. The magic eight-ball and I will try to keep the relegators away while you move. Once you're out of there, we'll shut the system down. Well? What are you waiting for, a kiss on the cheek? Go!"

Austin and Maisie bolted back to the elevator and hit the 'Up' button. While they stood there waiting, both of them shuffled their feet and stared at the blinking floor numbers. Almost there, Maisie nudged Austin's arm. "You know this is a trap, right?"

"Yeah, but I have a plan," Austin assured her as the doors opened.

"To hell with your plan. You can barely control your powers, and you've never fought Solon before. Trust me, I know him better than anybody."

Austin grabbed Maisie by the shoulders. "Maisie, you have to trust me. Please, you never have to listen to me again. Just this once."

Gritting her teeth, Maisie silently agreed as they sprinted down another hall toward the chamber where the Template View was held. When they tried the door, it didn't budge. Locked. Waving to the camera hanging up in one of the corners, they watched the door unlock itself as they snuck in. Various styles of machinery filled most of the room. They treaded carefully to the middle where it hollowed out. In the center of the chamber, a glass tube hooked up to several cables and wires encased the Template View, stretching to the mechanics of the Genesis Engine.

It shone through the darkness as Austin and Maisie cautiously approached it. Maisie was reaching out to remove it when a voice cut through the air like a biting bullet. "I was hoping it would be you two. I kept the relegators away from this floor just so we could have it to ourselves. Sadly, you will not be around long enough to enjoy the privacy."

Austin noticed a shadow from the corner of his eye and shoved Maisie out of the way. "*Go!*" With yellow electricity sparking off his armor, he sped out of the room with a black cloud of smoke sailing behind him.

Alone, Maisie crept up and approached the power source.

THIRTY-FIVE

AUSTIN pushed his body to the breaking point trying to keep Solon away from Maisie and the Template View. In the corner of his eye, he spotted a black dart growing larger behind him. When he or Aviana ran, everything sounded like whirling arrows flying through the wind with cracks of lightning pulsing in the mixed sounds. When Solon ran, his momentum was without sound. Only smoke and dark energy flew off him.

Flying up the stairs and bursting out onto the roof of the Tower, Austin skidded to a stop. Behind him the enemy of the plenaries and creator of relegators faced him. In his armor, he stood almost seven feet tall, dressed in a black suit with a skull mask. His eyes glistened as pools of blackness bored into Austin. Black smoke gushed out of him as he stood there. Like a planet, he seemed to have his own field of gravity as everything, including Austin, was pulled toward him. The atmosphere around him dissolved into complete darkness as his silhouette resembled a nebulous shadow. His talon-like gauntlets, painted in dry blood, twitched by his sides.

"Solon Blak," Austin breathed.

The relegator inclined his head. "I've heard much about you, Austin Bennet. Let's talk." His voice sent chills down Austin's spine, reminding him of plenaries' modulated tones only throatier.

With a shout, Austin shot at him like a rocket, but Solon waved a hand lazily at him and he froze in midair. Grunting as he struggled against invisible bonds, Austin's eyes followed Solon as he approached him. With a shock, Austin realized he *could* see what held him. Black glass trapped him from the chin down to the tips of his toes as he tried to shatter it.

Solon read his mind. "It's not glass, but the two are very similar. I can manipulate the substance into anything with enough concentration." With a twirl of a pointed finger, he created a knife, identical to the one that killed Wade.

Austin eyed the blade as Solon pointed it under his chin. "Do it then."

"Oh, I could." Solon released the knife as it dissolved back into black powder. His armor absorbed the particles as he made a turning gesture toward Austin. Despite his protests, Austin turned right where Solon faced. "I imagine they told you I was responsible for the extermination of the plenaries."

Austin said nothing.

"I take your silence as a yes," Solon continued. "Did they also tell you the real reason why I divided the humans and plenaries? No? Before the Excretion Act, before the United Alliance rose to power with the relegators, I had come to a realization. Why was our realm divided into humans and plenaries? Why should one race be more powerful than the other? Humanity never quite evolved like the plenaries. I hated that.

"If there is one thing I despise, it's weakness. That's when I asked myself, why should we leave mankind to suffer in its inferiority? Wouldn't it be better to remove the realm's rejects altogether? I alone knew it would be best to put you out of your misery. When I approached the elders about my plan to wipe out your kind, they rebuked me."

"And so you crawled to the United Alliance instead." Austin grimaced as his bonds tightened.

Solon waved a hand across the city. "Humans are always looking for someone to look up to, someone to protect them. I created the relegators as the Alliance's own blade against the people who betrayed me. Over the years, the Alliance foolishly allowed my forces to grow in numbers. The relegator population is almost the same size as the plenarie population was decades ago. When we are ready, this world will evolve into something greater. An empire beyond the limitations of mankind. And this machine will help us progress quicker. Is that not better than the world we live in now?"

Energy crackled under Austin's impenetrable shackles. "I don't give a crap about your misunderstood villain speech! You're just the next in a line of psychopaths trying to change the world with violence." Austin choked as Solon thrust his hand up and closed his claws around his neck. Black dots danced in his eyes as his vision caved. "You can drop the act," he wheezed. "I know you're not the real Solon Blak anyway. He was killed by Alton Malachite!"

Solon released Austin from his death grip as he stepped

away. While Austin coughed for air, Solon willed the substance to slowly crush him. "I think we have talked enough."

"You... are not... Solon," Austin rasped. "I know... you... are Ryker Darkthistle."

The bonds pressing against his body froze. They melted away as Austin dropped to the ground, moaning. Before he could recover, Solon had a foot against his chest. "Last chance, Austin. You can join me or die with the rest of your friends. That's right, I know you and Maisie didn't come alone. Before I met you two, I already gutted a friend of yours downstairs. When I'm done with you, I'll slaughter the rest of them myself!"

"I will never join you," Austin hissed at him.

"Then you will die."

Austin screamed as Solon plunged a knife into his chest, turning it as he raised another above his head.

Maisie and Austin had just left the control room when Reuel checked the cameras. He spotted Braylin in the garage, rigid as a statue by the entrance. While Orion hacked into the mainframe, Reuel kept an eye on Austin and Maisie until they reached the door. After one of them waved at the camera, he unlocked the door and opened it for them. When he checked back on Braylin, he frowned as the screen glitched.

As the monitor cleared up, Reuel jumped out of his seat. Braylin was sprawled on the ground unconscious. A familiar shadow disappeared out of the camera's sight as one of the elevators activated. Arming himself with one of the emergency pistols by the controls, Reuel closed the door and locked it. While he aimed his weapon at the door, he heard the elevator ding as it opened on the other side. The sound of someone clanking toward the door made him flick off the safety as he waited for them to open the door.

"Maisie? Are you in there?"

"Aviana?" Reuel typed a command into the panel and reopened the door.

Sure enough, Aviana stood in front of him wearing her own armor. Behind her, Alton Malachite guarded her back with a sword coming out of his right gauntlet. When she laid her eyes on him, Aviana removed her helmet and made it vanish. "Oh, it's you. Where are they, relega—"

BOOM!

Aviana yanked Reuel out of the way as Orion exploded behind him. Running up to the control panel, Reuel swore every curse he knew. The Tower's firewalls had fried the robot, locking the plenaries out of the system. Alton glanced at the controls and then quickly pressed a few buttons and flicked a switch or two. Typing as fast as his metal fingers allowed him, Alton muttered while he fought to override the system.

Backing away, Reuel wiped his forehead and sighed. The elevator dinged again. As the doors opened, he slammed his hand on the panel and jumped out of the room as the door dropped down. He shot the panel on the side and faced Solon Blak.

"Hey, what are you—Reuel! What's going on out there?"

Reuel opened fire as Solon marched toward him. He heard Aviana scream from behind the door as he watched the bullets bounce off Solon's armor like foam pellets. When his gun clicked empty, he threw the weapon at Solon and blocked the sealed door with his body. Crushing the gun under his foot, Solon pinned Reuel against the door and pushed him up until they were eye level. "I should thank you, Reuel."

"Thank me?" Reuel gasped.

Solon cackled. "Why do you think I came to your apartment and told you about my plans? I knew you would run to the plenaries. It was the perfect distraction so I could sneak into the Sacrarium and take back the orb and steal the Template View. And just as I predicted, you brought them here, a pathetic attempt to redeem yourself, I'm sure. You are nothing but a traitor, but a useful traitor nonetheless. Unfortunately, your services are no longer required. Goodbye, Reuel."

Reuel cried out as Solon slashed his claws through his armor and into his stomach. Throwing him onto the floor, Solon tapped on the door with his blood-stained index finger. "Don't go anywhere, I'll be back in a minute." Solon stepped over Reuel's curled up form and vanished into smoke.

After Solon left, Aviana opened the door a crack and pulled Reuel into the control room. Once she resealed it, she propped him against the wall and checked his injuries. Reuel could taste blood in the back of his throat as he coughed. Pressing her hands over the gashes, Aviana glanced around, searching for a medical kit.

"Aviana…"

"Sshhhh." She tried to calm him. "It's all right, you're going to pull through this. You hear me?"

Reuel shook his head. "No, no I can feel it. Everything's slipping away…."

"Focus on me, Reuel. We can get Maisie. She'll heal you and then we'll all go back to the Sacrarium."

"My brother"—Reuel grabbed Aviana's arm—"Jackson, he doesn't have anyone else. Aviana, promise me you'll find him and take care of him. Please."

Aviana blinked a tear away. "I... I promise."

"Thank you," Reuel sighed softly. He winced as he leaned forward and kissed her on the lips. Holding on to him tightly, Aviana sobbed as his grip on her slipped. A smile touched Reuel's relaxing face as he closed his eyes and stilled. Lowering him to the floor, Aviana pressed her face into his chest and continued to cry.

"Oh dear." Up in his chair, Alton gazed at the screen as multiple warning symbols spammed the monitor. He tried entering a few more commands, but the system booted him out. "The system locked me out and the Genesis Engine is powering up. If they do not remove the View, I will not be able to shut the machine down! Unless..."

Aviana wiped her nose and sat next to her father. "Unless what?"

"Alliance Tower has backup generators," Alton rambled. "If those haven't been locked down yet, I can use them to overload the whole system and maybe even destroy the building. But—" Alton looked at Aviana. With a heavy sigh, he flipped more switches and typed a new command into the computer. "I need you to go outside the control room and walk over to the elevator. There should be an electrical panel near the door. Open it and I'll tell you what to do next."

Nodding, Aviana opened the door and sprinted down

the hall. "Papa, I don't see—" The door to the control room slammed shut behind Aviana. Pounding her fist against the metal, she screamed at Alton. "*Papa!* Let me in!"

"I am sorry, my daughter." Alton's voice echoed behind the door. "I cannot access the generators without additional power. I can use my pendant to boost the computer long enough to input my self-destruct command. My temporal energy will overwhelm the controls—this whole room will go up in smoke long before the rest of the building blows up. You have to find the others and get them out of here before it is too late!"

"No! I won't leave you, Papa. You'll die!"

Alton ripped open the computer and pulled out a couple of wires. Connecting them to his pendant, he gasped as the energy drained from his body. When the computer returned online, he activated the generators and set them to maximum power, then bypassed the safeguards. As the generators continued to power up, the walls around Alton sparked and smoked. Leaning back in his chair, he watched as the screen alerted him that the Engine would overload.

"Time to rest this old body of mine."

The green light streaming through the cracks of Alton's armor died out, leaving a hollow body of broken plenarie armor. With a groan, the armor fell backward, exhaling a small puff of air like a final sigh as it shattered on the floor.

On the other side, Aviana slammed her hand on the door in tears. "Alton… Alton…," she cried out as the metal burned her hand. Clutching it to her chest, she summoned her helmet and darted to the stairs.

THIRTY-SIX

As Solon's second knife slashed downward, Austin shouted as he raised his right hand. A bolt of lightning blasted Solon's fist, knocking the weapon away as he snarled. His concentration broken, both knives melted back into the sand-like dust and disappeared. Tapping into his powers, everything slowed down as Austin kicked Solon in the chest and rolled away. Solon stumbled backward, and Austin's electricity flickered across his armor as he dropped to a knee.

After Austin struggled to his feet, he tapped on Lada's pendant. As soon as he did, the armor gradually repaired itself and covered his injury.

Below him, Solon merely chuckled. "Did you come up with that trick yourself? I have a few of my own." When he returned to his full height, Solon clenched his fists and absorbed Austin's electricity. Admiring his hand, he showed it to Austin. It vibrated, just as Austin's did whenever he moved at superspeed. "I guess they forgot to tell you about my other power. I can absorb other plenaries' abilities. It's not a permanent absorption, but it gets the job done."

Austin roared as he flew at Solon again. Instead of trapping him, Solon charged at him as well. The two collided in midair as Solon's blow shattered through Austin's. Scrambling to his feet, Austin threw an uppercut. With speed to rival Austin's, Solon caught his fist and closed his hand to crush it. While he squeezed it, he pulled his other fist and knocked Austin over with another punch. His visor cracked, Austin jumped back up and threw a fist against Solon's torso. He screamed as his wrist crunched against the metal. In his hesitation, Solon grabbed the back of his head and slammed Austin's face against his knee.

"Power can make you strong, but strength is nothing compared to skill and experience." Solon peeled the remains of Austin's helmet away, revealing his bleeding and bruised face. Gasping and spitting out more blood, Austin tried to crawl to his feet. Above him, Solon walked around, shaking his head. "I should have just killed you first. Your friends would have been more of a challenge for me."

"You… will never… win," Austin moaned.

Solon dragged him up by his hair. "If I had a pendant for every time someone told me that." As he pulled him toward the edge of the Tower, Austin tried to break his grip. When they looked over the side, Solon leaned him over the edge. "I don't have time to play all day. I can drop you right now, let you plummet to your death, or I can finish that hole I carved into your chest. Any preference?"

"Yeah." Austin closed his eyes, concentrating. "You can

take the jump yourself!'"

Vanishing in a burst of yellow light, Austin reappeared behind Solon and kicked him over. Before he could catch himself, Solon toppled over the side. Under the armor, Austin's wound bled out. As he limped to the stairs, he shouted out as Solon suddenly yanked him off the ground.

"You can pocket-jump too, eh?" Solon grinned at him, holding him by the neck. Austin slammed his foot backward, but the relegator didn't even flinch. "Is it true you were paralyzed before you got your powers?"

Austin tried to teleport again, but he was too drained. If he wasn't careful, he wouldn't be able to fight back using his powers at all. After trying to shake himself free, Solon's glass-substance enclosed Austin's body as he raised him above his head.

"Your powers healed your spine, let's see if you can recover twice." Solon slammed Austin's back against his knee.

Crunch!

Austin's screams drowned out the sound of his spine snapping. The agony overwhelmed half of his body, but from the waist down he felt nothing. As he glanced down at his legs, he couldn't stop shaking his head, unable to process the sense of being paralyzed again. Crumpled beneath Solon, Austin's eyes stung as he gritted his teeth and tried to drag himself away.

The relegator tilted his head at him. "Still kicking, are we? Well, crawling, I should say."

"You can hurt me all you want." Blood dribbled from Austin's mouth as he panted. "I won't let you get away with it.

Nobody else is going to die by your hand."

Solon pushed Austin onto his back. Tightening his claws around the pendant, he ripped it out of Austin's chest. While he turned it over, Solon glanced back at Austin. "You should choose your words more carefully."

As he closed his hand, the pendant splintered like shattered glass. Without Lada's device, every nerve in Austin's body burned as the energy bottled up inside him. Looking up, he cried as he watched the Genesis Engine pulse to life as energy spiraled out of the tower into the sky. Clouds above the city darkened as thunder and lightning clapped and crackled above their heads.

Austin's armor trembled as his body all but combusted under the uncontrolled overflow of electricity. Stealing a glance at his hand, his heart almost stopped, watching it disintegrate. With the pendant broken, his body would burn out before he could bleed to death. Outbursts of lightning flew off him as more of his body faded in a blowout of light. A faint humming flooded his ears, getting louder and louder as everything around him blanched out into white light. When Solon tried to back away, Austin snatched his ankle and wouldn't let go.

"*Idiot. Let me go!*"

Austin grinned at him as he ruptured in a final blaze of yellow light. In a fleeting second, he felt every part of his body blaze into nothing and the world around him disappeared.

Dodging relegators and speeding up the stairwell to the top

of the tower, Aviana stumbled as an explosion rocked the building.

That wasn't from the generators.

Aviana picked herself back up and finished the last flight of stairs leading to the rooftop. A crater burrowed into the center of the deck, fractures zigzagged from the smoking hole toward the edges of the building. The Genesis Engine still operated as the black sky flashed different colors of lightning toward the city. Someone limped out of the crater and stepped away from the smoke and ashes. His right leg's armor torn apart, Solon favored his left when he stood across from Aviana.

"*You!*" she spat as she yanked her sword out.

Zooming at him, Aviana swung her weapon in a wide arc. His movements slower, Solon's right hand was impaled by the blade as he blocked it. As Aviana tried to pull it back, he moved closer, pushing his hand down the metal until he touched the hilt. Yanking it away, Solon pulled the sword out of his palm and threw it over the side. Weaponless, Aviana bellowed a war cry as she lunged at him. He uttered nothing as he dodged her attack. When she flew past him, Solon snatched her out of the air by the head. Kicking and punching wildly in the air, Aviana cursed at him. "*Let me go. I'm going to kill you, Ryker! I'm going to tear you apart!*"

"Goodbye, Aviana."

In a swift strike, Solon slammed her head against the roof of the Genesis Engine. Her screams cut off as she dropped like a rag doll. Aviana hung limp in his arms when he heaved her up and walked over to the edge.

"It will be quick, I promise you," Solon rumbled as he

threw her.

Tumbling through the air unnoticed, Aviana's body hurtled toward the ground. His good hand pressed against his right thigh, Solon dragged himself to the stairs. Once he took care of Orchid, nothing could stop the Genesis Engine. But as the relegator trudged down the stairs, he hadn't noticed the clouds slowly clearing up and stars shining through the darkness.

Maisie blinked the sweat out of her eyes while she worked. Removing the Template View was as painstaking as she'd predicted but taking longer than she'd assumed. If she unplugged the wrong wire—BOOM! If she pulled the orb out too soon—BAM! When the chamber lit up as the power surged, Maisie almost blew herself up. Carefully, she disconnected the last of the wires taped into the View's shell.

Maisie was reaching out to remove it when a voice from the past echoed in the room. "None of this would have been possible without Cayden Orchid. Which is why I saved his successor for last." With inhuman agility, Solon pulled her away from the Template View and lifted her into the air. Drawing her close to his mask, Maisie could see her pale face reflected in his empty black eyes. "You won't escape death twice, Orchid."

THIRTY-SEVEN

THE last time Austin woke up this groggy, he and Kate had binged-watched the four seasons of *Sherlock* and eaten nothing but potato chips and Oreos the night before. Austin moaned as he forced his eyes to open. He quickly shut them as blinding light danced in his eyes. Cautiously squinting, Austin sat up and looked around. Nothing stretched to infinity in every direction. Once he got to his feet, he noticed instead of armor, he wore a clean T-shirt with jeans. The wound on his chest had vanished along with all his scars.

Cupping his hands around his mouth, Austin shouted, "Hello!" His voice echoed as he tried again. "Hello!"

As the light strained his eyes, he rubbed them and tried to rationalize where he was. Did he die? Is this death? Just endless nothingness for eternity? Looking back, he remembered exploding in a flash of yellow light. Did he blow up Ryker too? Did his friends succeed? He closed his eyes, massaging his head as questions piled one after the other in his head.

"Austin?"

His eyes snapped open as he stood face-to-face with himself. After staring for a while, Austin realized it wasn't himself. The man in front of him stood taller with toned muscles and tanner skin. His eyes blazed a darker blue than Austin's, and his shorter hair shone a brighter shade of blond. The stranger wore a simple white collared shirt with black jeans rolled up around his ankles.

"Wade Chiffon?"

Wade dipped his head. "It's great to finally meet you face-to-face, Austin."

"Are we dead?" Austin asked while glancing around.

"Merely between this life and the next."

His gaze cast down, Austin mumbled, "But you died. Didn't you?"

"Yeah, I guess I did." Wade laughed. He seemed surprisingly cheerful for a dead person.

"This is like a halfway point between our worlds." He waved a hand around the area. "I haven't passed on quite yet. Unfinished work you could say. There's a part of me that's still alive—er—*was* alive until a few minutes ago."

Austin pointed to his brain. "You were the voice in my head?"

Snapping his fingers, Wade smiled. "Bingo. Yeah, it wasn't easy, mind you. I can only explain so much to you, Austin. You're only just beginning. Me? Time isn't relative where I am right now. I've seen how it all starts… and where it all ends. If I told you too much, it could change what has yet to come or make it worse."

"But what happened?" Austin questioned. "I still don't fully understand what happened back in June."

Wade looked around. "Guess there's nothing to sit on here, huh? Anyway, when Ryker and I moved to the Sacrarium, we'd just lost our families. Ryker was always a little distant, but he got along fine with Maisie and Braylin, and I got close with Alton and Aviana. But then Ryker started becoming isolated again. I was worried about him and someone warned me that he might be working for the relegators. That's when I caught him trying to steal the Template View."

Austin recalled the dreams he'd been having. "And that's when you two fought, right? That night in June?"

"Yes… that's when we fought. I almost had him when he surprised me with a knife. After we crashed in that field, one of Ryker's daggers was in my chest. When he disappeared, my body tried to reincarnate, but something from his blade wouldn't let my body heal. Reincarnation was no longer an option. That's when I saw you. When we collided, my energy fused with your body. My powers, my lightning, and even some of my mind got snagged in the back of your brain too. Crazy, huh?"

"So my powers *did* come from you. What happened to your pendant? Every time I used your powers, these scars spread on my chest." Austin pointed to himself.

"Yes they did. That's because my pendant was lost in the process," Wade explained. "I don't think you had my polestar, but there must've been enough of me inside you to produce the plenarie energy. The only explanation I can think of is consigned reincarnation. The process only works though if the plenarie actually passes on. And since part of me was still inside you, you weren't fully converted. On the plus side, there was just enough of my consciousness to speak to you from time to time."

Austin nodded as he placed his hands on his hips. "I don't want to sound like an ungrateful jerk and all, but I'm dead now, right? What was the whole point of me helping your friends if I only died trying in the end?"

Wade shrugged. "I don't know, man. You were meant to survive that night, and it doesn't matter whether you're a human or a plenarie. The plenaries didn't want to fight anymore, but you stepped in without hesitation, and you motivated them in a way I couldn't. That's pretty heroic."

"Yeah, sure," Austin snorted, "but it's like Aviana said. I'm no hero. I failed and now they're probably dying as we speak. I'm sorry, Wade, but you died giving your powers to a useless nobody."

Wade grabbed Austin by the shoulders. "Hey, I wouldn't go back and change anything even if I could. I may know what lies ahead, Austin, but the choice is still yours to make."

"Choice? What choice?"

Letting him go, Wade stepped back and waved a hand to his right. At first, there was just a small speck. The portal grew bigger and bigger until it reached just the right size for a person to jump through. On the other side, Austin saw the Genesis Engine in the middle of the city. Turning back to Wade, he raised an eyebrow. "I can go back?"

"That's up to you," Wade replied. "Your choice. I'm just about done here, it's almost my time to move on. You can come with me if you want, but remember this, Austin, our friends need you. They always will."

"Wade? Wade!" Austin shouted until Wade completely disappeared.

When the plenarie disappeared, Austin rubbed his forehead. There was still so much he didn't understand or know. He stared at the portal, deep in thought. He'd failed once, who's to say he wouldn't fail again?

"I can't do this." Austin sighed to himself. Shaking his head in dismay, he stepped away from the portal as it closed.

THIRTY-EIGHT

MAISIE'S struggle against Solon Blak weakened as he crushed her throat. Her pulse fluttered feebly against his metal claws, her vision darkening. Giving one last effort to pry his fingers apart, her head sagged as her limbs fell to her sides, dangling. Solon held her neck still as his other hand wrapped around her face to break her neck.

WHAM!

Something slammed him aside, knocking him away from the unconscious girl. When he whipped around, Solon's eyes widened. The portal closed behind Austin as he stood in front of Maisie. In his hand, a yellow and silver pendant glittered in his palm. When he lifted it to his chest, plenarie armor constructed itself across Austin's body. Yellow light glowed between the plates and brightened the oval symbol on his chest plate. As the helmet enveloped his face, the visor flickered to life as it also displayed yellow aura energy. When Austin spoke, his voice boomed, modulated and deep like other plenaries'. "We're not done yet."

"You're harder to kill than I expected," Solon admitted. "But you will still lose."

Austin opened his arms out wide. "Care to test that theory?"

Before Solon could react, Austin plowed him through the wall. The renewed Austin tackled him out of the building, his fists popping like a machine gun with every blow against Solon's body. Just as they were about to splat on the pavement, Austin pocket-jumped and disappeared. Solon, on the other hand, slammed on top of a van, the armor barely protecting his body. Rolling off the vehicle, he zoomed into the city with Austin in hot pursuit. As he ran, Austin felt rejuvenated. Energy pumped through him without strain, his speed propelled him forward like a missile. No pain or exhaustion touched him as he sped after his target.

Take a left, ordered a familiar voice.

"Wade? Is that you?"

Of course not. I am Orion. I have been uploaded and integrated into your armor to serve you as a guide. Wade sends his regards, Orion's voice replied.

Taking a shortcut courtesy of Orion, Austin sidelined Solon on a street, throwing him down the road where he crashed into a parked truck. After he pulled himself out of the wreck, Solon ripped a door off its hinges and threw it at the approaching Austin. As Austin surged forward, the door pinwheeled straight at him, flying closer and closer. Dropping to his knees and sliding, Austin ducked and dodged the door and continued to charge at Solon.

When they collided, every window on the street shattered

as the shockwave vibrated down the city block. Both were almost evenly matched as they exchanged blows. Finally, Austin got lucky and reached under the Solon's swinging arm and nailed him in the jaw with an uppercut. Stunned for a moment, Solon flew off the ground after Austin nailed him with a bolt of his own lightning. Crouched on his hands and knees, Solon cradled his blasted chest with an arm. A layer of his armor blown away, Austin spotted exposed layers of machinery wrapped around Solon's chest. He moved to slam him down with his knotted fists but Solon leapt back and dashed away.

Cutting through the city and zipping around buildings, cars, and narrow streets, Solon couldn't shake Austin off. When he curved around a corner, Austin teleported in front and grabbed him. Together they vanished into darkness and reappeared inside the Alliance Tower. On the floor, Solon cursed at his damaged armor.

Folding his arms, Austin gazed down at him without pity. "It's over, Ryker. You won't get away this time."

Solon tightened his fists as he snarled, "Back from the dead or not, I still overpower you one-on-one."

"In that case, you might want to take a recount."

Aside from the bleeding nose and a bruise on her head, Aviana Blu looked ready for her rematch with the relegator. She leaned her sword against her shoulder, blue energy glowing from the blade as she swung it around and pointed it at Solon. Beside her, Braylin posed to fight as well. One of his eyes had sealed shut, but he looked absolutely livid.

"Three to one? I like these odds."

Outnumbered and surrounded, Solon actually chuckled behind his dented mask. "Your confidence in numbers won't save you. You think you've won?"

Suddenly the Genesis Engine began to shake and shudder as the walls exploded with fire. Everyone stumbled as the floor rocked and cracked down the middle.

"Alton rigged the backup generators to blow!" Aviana yelled. "This whole building is going to blast apart!"

In the confusion, Solon stumbled toward the middle of the room where the Template View rested in the heart of the machine. The wiring unplugged, he smashed the glass casing and removed the View from the machine. With a quick flick of his hand, Austin shot a spark at Solon's hand holding the View. After his bolt blew the metal hand apart, Braylin dived to the floor and caught the orb before it shattered on the ground. Black smoke swirled around Solon as he and Austin locked eyes. "Another time, plenarie."

When the relegator vanished, Braylin handed Austin the Template View and hoisted an unconscious Maisie over his shoulder. "We need to get out of here!"

Austin looked around him. All the mechanics of the Engine were short-circuiting and about to blow. Even if they could escape, there were still the rest of the relegators in the building. "We have to get everyone out of the building," he shouted to his friends.

"There's no time!" Braylin yelled. "We need to teleport to the Sacrarium now!"

As the upper half of the machine exploded, lightning shot into the sky reigniting the energy thunderstorm. From the blackening clouds, multicolored bolts of energy rained down, striking places around the city.

"We can't just leave them to die!" Austin shouted. "They didn't have a choice, Braylin. We do. We have to save them. Because we can!"

"We don't have time to argue," Aviana reminded them.

"You're right," called a voice.

A flash of light flooded the room as another portal opened. Summoning his armor, Wade removed his helmet as he ordered, "Braylin, take Maisie and get yourselves out of here. Austin, Aviana, and I will get the relegators out of here and protect the civilians."

Too dumbfounded to speak, Braylin grabbed Maisie and threw his pendant on the floor. Together they vanished in a blast of white light.

While they teleported, Wade ran up to Austin. "If anyone is still in the top levels of the building you have to run them out of here. I'll take care of the rest. *Go!*"

Austin nodded and popped away with a snap of electricity. After Austin left, Wade shook Aviana by the shoulders. "Aviana, I need you to get anyone around the building's perimeter away from the explosion. I'll help Austin get the rest of the relegators out of the Tower."

Aviana did not move as she stared at him, pale as a ghost. "Wade?" she sobbed.

Discarding his helmet, Wade pulled her close and hugged her. Breaking apart, Wade tried to move Aviana, but she wouldn't budge. With a pained expression, he grimaced. "You can't stay here, Avi."

"*No!*" she cried. "I can't lose you again! I lo—"

Wade shushed her, tearing up as well when he gazed at her. "I know. And I'm sorry, but I can't stay. I've only come back to save you this last time."

"Please!" she sobbed. "Just stop, don't leave me!"

"Sorry, Avi, gotta make me." He smiled sadly.

Holding her face gently in his hands, Wade kissed Aviana on the lips as tears streamed down both their faces. The eternity they both felt in that short second ended when Wade pulled away. For three years, Aviana had been trying to get Wade to kiss her. She held on to him tighter, her wet golden-brown eyes staring into Wade's dazzling blue ones.

"Go now, Aviana," Wade begged.

Aviana tried to say the words, but she choked and couldn't force herself to make them out. But she didn't have to. Taking her hands one last time, Wade leaned in and whispered in her ear. When he backed away, more tears rained down Aviana's face as her cheeks glowed and her puffy lips formed a trembling smile. Still holding her cupped hands, Wade pressed something into them and closed them together. He flashed her a devilish smile and winked. After he shooed her away, Wade turned around, facing the detonating machine with grim determination.

Austin ran more than a dozen relegators out of the Alliance Tower before it crumbled. More relegators had been rushed out by yellow and blue blurs until the streets were packed with the black-armored soldiers. Austin and Aviana moved close-by civilians to safety before chunks of the Tower crashed into the roads. Just as Austin returned a child to a sobbing mother away from the chaos, the Genesis Engine illuminated the city as a pillar of light before it collapsed completely. When the dust settled, crowds of humans and relegators huddled around the disaster zone as the three plenaries snuck away.

Away from the streets, Austin gave Wade and Aviana a moment and checked the Template View for any scratches. Wade kissed Aviana's hand before waving to both of them and fading away. Walking back to Austin, Aviana wiped her glassy eyes as she kept her fist closed tightly. Austin almost asked her what she held, but he shut his mouth instead.

"Well, that was quite the spectacle!"

Aviana and Austin spun around. Dressed in a modest gown, Lada folded her hands and smiled with her silver-toothed grin. Handing Aviana the Template View, Austin approached the High Sultana. "I see you decided to make an appearance."

Aviana stepped between Austin and Lada. In case the message wasn't clear enough, she grabbed the hilt of her sword and pulled it out slightly. "We should get going, Austin."

"Oh, Aviana." Lada giggled. "He did not tell you?"

"Tell me what?"

Austin looked at his toes. When Aviana glared at the High Sultana, she shrugged innocently. "Austin made a deal with me, dearie. One of my pendants with a few adjustments. Along with a second trip to my cogitari chamber as an added bonus."

"In exchange for?" Aviana questioned.

"Austin has agreed to return to my realm to serve as my own personal guardsman. He will be well taken care of, I

promise you," Lada assured her.

Aviana pulled Austin aside. "Austin Bennet. What. Did. You. Do?"

"I did what I had to. Say goodbye to the others for me, okay?"

Aviana startled to splutter, but Austin walked past her. Smiling down at him, Lada offered him her hand. Before he took it, Aviana slapped his hand away. "You are not going with her! How am I supposed to explain this to the others? To Kate?"

"Time to go," Lada interrupted.

Austin paused. Biting his tongue, he gave Lada an apologetic glance.

"Do not give me that look, Austin Bennet." Lada's hair swirled around her crossly. "A deal is a deal."

Austin bowed his head toward her. "Lada, I have every intention of keeping my promise to you, but Solon Blak is still out there. I can't just leave the world behind and forget about him."

"Your plenarie friends cannot take care of him?" Lada pouted.

"Not without Austin." Aviana crossed her arms, she matched Lada's cold glare with one of her own. When Lada tried to step closer, she drew her sword and pointed it at her chest.

The High Sultana bared her teeth with a hiss. Her voice boomed as she towered above the two of them. "*You dare to defy me?*"

"Lada, please. I can help them bring Solon to justice *and*

fulfill my promise to you. Just give me a little more time. If you helped us, we could catch him faster." Austin worried he might have overstepped with that last part.

Lada dropped her outstretched hand. For a moment, Austin thought she would sink her teeth into him when she leaned down and got in his face. "Believe me when I say it, you do not want me as your enemy, dearie. Tread carefully, Austin Bennet. I always get what I want."

And with that Lada stepped away and disappeared into a dazzling white light. Sighing in relief, Austin turned and grinned at Aviana.

She looked like she wanted to slap him. "If you ever do something stupid like that again, I'm going to pin you to one of the Sacrarium trees with *this* sword!"

"Better that than facing the wrath of Lada." Austin chuckled as he started to wobble.

Aviana caught him before he fell. "Easy there, I got you."

"Just… just a little nap," Austin mumbled. He closed his eyes once and didn't open them again for a while.

THIRTY-NINE

LOUD whispers slipped into Austin's subconsciousness and shook him out of his deep sleep. Back in his bed at the Sacrarium, he recognized the worried tone of Kate's voice as well as the low, rumbling voice of Braylin. Austin coughed as his eyes fluttered open.

"Austin." Everything blurred out of focus as Austin's body was crushed under tight embraces.

"Girls, give him some breathing space." Braylin laughed.

Austin gasped for air as Maisie and Kate backed off his bed. When his vision cleared, he looked at his friends. Maisie had faint bruise marks around her neck while Braylin still sported a black-eye. His best friend rubbed her irritated eyes as she placed her hands on her hips. "You gave me a freaking heart attack, Austin."

"You were the one who was crushing me," he wheezed. Turning to Braylin, Austin asked, "How long was I out?"

"Two days," he answered. "Maisie said relegator pickup

crews already started clearing away the remains of Alliance Tower. They told the press it was just a design flaw. As far as the world knows, that storm was just a weird coincidence." Seeing the question forming in Austin's eyes, Braylin added, "There's been no word or sign of Solon Blak."

Austin pushed himself up on his elbows and blinked hard to get rid of the stars he was seeing. When he looked at all of them, he could tell they still held something back. "Is there something else?"

Kate squealed with delight as she bounced on the balls of her feet. Rolling his eyes at her, Braylin explained, "After we brought you back, we did a test on your blood, DNA, and—"

"Just get to the cool part, Braylin," Maisie interrupted.

Braylin sighed. "Okay, fine. Test results came in… and they were positive for plenarie energy."

"And that means?"

Maisie grinned at him. "It means you're a full-blooded plenarie like us!"

"How?" Austin laughed in disbelief. "Why?"

When he tried to get up, Braylin pushed him back down. "Not so fast. You aren't going anywhere for at least another night."

Groaning, Austin tapped his forehead. "Care to knock me out again?"

"I think you've had enough head trauma for a while." Braylin chuckled.

Nodding, Austin closed his eyes as his friends left him to rest. For the first time in a long while, he slept dreamlessly as he lay in bed. He knew that after the explosion, his connection to Wade had been severed. Waking up with a small headache later that night, a soft tapping on the other side of the door alerted him to someone else's presence. The door slid open slowly as the entrant tiptoed to his bedside. Even in the dark, Austin recognized the sea green eyes looking at him.

"I wanted to give you something, I just finished it." Maisie smiled.

Austin sat up and took the small wrapped object from her. "The piece of tech Alton modified for you?" Tearing through the tissue paper, he gasped. Completely restored, his mom's phone glimmered without a scratch and with a new lock screen wallpaper. Maisie had taken the liberty of putting a selfie of herself sticking her tongue out as the new picture. "How did—I thought I'd lost this forever."

Maisie shrugged. "Well, I found it in your old clothes the day you first came to the Sacrarium. Alton helped me repair it and change the battery with a temporal energy one. It... it took a little longer to finish fixing it without him, but I was able to get it to work last night."

"Maisie, I..." Austin closed his fingers around the phone. "Thank you."

"Mhmm. Sorry if I woke you up, I'll just—oh okay and we're hugging now."

After Maisie relaxed and hugged him back, Austin scooted away and lay down. "Nice jacket you got there."

"Oh yeah." Maisie tugged at her sleeve. "Confession time, this actually is your jacket. By the time I remembered I was still wearing it, I was back at the Sacrarium. I didn't know who you were at the time, so I kept it. I can take off the patches, but unshrinking it is gonna be a lot harder."

"It's fine, you can keep it."

"Really?" Maisie offered it to him. "You sure?"

Austin pushed it back toward her. "Yeah, just take good care of it for me."

Slipping the jacket back on, Maisie edged to the door. "I will. Thank you. Okay, Braylin's gonna lecture me if he catches me keeping you up."

"Thanks, Maisie."

"G'night, Austin." Maisie smiled as she closed the door.

A couple days later, Austin was the first to wake up at the Sacrarium. With the Template View restored, Vera had returned as well as the other felera spirits, resuming their daily tasks at the Sacrarium. Slipping out of his room, Austin headed to the Athenaeum, taking a detour through the bedroom hall. Glancing on the right, he eyed the dark purple, red, and blue symbols scribed onto the doors. He recognized the blue representing Aviana's room, but frowned as he looked at the red pendant symbol. Whose room was this? He'd never seen a plenarie with a red energy aura before. The door with the dark purple symbol Austin now knew was Ryker's.

Touching the handleless door with his hand, he willed it to open. Nothing. The room had sealed itself like Wade's had. Austin closed his eyes, imagining the room on the other side of the door. When he pocket-jumped to the other side, he almost tripped over himself. Lights automatically turned on at Austin's presence as he dusted his jeans off. Like Wade's, the messy bed hadn't been slept in for a long time. On the wall across the bed, a large bookshelf grayed with dust, and the books sitting in it appeared untouched as well.

Austin walked over to the bedside table. On the dusted surface, three pictures sat together. Blowing on them, he picked up the largest one and peered at it. A copy of Wade's photo of the five friends smiling at the camera. After setting it back down, Austin grabbed another frame and brushed his thumb across the glass. Wade and Ryker had to be about ten in this one. Both rough-housed playfully as they beamed at the camera. How could one of these boys kill the other? If there was some sign that Ryker would become Solon Blak, Austin couldn't find it. He looked so happy in the old photos. Had he known he would turn evil? That he would kill his best friend?

Setting the picture down, Austin gingerly lifted the last photo. The picture framed a portrait of a girl. She looked really familiar, but why? Then Austin remembered, he'd seen her in Aviana's memories. She had been with Ryker when he talked to Aviana. Just as he remembered her in the memory, the girl had straight brown hair flowing down to her chest. Her eyes, a chilling arctic-blue, had mischief twinkling in them as they stared at Austin. In the photo her mouth curved into a beautiful smile, and Austin felt warm just looking at her.

Taking the photo out of the frame, he heard the crinkle of paper underneath him. When he lifted his foot, he found half a yellowed page ripped at the top. Hastily stuffing it in his pocket, Austin ran out of the room to find someone. He noticed someone making clanking sounds in the kitchen while he sprinted down the hall. After he barreled into the kitchen, he found Aviana putting dishes away behind the counter. "Aviana?"

She jumped with a squeak, almost dropping the bowl she'd lifted. "Austin! Sorry, I didn't know anyone else was awake."

She looked better today. The bruises and cuts on her face were gone and she'd returned to her physically perfect, annoyingly rigid self. Austin and Aviana hadn't talked much since the Genesis Engine. Neither of them had been eager to talk about their argument. But today Aviana looked more at peace with herself. Her hair was starting to curl again, and her eyes were softer, gentler when they looked at Austin.

"Can I ask you something?" Austin asked.

Wiping her hands on the apron she had tied around her waist, Aviana nodded. As they sat down at the kitchen table, he showed her the picture. Aviana's eyes widened as she picked it up. "Where'd you find this?"

"It was in Ryker's room."

"It's been locked since he left," Aviana protested.

Austin shrugged. "I pocket-jumped through the door. So, who is she?"

"That's Emily Claret," Aviana enlightened him as she held the photo up. "She's a plenarie—Ryker's girlfriend. When he lived here, she eventually came along and stayed with us. After Ryker and Wade disappeared, she just left one night and never came back. We tried to track her down, but she was always one step ahead of us. She doesn't want to be found."

An idea took shape in Austin's mind. "If we could find her, do you think she might know where Ryker is?"

"Have you started breakfast yet, Aviana?" Maisie called out.

Aviana quickly hid the photo in her dress as she smiled wearily. "I've been up for five minutes. How would you and Braylin cope without me?"

"We'd probably starve." Maisie shrugged.

After breakfast, Austin returned to his room for a fresh change of clothes. He tugged on a shirt as someone knocked on the door. "Come in." When the door opened, he was surprised to see Aviana of all people. "Did I not wash my plate or something?" he joked.

Stepping into the room, Aviana closed the door behind her. She followed him to the bed and sat on the edge of it. "I've been meaning to talk to you about something. I wanted to apologize to you."

"*You* want to apologize to *me*?"

Aviana smiled weakly. Her attempt to look sheepish was horrible, but Austin sighed as he gazed at her beauteous face. "Oh, come on, I'm not that bad, am I?"

Austin thought it was in his best interest not to answer that. "Does this mean you'll be nice to me now?" he blurted. "'Cause if so, that's going to be a little weird."

Aviana laughed as she wiped her eye. "I can't promise I'll be nice all the time." Another shock came when she hugged Austin. Backing off, she spoke in a snippy tone. "Don't get used to that. You still annoy me, Austin Bennet."

"Right back at you, Blu." He grinned.

Aviana rolled her eyes as she left the room. His hands in his pockets, Austin followed her out and remembered the wadded-up piece of paper from Ryker's room. Pulling it out and flattening it, Austin's eyes widened. It was the missing half of the page from the Plenarie Tome! After he closed the door, Austin opened the Tome and slid the page back into place.

Solon Blak—Solon Blak, his true identity unknown, rebelled against his people and desired the Template View for himself. He hoped that with it, he could destroy his enemies and rise as the master of the four realms with his army of rogues. The corrupt plenaries, soon to be named relegators, were the followers of Solon Blak throughout the purge. While Blak still possessed a pendant, he wore his own self-designed armor that could manipulate his aura into a combination of black smoke and electricity. He perished in the last days of the purge, but—

—this may no longer be true. It is unknown how he survived the destruction of Villhilium, but a relegator, who claimed to be Solon Blak, attacked and killed a plenarie in an attempt to steal the Template View. He disappeared after that, his current whereabouts are unknown.

Below the missing half of the paragraph, someone had scrawled an additional message. The writing, Austin noticed, was very neat and slanted. It might have been a woman's, but Austin guessed it belonged to a man based on the initials signed in the corner of the page:

The relegator returned. My friends and I here at the Sacrarium were recently almost killed by him. After our encounter, I compared notes with Alton on his memory of Solon and my own observation of the relegator who claimed to be him. Some of the facts do not line up. Currently looking into the matter myself to see whether this is indeed the real Solon Blak, or one of his surviving minions. I've also made an additional note concerning the true identity of this relegator, if he or she is not, indeed, Solon Blak.   — R. A. D.

Austin reread the page several times. So, Solon had made another appearance before June and killed one of the plenaries, but who? And what about Ryker's note? Why would he write that if he was the new Solon Blak? Closing the book, Austin held it under his arm and walked into the hall. When he knocked on Braylin's door, nobody answered. Someone grunted on the other side as Austin tried again. "Braylin? Hello?"

Without warning the door flew open. Austin staggered back in surprise, raising the Plenarie Tome to cover his face. Wrapped around each other kissing, Braylin and Kate quickly broke apart once they noticed him.

"Austin!" Kate's face blossomed like a bunch of roses. "Do you mind?"

"Jeez, Kate. Just get a room."

"This *is* my room," Braylin pointed out.

Austin suddenly remembered how short he was compared to Braylin. Backing away, he shielded himself with the book, just in case. "Right. Sorry, guys. Um... can you, er, put that on pause for a moment? I need to show Braylin something."

Kate tried to melt him with her trademark glare while

Braylin gave her a *what can you do* shrug. After he moved to let Austin walk in, Braylin cleared some space on his bed to put the book down.

"I saw this ripped page in the Tome," Austin explained as he flipped past the cover. He showed Braylin the missing page and the piece of it he'd just discovered. Braylin read the text over Austin's shoulder, his brow creasing. Squeezing herself between them, Kate took a peek at the page and tilted her head. "R-A-D? Does that stand for 'really annoying douchebag?'"

"Those are Ryker's initials." Braylin traced his fingers along the lines, his eyes narrowing.

"You guys have fought Solon before, haven't you? And Ryker was with you."

"We have." Rubbing his chin, Braylin turned to Austin. "Ryker Darkthistle wasn't with us though. That day we were out of the Sacrarium, he stayed behind because he said it was too dangerous. That's when we were ambushed and almost killed."

"How did you escape?" Kate gasped.

"Ryker. When we didn't return, he tracked us down. He and Emily saved us and we all barely made it back to the Sacrarium before the relegators got us."

Austin pointed back to the book. "See? There's something fishy here. Ryker wrote about what happened, but why would he speculate the identity of Solon Blak if he was Solon? The only other person we know who has gone by the name Solon Blak was Maisie's brother."

"*What?*" Kate's jaw dropped. "Maisie has a secret brother? Am I the only one here getting goose bumps? Maisie's got a secret brother who's a supervillain? Is he hot?"

"No, he's dead." Braylin frowned.

"Something isn't right, and all we have is this scribbled note from Ryker. That's why I thought we could talk to Emily Claret."

"Ryker's old girlfriend?"

Austin nodded, rushing to continue. "Besides Wade, I bet she knew him better than anyone. She might know what he's got planned next, or maybe she knows where he's hiding."

"Except we have no idea where she is." Braylin waved with a sigh. "None of us could track—" The plenarie froze, then his eyes rounded as he slowly nodded. "Actually, there is someone who might be able to find her. Amari is an excellent tracker. He can help us find Emily. But we better hurry."

"Why?" Kate frowned.

"Because," Austin gasped, "if Emily knows anything important about Ryker, you can bet we won't be the only ones looking for her. I just hope we find her before Solon does."

FORTY

JACKSON sat alone in the cramped apartment. Up on the couch, he held his brother's helmet tightly, glancing at the door every time something creaked. When someone knocked, Jackson hopped off the couch and dashed to the door. Flicking all the locks open and throwing the door ajar, his heart stuttered when he realized it wasn't Reuel.

"Hi, Jackson." Emma smiled and reached down to ruffle his hair.

Jackson ducked away from her hand and stepped back. His eyes watered as his bottom lip trembled. "Where's my brother?"

Kneeling down in front of him, Emma reached out. "Oh, Jackson, I'm so sorry. There… there was an explosion inside Alliance Tower. The whole building is gone."

Reuel's helmet slipped from Jackson's hands. As it bounced on the floor, Jackson threw himself into Emma's embrace and cried into her chest. Holding him tightly, Emma rubbed his back as she kissed his forehead. "I'm here to pick you up. We're going to leave this city and go somewhere safer for both of us. I'll take care of you, Jackson, I promise."

Before they could leave New Jersey, Emma told Jackson someone wanted to meet him. Someone who knew Reuel. Emma held his hand as they walked through the lobby of a fancy skyscraper and rode the elevator up to one of the highest floors. His arms wrapped around Reuel's old helmet, Jackson followed Emma into a room with a giant desk overlooking the city. From the view he could spot where Alliance Tower once stood. Sitting in the leather chair behind the desk, a man in his late twenties greeted them.

"My name is Dominic Harrison. I'm the new Head Director for the United Alliance." He said the title like he wasn't used to it. Dominic straightened his glasses as he folded his hands.

"You knew my brother?" Jackson asked him.

"No. That would be me."

Dominic cowered behind his desk as a tall relegator walked into the office. When the relegator stood in front of Jackson, he dropped down to a knee and looked him in the eye. Taking a step forward, Jackson showed the terrifying stranger Reuel's helmet. As he reached for it, the relegator's metal claws peeled away, uncovering his real hands. The relegator's face reminded Jackson of the robot from *Terminator*. That movie always scared him, but Jackson didn't cry and he wouldn't be afraid. He would be brave, just like his brother.

"Your brother was my friend." The relegator sighed as he

returned the helmet. "He died trying to save everyone from—no, I shouldn't tell you. It's too soon."

"Please, Mr. Relegator," Jackson begged him. "What happened to Reuel?"

The relegator closed his fists, turning away. "He... he was murdered. A plenarie who goes by the name Austin Bennet killed him."

"Did you catch him?" Jackson rubbed his eyes so he wouldn't tear up again.

"I'm sorry." The relegator laid a hand on his shoulder. "Austin got away with some other plenaries who blew up the Tower. We tried to stop them, but those plenaries are like monsters. They don't care who they hurt when they fight for their cause. Especially heroes like your brother." Jackson sniffed as he stared at his reflection in the helmet's glass. Reaching out, the relegator wiped a tear away. "We will get your brother justice, Jackson. I promise you, Austin Bennet will pay for his crimes."

Jackson said nothing. Beside him, Emma brushed the hair out of his eyes and pulled him close. "Wait for me outside, Jackson. I just need to speak to the relegator for a minute."

After Jackson left the room, Solon brought out a transparent orb. Tossing it between his hands, he began to pace the room. "You will be flying out tonight, then?"

"Since your little Genesis Engine scheme bombed, yes."

Solon laughed as he shook his head. "There you are wrong, my dear."

"Care to explain?"

"I predicted the outcome of the Engine failing, which

is why I had a second initiative." He lobbed the orb at her. "Remember this? The last time you saw it, it was orange and crackling with energy. Using the Template View to metamorphose everyone into beings of equal power was only one of the Genesis Engine's purposes. Like insects drawn to a fly zapper, the plenaries took the bait and focused only on destroying the Engine. It gave me the distraction I needed to use this energy elsewhere."

"Elsewhere?" Emma repeated.

Solon opened the door and invited her to leave. "The plenaries have been drawn out, and now they will be looking for allies for their cause. While they scramble their forces together, the relegators will overthrow the United Alliance and take control of this realm."

Walking out, Emma stopped and turned on her heel. "Ry— I mean, Solon?"

"Yes, Emily?"

"They'll be looking for me. You know that, right?"

For a moment, Solon said nothing. When he closed the door, he murmured, "You know what to do. The pawns have come into play." After he shut the door, Solon marched up to Dominic's desk. "Let's talk business, Head Director."

ACKNOWLEDGEMENTS

Every day since I started writing *Echo of a Hero*, I prayed that God would inspire me and bless my writing with His favor. Thank you, Heavenly Father, for hearing my many prayers and making this dream of mine a reality. None of this would have been possible without You. Praise God! For He hears and answers those who call upon Him in His name. Whatever lies ahead in the future of this series, God, I know You will always be there for me.

I want to thank someone who has listened to every idea of mine since the beginning, my awesome brother Prescott, for all the feedback he's given me. Some characters would have turned out very differently without your advice and insightful criticism. I'm so thankful for all those long nights we spent in our rooms upstairs, talking in the dark and discussing this series and the development of the characters who came out of it.

I never would have been able to publish this book without the help of my parents, Michael and Candy Myles. Dad, thank you so much for helping me fund this special project of mine. Your first investment gave me the momentum I needed to take this book to the professional level. Thank you both for always supporting me and believing in me. I love you guys so much and I'm so grateful for everything you've blessed me with.

To the best grandma in the world, it always brightened my day when you asked about my book. Thank you, Noni.

I want to thank Savvy, my manuscript's first editor, for pointing me in the right direction and giving me writing advice I will never forget. You inspired me to put my own ideas and daydreams into ink and paper the day you published *The Thirteenth Hour*.

To my other sister, Livvy, I'm so grateful for your encouragement and entrepreneurial spirit and advice. Your infectious, can-do attitude always keeps me motivated.

I can't thank Olivia Ventura and the rest of the team at Hot Tree Self-Publishing enough for everything they've done to make this book the best it can be. You guys rock the house! Thank you, Olivia, for taking *Echo of a Hero* under your wing and never failing to answer my countless emails. To the beta readers and editors, I just want to say your positive feedback and excitement for this book were wonderful surprises to read. Thank you, Carrie Champion, Randie Creamer, Kolleen Fraser, Andrea Robinson, Mandy Pederick, and everyone else for all the notes and fixes you made to make this book a masterpiece.

A special thanks to RMGraphx for creating such a fantastic cover. All of the time, detail, and heart you put into this work of art speaks for itself. Seeing my book brought to life by your talents makes me dream of the day I'll get to walk into a bookstore and find it on display. I can't wait to work with you again on the next book's cover! I also want to thank the IngramSpark team for all of their support and help in making this book a published work. Self-publishing would be a lot harder if you guys weren't out there.

To one of my best friends, Zoë, I just want to say I wouldn't be here without you. From the moment I first told you I was writing a series, you were always there to listen to my ideas and love all of the sketches I shared with you. You're the best kind of friend an introvert like me can ever have. I'm so grateful that God brought you into my life.

And last but most certainly not least, I want to add how blessed I am for the real heroes: the readers. You guys are the best. Thank you for enjoying reading this book as much as I have writing it. Welcome to the family; Austin and his friends will be waiting for you at the Sacrarium when you return for their next adventure in book two.

ABOUT THE AUTHOR

Pearson Myles has been writing stories since he was sixteen years old, drawing inspiration from his childhood adventures traveling across the United States with his family. He especially loves the slopes of Denver, Colorado, where he wrote his first draft of *Spirits of Power*. Pearson is a huge fan of books and has read *The Hobbit* and the *Harry Potter* series far too many times to count. When he isn't reading or writing, Pearson is training as a martial artist in Tae Kwon Do. *Echo of a Hero: Spirits of Power* is his first novel.

WWW.PEARSONMYLES.COM

9 781732 450608